Anne sto...
doorway,...

Her first impression was that Jason was
wearing nothing under his apron. On second
glance, she realized that he had on a rather
skimpy pair of tan bathing trunks. From
where she stood, Anne had an unobscured
view of his legs and the play of muscles across
his back and, in between, a nicely shaped
derriere.

Oh, good heavens. She wasn't used to
thinking about men this way. And Jason
was—well, he lived here, for heaven's sake!

She sought a way to make a joke out of her
embarrassment. "I don't know why I bothered
to study anatomy. You're a complete lesson in
yourself."

Jason finished grating cheese. "I was
sunbathing and the time got away from me. I
meant to put some clothes on before you got
here."

'Oh, don't get dressed on my account." Anne
waved her hand airily, feeling as if she'd fallen
down the rabbit hole....

ABOUT THE AUTHOR

Jacqueline Diamond likes to do just about anything that doesn't involve physical exertion. She enjoys reading, getting to know interesting people, eating her husband's cooking (she cooks during the week and he cooks for company) and writing—fourteen novels so far. She's spent more than ten years working as a news reporter and editor, including four years with the Associated Press in Los Angeles. Jackie lives in La Habra, California, with her husband, Kurt, and their son, Ari.

Books by Jacqueline Diamond

HARLEQUIN AMERICAN ROMANCE
79–THE DREAM NEVER DIES

An Unexpected Man
Jacqueline Diamond

Harlequin Books

TORONTO • NEW YORK • LONDON
AMSTERDAM • PARIS • SYDNEY • HAMBURG
STOCKHOLM • ATHENS • TOKYO • MILAN

For Ari

Published April 1987

First printing February 1987

ISBN 0-373-16196-4

Chapter One

The cesarean section had gone well. After her patient was wheeled out to the recovery room, Anne stopped by the nursery to check on her newest arrival.

The tiny red creature, given a clean bill of health by the pediatrician, lay wailing lustily while a nurse cooed soothingly.

Anne rubbed the back of her hand wearily across her forehead. For a moment, she couldn't even remember whether it was a boy or a girl. Oh, yes, a girl, although she'd scarcely had time to check as she lifted it from its mother's womb. It was a little girl, with a big head, who hadn't wanted to arrive in the world the usual way. Maybe that's where the term headstrong had come from.

She smiled to herself. She'd have to tell that one to her partner, John Hernandez. He'd been accusing her of losing her sense of humor lately.

Stretching her cramped shoulders, Anne made her way to the telephone at the nursing station and called her receptionist to check for messages.

There was nothing urgent, Ellie said, just a few routine matters that Meg, the nurse-practitioner, had been able to handle.

"And don't forget you have to be home by six." Ellie was only twenty-five, but she had a motherly air that managed to make Anne feel like a child sometimes, especially when she was tired. In addition, they'd become good friends outside the office, so Ellie wasn't shy about teasing. "I know you usually forget about anything that isn't work related."

Absentmindedly, Anne fingered the name bar attached to her white coat, the one that said Anne Eldridge M.D. and had thrilled her so much the first time she wore it, which felt like eons ago but was really less than eight years. "Actually, I was thinking of coming back to the office to pick up some of the new journals; I'm a little behind in my reading. Refresh my memory; what's going on at six o'clock?"

"Four would-be housekeepers will be descending on the Eldridge residence. If you're not there, who knows what they might do?" Ellie chuckled. She'd been in a good mood for the last few months, ever since she got over her morning sickness. It sometimes seemed to Anne that everybody in the world was pregnant. Everyone except Anne, of course.

Now she groaned. The last thing she felt like doing tonight was talking with a bunch of matronly women about their references as live-in housekeepers.

But duty called, and whenever it did, Anne Eldridge could be counted on to snap to attention. "I'll be there," she promised, and hung up.

Oh, Ada, how could you do this to me? she wondered as she trudged out to the doctors' parking lot and shrugged off her coat to reveal the crisp, no-wrinkle sheath dress underneath.

Her Oldsmobile—a model chosen for its reliability and practicality—seemed to know its own way home from Irvine Doctors Medical Center. The air conditioner purred quietly, blotting out the warmth of a Southern California June day.

Actually, it was all the fault of the state lottery, Anne reflected as she drove.

Her longtime housekeeper, Ada Allen, had been an avid player. Last month, she'd finally hit pay dirt—twenty-five thousand dollars—and announced she was moving to Northern California to be with her daughter and grandchildren.

Was it possible to find another woman so efficient, so self-contained, so unirritating at the end of a hard day?

Turning onto one of the wide, straight boulevards of the planned city of Irvine, Anne mentally reviewed the course of her day. It was Wednesday, she reminded herself; halfway through the week.

She'd been on call the previous night and had delivered a baby at 5:00 a.m. There hadn't been time to go home before making her rounds and then reporting to the office for the usual prenatal checkups and Pap smears. After a lunchtime meeting of the hospital's perinatal committee, she'd performed two D & Cs and then the C-section.

Anne's partner, John Hernandez, was a perinatalogist, specializing in complicated pregnancies. Although Anne chiefly handled the less difficult cases, she often found herself filling in for him on C-sections and other surgeries. In truth, she admitted to herself, it gave her a sense of achievement when she was able to save a baby who, without careful monitoring and care, might have been lost. But it was hard, intense work, leaving her drained at the end of a long day.

No wonder Anne's shoulders ached and her feet felt swollen, even in her sensible flat shoes, and all she wanted was a bath and to be able to go to bed early.

Anne experienced only a trace of her usual surge of pride as she turned into the road she lived on, with its elegant and costly two-story houses, all tidily landscaped.

She'd come a long way from the dreamy-eyed girl she'd been as an undergraduate at UCLA, when she'd toyed with the idea of becoming an actress and working side by side with the handsome, single-minded actor whom she'd nearly

married. But on days like today, Anne wondered if maybe
she hadn't come a little too far, if she might not have been
happier if she'd found time along the way for a husband and
a child, like that squalling bit of humanity back at the hospital.

Oh, nonsense. It was just her puffy feet talking.

It was only five-thirty. Well, at least she'd have time to
catch her breath before confronting a roomful of would-be
housekeepers.

THE TRAFFIC WAS GETTING heavy by the time Jason Brant
piloted his restored 1964 Mustang convertible through
Newport Beach on the way to Irvine. He'd made a leisurely
journey down the coast from Santa Monica, enjoying the
smell of the salt breeze, the sight of bronzing bodies strewn
about the sand and the cheerful shouts of teenagers as they
darted across the road to the funky shops on the other side.

But now he was headed away from the coast, and the
landscape was changing.

What must once have been scenic coastal bluffs and fields
of orange groves were now covered with condominiums and
houses of cookie-cutter similarity. Everything looked as if
it had been lifted bodily from an architect's rendering, even
the wandering paseos that were supposed to be an improve-
ment on old-fashioned sidewalks but instead looked con-
trived, at least to Jason.

He smiled and shook his head. Still the young renegade
even at thirty-five, he scolded himself. How could his editor have thought otherwise? The man just didn't understand that political significance began at home. Literally.

Actually, Jason knew, he ought to be angry. His publisher had no business refusing to give him an advance until
his latest book was completed. By all rights he ought to take
the book elsewhere, but he liked his editor, and the company's printing was top quality, which was important with
photography.

Besides, having to conserve his funds had given him a splendid idea, one that dovetailed neatly with his plans for the new book.

What had finally decided him was the ad. "Housekeeper to Irvine physician. Live-in. Refs. reqd." He'd have to fudge on the references, but he'd gotten the impression that the doctor was single, when he spoke to the secretary, and he figured the guy would probably be relieved to have another man around, instead of some motherly woman who'd turn up her nose at overnight female guests or smoky, early-hours poker parties.

Or whatever games rich doctors in Irvine played these days.

Jason grinned ruefully. He'd have to watch himself. He still retained his hungry-days prejudices against rich folks, even though he wouldn't mind qualifying for that description himself. But, despite the warm reception of his first book, *The Private Life of a Revolutionary*, photography wasn't a field in which one was likely to make a fortune. That was all right with Jason. He was glad just to be able to make a living doing what he loved best.

It had been the greatest challenge of his life, spending three months at a training camp for revolutionaries in the Middle East. Jill had claimed she understood why he had to do it; only afterward, looking back, could he clearly see how unhappy she'd been with his long absence. He couldn't really blame her for leading such a wild life in New York, even though her spending sprees had nearly cleaned out their savings account.

Then there'd been *The Private Life of a Politician*. That time, Jill had gone with him on the campaign trail with a congressman, a low-key bigot whose hypocrisies Jason had managed to portray with his camera, even without the man's realizing it. Jill had enjoyed that trip, mainly because of all the parties and occasions for showing off her elegant wardrobe. She'd changed, he realized then, from the idealistic girl he'd met in college.

Maybe that was when their marriage had begun to come unglued. Or perhaps it was afterward, when Jason had begun to feel it was time to settle down, buy a house, think about starting a family. Jill wasn't ready for that, she said. He'd offered to compromise, but she'd decided it was time to strike out for herself and had gone to live with friends in New York. He didn't fight the divorce; sometimes people just drifted apart, he told himself, although the failure hurt.

The truth was, he decided as he turned onto a small residential street, that despite his spirit of adventure, he'd been the one who tried to make a home wherever they were. If it hadn't been for Jason, there never would have been a dinner cooked or laundry done or any of those other things wives were supposed to be so good at.

No wonder he felt qualified to apply for a job as a housekeeper.

Jason double-checked the address as he pulled up in front of a two-story house that looked very much like all the others on the street. Yep, this was perfect.

It was a long way from the slums of Tijuana, or even the rundown areas of Santa Ana, to this bastion of upper-middle-class achievement—a route that probably half or more of the maids had traveled. It was a contrast he meant to capture with the set of camera lenses that lay hidden in his trunk.

Underneath the upper-middle-class luxury of Orange County, Jason knew, lay deprivation and fear for some. In order to earn enough to support their families, maids often had to leave their children with relatives and live in their employer's house. Fearful of losing their job, they often worked long hours for low wages. Perhaps such conditions weren't unusual in the rest of the world, but it angered Jason to find such misery in his own country, amidst wealth. The conservative residents of Orange County talked a lot about their patriotism and their ideals, but they didn't always live up to their rhetoric. He supposed he wanted to hold up a mirror to the employers even more than he wanted to expose the situation to the general public.

Jason checked his watch. Five past six. Well, that wasn't bad timing, considering the leisurely course he'd taken. He strolled up the walk and pressed the doorbell.

A grey-haired, thin-faced woman answered. "Yes?"

"I have an appointment with Dr. Eldridge. About the housekeeping job."

The woman looked puzzled but stepped aside to let him enter. "We're supposed to wait in the living room. The doctor asked me to answer the door." From her aggrieved tone of voice, it sounded as if answering the door had been a great deal of trouble.

Jason felt a momentary pang of guilt as he entered the house and followed the woman. He certainly didn't want to deprive someone of a job she needed badly. On the other hand, this woman already looked defeated.

As Jason stepped into the living room, he made a mental note of the plush carpet, the high-beamed ceiling and over-size fireplace and the costly, subdued furnishings with co-ordinated paintings, undoubtedly selected by an interior designer.

This confirmed his mental picture of Dr. Eldridge as a middle-aged man who was probably divorced and who spent most of his spare time at the racquet club, or chasing women, but who also worked sixty to eighty hours a week to rake in the money. Not someone who spent much time making a house a home.

Which suited Jason just fine.

The doctor had thoughtfully set out some magazines—*Discover*, the science magazine, and *National Geographic*. He wondered if the guy ever bothered to read them himself.

Two other women, in addition to the one who'd opened the door, were staring at him curiously from where they sat on the couch. He pretended not to notice their scrutiny.

Jason had just settled down with a copy of *Discover* when an inner door opened and a plump woman stepped out, nodding obsequiously. Behind her was an attractive woman whom he guessed to be in her mid-thirties.

So the doctor was married, after all. He swallowed hard against his disappointment. That meant he probably wouldn't have a chance at the job.

The younger woman glanced at him in surprise. "Can I help you?"

He explained why he was there.

"I see." The woman frowned and tapped her foot lightly on the carpet. "Well—all right. You'll have to be last to be interviewed, though. The others have been waiting."

"Fair enough." He grinned. She didn't grin back.

Jason watched as she turned to summon one of the other applicants. Mrs. Eldridge was tall and capable looking— qualities he appreciated after Jill's flightiness—with a trim figure and dark-blond hair pulled back into a bun.

All in all, she was a damn good-looking woman. Yet the plainness with which she was dressed and the starchy way she moved hinted that she was largely unaware of her own allure.

No doubt Dr. Eldridge didn't pay much attention to his wife. Idly, Jason wondered if they had children. He wouldn't mind that; he liked kids, and he'd enjoy looking after them, as long as they weren't spoiled brats. With this woman for a mother, he had a feeling they wouldn't be.

Patiently, with the magazine in hand, he sat back to wait his turn.

EVEN A DOSE of Extra-Strength Tylenol wasn't doing much for Anne's headache as she questioned the last of the three women in the tight confines of her home office. The man,

of course, was out of the question for the job, but since Ellie had arranged for him to drive all the way out here, Anne
knew she had to give him the courtesy of an interview.

"I don't do windows or move furniture, anything heavy
like that." The thin-faced applicant, sitting ramrod straight
in her chair, reminded Anne of the farmer's wife in the
painting *American Gothic*. "And I must have my weekends off."

Anne tapped the erasered end of the pencil against the
woman's résumé. "Naturally, you would have two days off
per week, but my former housekeeper occasionally rear-
ranged her schedule when I was entertaining...."

"I have other commitments." The woman glanced down
at the disorder of bills and circulars on Anne's desk, her
nostrils flaring slightly.

"Now, about cooking..."

"My day begins at eight and ends at five, like anybody
else's." The applicant stared Anne straight in the eye. "I
believe in sticking to schedules."

"I see." Anne groaned inwardly. The first candidate had
lacked references, spoke little English and didn't appear to
know much about housekeeping. The second lady chatted
on and on endlessly, a habit that would drive Anne crazy
within a matter of days, and also had revealed a number of
personal details about her previous employer. The last thing
Anne needed was to have her private life discussed all over
the neighborhood. She'd sent both women home with her
thanks and a promise to call them within a few days. If she
got really desperate she might have to hire one of them, although she certainly hoped not.

But this woman was intolerable. Anne would be glad to
give a housekeeper extra time off during the day just so there
was a hot meal waiting when she got home from work.
What she really needed, she told herself wryly, was a wife.

"Well, thank you." Anne stood up, bringing the interview to an end. "I'll be notifying everyone within a few days."

"I'd like to know by Friday, if you don't mind." The woman collected her purse.

"Very well." Anne wondered what it was this woman did on weekends that was so inflexible. Her imagination conjured up a murderer son who required weekend visits in prison, or a ring for which this woman smuggled in drugs from Mexico....

She certainly was tired to think of such nonsense, she scolded herself as she showed the woman out.

Anne took a moment to reapply lipstick, then chuckled at her own vanity. True, the man—Jason Brant was his name—was well-groomed and rather nice looking, but she was interviewing him as a prospective employee, not as a boyfriend.

The résumé he'd mailed to Ellie was rather scant, and under references he'd put merely: "On request." Her instinct was to dismiss him quickly, but she suspected a well-to-do physician would be a likely target for a discrimination suit if the man didn't feel he'd been given a fair hearing.

Fine. She'd question him, just as she'd done with the others. And then she'd ask Ellie to put the ad back in the paper.

Chapter Two

The office seemed to shrink to even tinier proportions than usual as the man relaxed in the chair opposite Anne, his long legs stretching so close to hers that they nearly touched.

"Have you worked as a housekeeper before?" She couldn't help noticing the intelligent glimmer in his dark-brown eyes, a hint of humor and of something deeper that intrigued her. And then there was the softly mussed but well-cut brown hair that looked as if he'd just gotten out of bed, as if someone ought to run her fingers through it....

Anne was surprised by her own thoughts.

"Only unofficially." His calm self-confidence made her feel as if he, not she, were conducting the interview.

"Unofficially?"

From an expensive leather portfolio, he produced several letters. Curious, Anne inspected them. One was from a lawyer, attesting that he'd eaten Jason's cooking on a number of occasions and found it excellent. Another was from a woman named Jill Brant, attesting to Jason's skills as a housecleaner and launderer.

"Is Jill Brant a relative of yours?" She handed the letters back to him.

"My ex-wife." He spoke easily, amusement quirking the corners of his mouth.

Anne started to choke and ended up coughing. "You brought a recommendation from your ex-wife?"

"Who knows my housekeeping skills better than she does?" Jason spread his hands expansively. He had nice hands, Anne noted from the corner of her eye—slightly roughened, as if he knew the meaning of real work, but well kept and clean under the nails.

She blushed, hoping he hadn't noticed her inspection and half-aware that she was focusing on the peripheral portions of his anatomy to keep her gaze from the lean rugged length of him. There was something unsettling about the man. Why did she keep getting the feeling that there was more to him than appeared on the résumé?

"Why do you want to work as a housekeeper? Don't you have some other occupation? I mean, it is a bit unusual for a man to seek a job like this, particularly when he has no previous experience." She was pleased by the professional, clipped tone of her voice. All business.

"Well, I have done some professional photography, but my divorce pretty well cleaned me out financially." The strong bone structure of his face and slightly pronounced jaw were offset by the velvety softness of his eyes, she noted before dragging her attention back to his words. "I thought this would be a secure setting, doing work I enjoy, while I indulge in taking the kind of photographs that interest me."

"I see." It was out of the question, of course, but how was she going to tell him that?

Before she could find the words, Jason took the initiative. "Tell me more about you and Dr. Eldridge, about your life-style. Do you have children?"

"I beg your pardon?" She gaped at him for a moment.

It was his turn to look confused. "Excuse me. I just assumed you were Mrs. Eldridge...."

Anne felt the heat rising to her cheeks. "My friends call me doctor."

He ducked his head, a gesture she found appealingly boyish. "And I thought I was the most liberated male in Southern California. My apologies, doctor. Somehow I was picturing a man."

At least he'd brought the subject of gender out in the open, she reflected. "And I was picturing a woman."

"For the job?"

"As you can imagine, a single woman like me would find it awkward to have a man around the house." Anne took a deep breath. She wished he wouldn't stare at her so intently, as if he were regarding her in a new light, as if . . . as if he'd become aware of her as a woman. An unmarried woman. "Besides the way it might look to others, there are questions of privacy."

Instead of taking the hint and agreeing with her, Jason shook his head. "I'm sure you have some living quarters set aside for the housekeeper in a place this big."

She admitted there was a bedroom and bath off the kitchen, while her own quarters were upstairs. "Nevertheless, I'm naturally in the habit of wandering around in my bathrobe." She cut off the words abruptly. Why on earth was she disclosing such personal details to this total stranger?

"On the other hand, you might want to consider the advantages." He leaned forward, his eyes catching hers and locking them in an intimate way. "The added security of having a man on the premises, for example."

"I have an excellent burglar-alarm system." *Besides, what am I going to do for protection when the most dangerous man around is already living here?*

"And there must be times when furniture needs to be moved or there's other heavy work that most women couldn't handle."

"I've never denied that men could be useful for their brawn." Anne smiled to take the edge off her words. "But my gardener comes once a week, and he handles any heavy work for a few extra dollars.''

"Then there's my cooking." The man certainly didn't give up easily! "You're probably used to rather plain fare from your housekeeper—meat loaf, or maybe enchiladas. Well?"

Reluctantly, Anne nodded. Ada's repertoire had extended only as far as frying chicken and broiling steaks.

"Cooking's always been a hobby of mine. French, Italian, Chinese—you name it." From the glow on his face, Jason was obviously enjoying this match of wits. "Let me tell you about my fettucine. I have my own pasta-machine, and I use heavy cream, lots of butter..."

"Cholesterol," Anne pointed out.

"Doctors never pay any attention to their diets. Everybody knows that." He leaned back, as if he'd won his point, which, in fact, he had. Anne thought ruefully of her own hasty lunches at the hospital cafeteria, usually involving overcooked green beans, a gravy-laden entree and Jell-O for dessert.

"Well..."

Unexpectedly, he sprang to his feet. "Like right now. You haven't eaten dinner yet, have you?"

"No," she admitted, reluctantly following him out of the office and down the hall to the kitchen. "I was thinking of sending out for pizza."

Jason's long legs cut across the expanse of off-white tile and he swung open the door of the side-by-side refrigerator-freezer. Fortunately, Ada had gone grocery shopping before she left on Monday, and it was well-stocked.

"You'll need to use up some of these vegetables before they wilt." Jason began removing packages from the shelves and laying them on the counter. "Got an apron?"

Anne pointed wordlessly to a towel rack at one side, and Jason equipped himself with a black apron trimmed in red and white. She knew she ought to stop him, but darn it, she was hungry. Maybe she could hire him for an interim period, a week or so, until she found a permanent house-keeper. "I suppose I could take you on temporarily...."

"I'll tell you what." He began unwrapping a package of Swiss steak. "We'll have a trial period of one month. If at the end of that time either of us is dissatisfied, we'll call it quits and no hard feelings. What do you say, doc?"

She chuckled inwardly at his use of the nickname, which managed to sound both respectful and irreverent at the same time. "Well, a month might be a bit long."

"Now, you have to be fair about this." Wielding a heavy knife that resembled a miniature hatchet, he began chopping the steak into narrow strips. "I'll be giving up my apartment in Santa Monica, so naturally I'd need to stay at least a month. But I'm willing to gamble that you'll keep me on permanently, once you get used to me."

With a sigh, Anne sank down into a chair at the kitchen table, watching the whirlwind of energy with which he chopped everything up and located the appropriate seasonings, from teriyaki sauce to fresh garlic.

She was too tired to throw him out of here and too hungry to resist the mouth-watering smells arising from the stove. A few weeks. What could go wrong in so short a time?

"Well, all right," she said. "But only for a month."

AFTER SO MANY YEARS spent traveling, Jason had reduced his possessions to the bare minimum—which included the pasta maker and a cappuccino machine that wheezed and groaned like a calliope but made delicious coffee.

He managed to stuff most of his possessions into his car and make it down to Irvine by Thursday afternoon. Anne—or should he call her Dr. Eldridge?—had informed him she'd be gone until late that night, lecturing to a nursing class, so he could move in at his leisure. She'd given him a key and the combination to the burglar alarm; trusting woman, he reflected.

As he turned the car away from the coast and into the predigested city of Irvine, Jason felt doubts begin to nag at him, doubts that he'd shoved aside last night in his elation at having landed this job.

The fact was, he was coming here under false pretenses. In much the same way that he'd exposed that politician for the hypocrite he really was, Jason intended to show this wealthy community its own darker side. Through his photographs, the public would see the harsh private lives of the servants who kept the rich people in comfort and ease.

He didn't like the feeling that he was double-crossing Anne.

She certainly wasn't like any other woman he'd ever met before—any more than she was like the imaginary middle-aged Dr. Eldridge who played racquetball and chased young women.

There was a fundamental honesty about her that appealed to him. And a sense of humor. And a wariness in those green eyes that made him want to win her over, to make her laugh and trust him.

So how could he violate that trust?

On the other hand, perhaps he was underestimating her, Jason told himself as he paused for a traffic light, one part of his mind noting that it must have cost the city well over a hundred thousand dollars just to install the computer-controlled lights and pressure plates at a single intersection.

Anne might make a lot of money, but he didn't get the impression she was obsessed by it. In fact, judging by her practical and not particularly stylish clothes and her long working hours, he suspected she got little enjoyment from her high income.

Perhaps she would understand, even sympathize with his project. But he couldn't tell her about it, not yet. She would never accept him as a housekeeper if she knew he was really there for another purpose. And he wanted the experience, wanted to know firsthand how it felt to launder and mop and dust day after day, wanted a common ground on which to meet the cleaning ladies in the neighborhood.

Pulling up in front of the house, Jason began unloading the car.

He certainly did like this kitchen, he reflected as he passed through it on the way to his cheerful bedroom, which looked out on a tiny manicured lawn and a bed of marigolds and pansies. The kitchen was huge and well designed, perfect for gourmet cooking; he'd long dreamed of having a facility such as this, with butcher-block counters, double ovens and a gleaming array of copper pots and pans.

His thoughts returned to Anne. Apparently she didn't cook, but Jason knew better than to equate domesticity with femininity.

What kind of a love life did she have? Obviously, no man had awakened the woman within her; he'd seen that at a glance. Yet there was enough sensuality left over, even unconsciously, to intrigue him. How would she look with her hair down, and a glittery dress revealing that splendid form, and a touch of the right eye shadow to bring out the green in her eyes?

Stowing his camera bags under the bed, he went out for another load and tried to get his thoughts back onto a more mundane level.

In all fairness, he admitted to himself as he carted in two suitcases of clothing, this elegant life-style had a certain appeal. He could get used to living in a fine house with five bedrooms and four bathrooms—Anne had given him a tour of the premises last night—as well as a video recorder, compact-disc player and two color televisions, including one in his own quarters.

It's only for a few months, he told himself firmly. But there was no rule that said he couldn't enjoy himself in the meantime, was there?

Anne had assured him he wouldn't need to start work until Friday, and as far as he could see, everything was spick-

and-span. Still, out of curiosity, Jason inspected the laundry room, which was connected by a chute with Anne's upstairs bedroom, and noticed a pile of delicate lingerie in rainbow pastels, peach and soft blue and aqua. Now, who would have suspected something such as that underneath that businesslike dress?

Grinning, Jason turned away. His new employer clearly had forgotten about this aspect of her privacy, and he certainly wasn't going to remind her.

He could go back to Santa Monica for a last load, but that would mean getting stuck in rush-hour traffic. No, he had the apartment through the weekend, and he could live without the remaining odds and ends for a day or so.

Deciding instead to enjoy the rest of the day, Jason changed into his swim trunks and walked out through sliding glass doors onto the redwood deck, its corners anchored by wooden half barrels spilling out flowering geraniums.

Spreading a towel on a chaise lounge, he was preparing to sun himself when he heard a yapping noise from the house next door and glanced over.

"You get back in there!" snapped a woman's voice with a slight Hispanic accent as a screen door slapped shut.

Jason swung to his feet and walked over to the low dividing wall to take a look.

Standing on the rear deck was a large-boned, dark-haired woman carrying a bucket and mop. Dancing about her feet was a second mop, which on closer inspection revealed itself to be an indefinable species of dog.

"Need some help?" Jason called.

The woman shot him a look full of frustration. "He's always under my feet. And try to catch him? Not me. I'm too old."

Jason vaulted over the wall and strode across the lawn to scoop up the eager ball of fur, which promptly licked his cheek.

"Thanks." The woman opened the door. "Just toss him in." Jason obeyed, and she managed to close the screen just in time to stop the dog from bounding out. He sat inside, peering out through the mesh, and yapped once, with a wistful note that made Jason wish he could let the dog out again.

The maid was wringing her mop. "You just move in next door?"

"I'm the new housekeeper," Jason said.

The woman straightened and regarded him dubiously, from his bare feet to his swim trunks to his uncovered chest. "Oh?"

"My name's Jason." He stuck out his hand and she shook it with her own, which was still damp from the mop.

"Rosa." She cocked her head. "Are you really the housekeeper?"

"That's right." He leaned against the wooden railing that ran around the deck. "Actually, I don't start work until tomorrow. Dr. Eldridge was kind enough to let me move in a day early."

Rosa frowned at her mop. "This is one of those new things? A man cleans house for a woman?" At his nod, she reflected for a moment and then said, "You want to come inside for some coffee?"

He accepted with pleasure and soon found himself sitting in a kitchen much like Anne's, except that it had been decorated with an unfortunate taste for cheap knickknacks and cartoon-covered curtains.

Rosa, he quickly gathered, was too Americanized to be an appropriate subject for his book. Her English was excellent, which meant she'd been in the United States most of her life, and he drew her out enough to learn that she had several grown children who held down responsible jobs.

But Rosa knew every other maid for blocks around and could tell him who was newly arrived from Mexico or Central America, who had children not living with them, and anything else he wanted to know. She was a gold mine of information.

It was too soon to admit his real purpose in being here, but an hour later, as he bid Rosa a reluctant farewell, Jason had a real feeling of accomplishment. With the help of his new friend, he should be able to find the right subject without difficulty.

Not bad for his first day in Irvine, he reflected as he jumped back over the fence and went to collect his towel.

It was too late now for sunbathing, he noticed with regret. But if he scheduled his chores well, he ought to have time for some tanning tomorrow before Anne arrived home for dinner.

Feeling quite pleased with himself, Jason went inside.

FRIDAY WAS ONE of those days Anne wished would end almost before it began. One of her first patients was an unwed teenager who cried when her pregnancy test came up positive, and Anne spent nearly an hour comforting her and talking. Finally she referred the girl to a service that offered free counseling and adoption referrals.

As a result, Anne was late for all her other morning appointments. The patients were annoyed, and her own usual even temper began to fray by noon.

Then one of her maternity patients developed complications, and Anne had to perform an emergency cesarean. The baby and mother, fortunately, were both healthy—probably in better shape than the doctor, she told herself wearily.

By six o'clock she was exhausted, hungry and crabby.

Anne had barely seen Jason the day before, merely calling out a good-night as she fetched a snack of milk and graham crackers to carry up to her room. Now, walking into the house, she was pleased to be greeted by the familiar lemon scent of cleansers and to see that the carpets had been vacuumed.

Maybe she hadn't made such a big mistake after all.

Her partner, John, had taken the whole situation as a lark when their receptionist told him about it yesterday, and at the hospital the other doctors had given Anne quite a bit of joshing about her new kept man. More and more she'd questioned the wisdom of her decision, but now, sniffing the aroma of ham and baked apples, she decided she could have done worse.

Heading for the kitchen, she stopped in the doorway, shocked.

Her first impression was that Jason was wearing nothing underneath his apron. On second glance, she realized that he had on a rather skimpy pair of tan bathing trunks that hid almost none of his lean body. From where she stood, Anne had an unobscured view of the dark fur on his legs, the play of muscles across his back and, in between, a very tight and nicely shaped derriere that twitched appealingly as he moved.

Oh, good heavens. She wasn't used to thinking about men this way. And Jason was—well, he lived here, for heaven's sake!

"I—" She cleared her throat as she sought a way to make a joke out of her embarrassment. "I don't know why I bothered to study anatomy. You're a complete lesson in yourself." Anne set her briefcase down on a chair.

"Actually—" Jason finished grating cheese and popped a leftover crumb into his mouth "—I was sunbathing and the time sort of got away from me. I meant to put some clothes on before you got here."

"Oh, don't get dressed on my account." Anne waved her hand airily, half of her mind wondering at her own light-hearted approach and the other half feeling as if she'd fallen down the rabbit hole and the whole world had turned topsy-turvy. "I'll just wander on upstairs and scrape off the day's grime."

"Dinner should be ready in fifteen minutes."

"Great."

When she came down again, Anne was relieved to see that Jason had changed into jeans and a formfitting navy sweat shirt that made him look like an athlete. She wondered at her own reaction. She hardly ever noticed how men were built—but then, baggy white coats didn't do much for a man's shape, and that was mostly what she saw.

The truth was, she acknowledged silently, that she wouldn't have been particularly stirred by Jason's looks if he were an airhead. But his efficiency around the house had already impressed her, not to mention his incredible cooking. And when she'd glanced into his room his morning, she'd noticed some striking photographs on the wall, scenes whose settings varied from everyday life in small-town America to the Middle East, shot with a keen eye for lighting and detail. When asked, Jason had modestly admitted shooting them and then quickly changed the subject.

Now, she saw, he'd set the table with a small vase of freshly picked flowers and a bottle of wine. "That's a nice touch," she said.

"I didn't know if you were in the habit of eating with the help, but since we're both hungry..."

"No, no, perfectly all right." She pulled out one of the rattan-backed chairs at the kitchen table. "Ada preferred to snack rather than eat full meals, but actually, I don't mind the company."

They didn't say much for a while, digging into the ham, baked apples, cheese-covered potatoes and salad. Anne wondered if her body might revolt against eating so much healthy food at one sitting.

As her hunger waned, her attention returned to Jason. Unselfconscious as a cat, he savored his food, apparently having worked up quite an appetite on her patio. At least, she assumed that's where he'd added to his tan, which was a degree or so darker than it had been on Wednesday.

Quickly, Anne dug into the remnants of her apple. Her train of thought was entirely too dangerous. Now, wasn't there something she'd meant to ask him, before she'd caught sight of his nearly nude body in the kitchen?

"Oh." She set down her fork. "I have a favor to ask."

"Shoot." He sipped at his wine.

"Normally, Saturday and Sunday will be your days off, but I hoped you wouldn't mind taking off Sunday and Monday this week. I've invited a dinner guest for tomorrow night, and I'd really appreciate it if you could cook. Of course, you're free to go out for the evening afterward."

Jason studied her with interest. "I wouldn't dream of it. Suppose you need a chaperon?"

Anne glared at him. "I hardly think that's likely."

"All the same, I did point out the advantages of having a male protector on the premises." He smiled lazily. "Don't worry. I'll fade right into the background. Your friend will hardly notice I'm around.

It was probably best to ignore his teasing tone. "I thought perhaps we could have something French. You did say that was one of your specialties."

"Leave it to me."

Irrationally, she found herself feeling embarrassed. What would Jason think of the rather pedantic Horace Swann, M.D., gastroenterologist cum laude and ad nauseam? Her own opinion was that Horace was not only balding and rotund but rather boring. Furthermore, his endless pontificating on intestinal disorders had a depressing effect on the appetite.

Still, he'd escorted her to a county-medical-association function, and she felt obligated to repay the courtesy. Besides, Horace might not be the most exciting date in the world, but he was better than sitting home watching TV.

Not that Anne didn't have other men she went out with occasionally. But not as many as she would have liked. First of all, she didn't meet very many unattached men; second, many of the ones she did meet preferred scatterbrained and doting women half their age; and third, her field of choice was rather narrow. How many men were there whom she could consider an equal? She'd discovered long ago that most men were intimidated by a woman doctor unless they, too, had advanced degrees and high earning power; that narrowed her selection of dates considerably.

"By the way..." Jason cleared away the dishes and poured them each another glass of wine. "No criticism intended, but I've been wondering how it is you grew up without learning to cook. Unless I'm mistaken about that?"

Anne shook her head. "I can make a few things, but nothing fancy. My mother was a tyrant in the kitchen. She still is, actually; when I visit my parents in Denver, she won't let me near a stove."

"Probably a wise woman."

"No doubt." Why did his comment bother her? Anne had never particularly wanted to be domestic. "Actually, I was pretty good at opening cans and heating the contents when I was in college."

"Stanford?" he guessed.

"Just plain old UCLA." This man must imagine she came from a rich family, Anne realized. "My father's a retired army officer and my mother teaches high-school English."

"Tell me how you came to be a doctor. Were you one of those little girls who listen to their dolls with a stethoscope?" His eyes seemed to shine at her across the table, or maybe, Anne reflected, she'd drunk too much wine.

"Actually, I started out wanting to be an actress."

Under his gentle prodding, she poured out the story of her college days and of Ken, a professional actor whom she'd met when she was nineteen. At first, she'd been thrilled by the idea of joint careers, of becoming another onstage couple like Jessica Tandy and Hume Cronyn.

That summer, she'd agreed to stay for a month with Ken at his Hollywood apartment. It was a rude awakening. His days were spent going out on fruitless auditions, trying to reach his agent by phone and rehearsing an unpaid role at a hole-in-the-wall theater. Anne quickly realized that she came in a distant second to his career.

Furthermore, by the time she'd wiped out her second colony of cockroaches in his run-down flat and helped Ken mail out the third bunch of photographs to producers who would probably throw them in the trash, she'd realized that the acting life was not for her.

Temporarily at a loss, Anne went home to Denver, where she volunteered to work at a women's health-care center. It was during those remaining summer months that she realized what she really wanted to do with her life.

"There's nothing more rewarding than helping other people." Anne rested her chin on the palm of her hand, gazing dreamily across the table at the quietly attentive Jason. "And obstetrics and gynecology is particularly satisfying because so often I see results right away, which rarely happens if you're, say, treating cancer or managing a patient's diabetes. Sometimes when I can correct an infertility problem or catch an abnormal Pap smear in time to prevent cancer, I feel like I've been given a gift, to hold lives in my hands and help pat them back into shape."

"That's a lovely image." His voice was deep and thoughtful.

"Unfortunately, sometimes things get so hectic I don't have time to think about the significance of what I'm doing." Roused from her reverie, Anne pushed back her chair and carried her dishes to the counter. "But I'm not complaining."

"Dessert?" Jason stretched as he stood up. "There's ice cream in the freezer." He walked toward her and reached around, rescuing her glass from the rim of the sink, where she'd accidentally set it. "I hope you're more cautious when you perform surgery."

"It's—a matter of concentration." Anne's breath came more quickly as his arm brushed her shoulder. Their bodies were only inches apart, his hip nearly touching hers through the simple sun dress she'd thrown on.

"I see." He paused, his mouth close to her lips, as if he were about to kiss her. "Is it really? I mean, a matter of concentration?" The boyish confusion only added to her sense of a growing intimacy between them.

"I think I'd better pass on dessert." Anne forced herself to step back. "Thanks anyway."

"My pleasure." He was still regarding her with a curious expression, almost of surprise. Or perhaps it was speculation.

"I—I usually sleep late on Saturdays, and then I have an appointment at the hairdresser's." The words poured out, creating an invisible fence around her. "I'll be on call in the afternoon, and I'll probably be catching up on my reading, so you're free to do whatever you like, as long as it isn't noisy." She suddenly realized that he hadn't asked if it was all right to bring dates over. Did he have a girlfriend? Why should she care whether he did? "Horace should be here around seven...."

"Horace?" Jason grinned unexpectedly. "That's really his name?"

"It runs in his family. For three generations." As he'd told Anne in great detail, she remembered. "You might need to do some extra shopping. I'll leave out grocery money." Resisting the urge to back up cautiously, she added a quick good-night and turned to go.

"Don't worry." Jason hadn't moved from his position beside the sink. "If you need any help getting ready tomorrow night, with zippers or anything, just let me know."

"Sure." Furious with herself for her own inexplicable panic, Anne fled out of the kitchen and up to the safety of her bedroom.

Why had she ever thought it was a good idea to hire Jason Brant, regardless of how well he cooked? He was entirely too disturbing, too masculine and too cocky.

And not her sort of man at all, Anne reminded herself. She'd always gone for the steadier sort, ever since she discovered how unhappy she would have been if she'd married Ken. Jason had something of the same zest for life, the same sense of daring—he ought to make a good friend and employee, she decided firmly. And that was all.

Chapter Three

Saturday was, on the surface, a quiet day. As she had planned, Anne slept late, got her hair trimmed and spent the afternoon reading medical journals.

Or rather, she spent the afternoon staring at the open pages of a magazine.

Her ears were following every movement Jason made. She knew when he went out to sunbathe, when he chatted with someone across the back fence, when he came in to change clothes and when he left to go to the supermarket.

After he returned, his soft whistling in the kitchen didn't annoy her the way whistling usually did. It had a Huckleberry Finn lightheartedness that reminded Anne of finding violets in the spring when she was a girl, and of squishing mud between her toes as she stood on the creek bed, fishing with her father.

Wait a minute. She'd never gone fishing with her father. They hadn't lived anywhere near any creeks that she could recall. And her parents would never have let her go barefoot in the mud.

This man was definitely having a strange effect on her.

There must be something to the old saying that opposites attract, Anne told herself, forcing her attention back to the printed page. No doubt it was the novelty of Jason Brant that fascinated her.

Like hell it was.

She was almost relieved when the telephone rang. She could use a nice, minor problem right now, a patient who needed to be checked at the hospital, something to get her out of the house.

But the answering service connected her with a maternity patient who had developed a sore throat, and all Anne had to do was telephone a prescription to the woman's pharmacist.

She should have known better. In obstetrics, emergencies happened only at two o'clock in the morning or on Christmas Day.

The hands on Anne's watch inched toward five-thirty. Too impatient to sit still any longer, she went upstairs to change for her date.

Originally, she had intended to wear a simple navy shirtwaist with pearls, but that hardly seemed festive enough to accompany what she presumed would be an elaborate French dinner. Besides, although she wasn't particularly crazy about Horace Swann, she felt an inexplicable reluctance to let Jason know that.

Instead, Anne decided on a dress she'd bought for her parents' thirty-fifth anniversary party, a flattering emerald crepe with a deeply slashed V-neck that was set off by a rhinestone-studded belt and matching shoes.

The intense color required complementary makeup, of course, so Anne dug through her cosmetics drawer to find the little-used palette of green eye shadows. Bright scarlet lipstick, a dab of blusher and eyebrow pencil—she sat back to regard herself. Satisfied, she brushed out her hair and fixed it in a sophisticated French twist, fastened with a jeweled comb.

Horace wasn't going to know what hit him, she thought as she pirouetted in front of the mirror. That was, assuming Horace would notice anything not shaped like an intestine.

It was still only six-thirty, but Anne decided her duties as hostess required that she go downstairs to make sure everything was in order.

Jason had straightened up the living room and put away her journals, she noted as she walked past toward the kitchen. And, spotting a vase filled with daisies, she had to admire his thoughtfulness in picking those up this afternoon.

Why didn't she ever think of things like that? Anne wondered as she headed down the hall. Unlike most women, she sometimes felt she'd been born without an ounce of romance in her soul. Even as a teenager, she'd never hung around the perfume counters trying on scents the way other girls did or bought hairstyling magazines and tried setting her hair different ways.

For some reason, the observation left her feeling vaguely dissatisfied, as if she'd slipped up somewhere. Anne shook away the thought and poked her head into the kitchen.

Attired in a discreet pair of slacks and a polo shirt, Jason was chopping shallots on the cutting board. Set out on the counter was an impressive array of spices, white wine, vegetables and chicken.

"You seem to have everything under control." Anne hovered a few feet away. "Is there anything else you need?"

Jason looked up. "Yes. You could sit down and keep me company." His gaze moved slowly across her face and down to the dress, lingered for a moment on the soft swell of cleavage revealed by the neckline, and proceeded down her stocking-smooth legs. "You look terrific. This Horace must be someone special."

"He's one of the most prominent gastroenterologists in Orange County." As she sat down, Anne realized that her answer must not have been what he expected, but what else could she honestly say? "What are you fixing?"

"Chicken in wine sauce with glazed carrots and new potatoes, followed by chocolate mousse. I hope that's all right.

You seemed to be willing to leave the menu up to me." He spoke over his shoulder while continuing to chop the onions deftly.

"Sounds terrific."

Silence stretched between them, broken only by the chunk-chunk of the knife against the wooden board. There was something appealingly offbeat about the sight of such a well-constructed male form clad in a black apron, attending to domestic duties, Anne mused. Somehow Jason managed to imbue every movement with intense masculinity; in fact, he appeared to have taken charge of the kitchen like a captain ruling a pirate ship. No potato would dare to emerge half-cooked beneath his command; no butter would have the nerve to blacken and burn.

The irony of his position struck her again. Jason just didn't seem like the type to be satisfied with a low-paying, dead-end job as a housekeeper.

On the other hand, Anne had known professionals who chose to work at a routine occupation for a while in order to concentrate on some creative project. Jason had mentioned something about taking pictures, she recalled.

"Tell me about your photography." She crossed her long legs, being careful not to snag her stockings with the rhinestone-covered shoes.

Jason stopped cutting the onions. For a moment, Anne thought she'd said something to startle him, but then she saw that he had finished his task and was transferring the shallots to a plate.

"Well, I've always been fascinated by how much people reveal of their inner personalities in the way they look and move and dress." His back still toward her, he began unwrapping a package of chicken. "I like to take pictures of people at their ordinary tasks and see how much I can reveal of what lies beneath—of their thoughts and fears and hopes. Not to mention vices."

"That sounds challenging." Anne wasn't sure it was possible to show so much with a still camera, but she was impressed by Jason's concept. "You said you did some professional photography?"

"Oh, from time to time." Expertly, he skinned the chicken and began removing it from the bone. "Actually, my ex-wife and I did some traveling, and I took photos wherever we went."

"I see." She supposed he must have sold scenic shots to travel magazines. That couldn't have paid very well, but he obviously wasn't unduly concerned with accumulating material possessions, a quality that was rare among the people Anne had met these last few years. It brought back, with a twinge of nostalgia, the dedication of her theater friends during the early years at college. "I take it housekeeping isn't something you plan to do permanently."

"Well, no." What expressive shoulders he had, Anne couldn't help noticing as Jason opened another package of chicken. What power he conveyed, even in such simple chores.... She bit her lip and returned to the subject under discussion. "Do you want to pursue photography full-time?"

"Eventually, yes."

She wished he would talk about himself more freely. Anne hesitated, not wanting to pry, but finally said, "Did you grow up around here?"

"Boston. My mother was ill a lot, so I learned to help out around the house." Jason removed the chicken to a pan and began scrubbing the cutting board.

The doorbell rang. Anne glanced at her watch and saw that it was seven o'clock on the nose. With a sigh, she went to greet Horace Swann, M.D.

STIRRING UP WHIPPED CREAM for the chocolate mousse, Jason kept his ears tuned to the desultory conversation emanating from the dining room.

What on earth did Anne see in a man like Horace? The bald head and paunch could be overlooked; in fact, Jason told himself, he would have admired Anne if he'd thought she loved a man despite his lack of good looks.

But even taking into account Jason's ignorance of medical minutiae, it had become apparent within the first half hour that Anne's dinner guest was a crashing bore.

To make matters worse, from Jason's perspective, the man hardly appeared to notice what he was eating, shoveling the food into his mouth between descriptions of his latest medical research. For the first time, Jason understood how chefs in restaurants felt when their best meals were sent back by some picky eater who wanted the steak burned and the potatoes fried in deep fat.

It was possible that Anne had merely accepted a date with the man from politeness, of course. But that didn't explain the stunning dress she'd put on or the carefully applied makeup.

Jason jabbed viciously at the whipped cream. Love might be blind, but he couldn't allow Anne to waste her time on a fool like Horace.

Spooning the cream onto the mousse, he carried the two dishes out into the dining room.

Anne smiled up at him. In the indirect light from the chandelier, he thought her eyes had taken on an animated sparkle. Could that be a result of the ramblings of her pompous windbag of a date? Surely not, but Jason wasn't going to take that chance. He was not only her housekeeper but her protector, after all.

"Dr. Swann." Jason stood respectfully behind one of the straight-back chairs. "I hope I'm not interrupting?"

"Oh, no, no." The rotund physician waved a hand expansively.

"Actually, I had sort of a personal question to ask you." He saw Anne's eyebrow arch upward but ignored it. "You see, colitis runs in my family, and I've wondered if I might have inherited it."

Immediately, Swann began questioning him about symptoms clearly unfit for dinner-table discussion. Jason answered gravely, noticing with some regret that Anne had barely touched her dessert. He felt more than a twinge of embarrassment at having raised such an indelicate topic, but it was right in line with what the gastroenterologist had been prating about all evening.

"As a matter of fact, I'm involved in some research on hereditary aspects of colitis." Swann waved Jason into a chair. "Tell me about your family...."

Silently asking his mother's forgiveness, Jason described her problems with colitis in detail, feeling Anne's outraged glare boring into him all the while. Well, it was for her own good, he reminded himself.

"Why don't we adjourn to the living room?" Anne stood up and led the way. Jason hesitated, but Horace caught his arm and pulled him along.

Once in the living room, the gastroenterologist whipped out a note pad and began taking down Jason's comments, continuing to probe with questions for the next half hour. By then, Anne was having a hard time stifling her yawns, and Horace took his leave. He pumped Jason's hand, thanked him for a splendid evening, said a cursory farewell to Anne and bustled off into the night.

Well, Jason thought as he turned to face Anne's wrath, things *had* gone a bit farther than he'd expected, but his ploy had worked, hadn't it?

"Very nice," she said.

Jason waited.

"Is this free with your housekeeping services, or do you charge extra for entertaining my dates?" Clearly she didn't realize that her folded arms merely emphasized the womanly swell of her breasts, or that the way her chin was tipped upward made her mouth look deliciously kissable.

On the other hand, he told himself, if he gave in to temptation, he was likely to find himself out on the sidewalk in the wake of the good Dr. Swann.

"I'm really sorry." He tried to inject into his voice the appropriate degree of contriteness. "It was a matter that had been on my mind, you see, and he did seem interested, but I didn't expect to monopolize his attention." That was true enough, he told himself, so why did he feel a twinge of guilt?

He hadn't meant to hurt her by driving away a man who was worthy of her. But Horace Swann clearly wasn't.

He couldn't imagine that tubby blowhard taking the willowy Anne in his arms, murmuring soft phrases into her well-shaped ears or pressing his lips to hers. Not for one second could he visualize that man nuzzling her slender neck, or tracing the sweet valley between her breasts with his tongue, or...

Oh, Lord. What was he thinking?

Suddenly Jason realized that Anne wasn't glaring at him anymore. Her mouth was twitching in an odd way, and it struck him that she was trying hard not to giggle.

"All's well that ends well?" he prompted.

She burst out with a chuckle. "He is ridiculous, isn't he? Oh, Jason! But you have to promise never to do anything like this again, or I simply can't keep you around."

He lifted his right hand as if taking an oath. "I will never again mention my mother's colitis at the dinner table."

"That isn't what I meant!"

"Or in the living room."

"Jason!" She clutched her sides, tried to give him a dirty look and went off into gales of laughter. "Horace had no idea you were putting him on! He was so earnest! He'll probably present a paper about you at the next convention!"

"Are you on call tomorrow?" he asked suddenly.

"Not until evening."

"How would you like to drive up to Santa Monica with me?" Now that the idea had struck him, it was obvious he and Anne were meant to spend the day together. "I've got to pick up a last load of stuff at my apartment. It's right on the beach, so if you want to bring a bathing suit, we could go for a dip."

Anne hesitated. "Actually, I didn't make much progress on my reading today, and I was planning to use tomorrow to catch up."

"Don't you think a break would do you good?" Jason could see she was about to argue, so he hurried on. "You need to be fresh to concentrate on your cases, you know. I'd say a little R and R was in order."

He could see the duty-bound physician in Anne warring with the lively young woman. Finally, she said, "Well, maybe just for a few hours..."

"Now go and get some sleep." He headed for the dining room before she could change her mind. "Leave the cleaning up to me. Breakfast is at nine."

"Jason." Standing there in the hallway with her eyes wide in the dim light, she looked like a little girl.

"Mmm-hmm?"

"Thanks." Anne's mouth stretched upward at the corners. "Tonight really was awfully dull until you came in."

He gave her a mock bow. "I aim to please, *madame*." Feeling a growing impulse to stride across the intervening space and sweep her into his arms, he forced himself to turn and hurry away.

This was becoming a dangerous assignment, Jason told himself as he cleared the dishes from the dining table. He'd never expected his rich physician to turn out to be a vulnerable and infinitely desirable woman.

Well, they were both adults, he reminded himself, fitting the plates into the dishwasher. Neither of them was going to get carried away. They could enjoy their mutual attraction as a harmless flirtation, and maybe in the process Ann would come to accept the feminine self she evidently preferred to lock away.

He was doing her a favor, actually. By the time Jason was through rescuing Anne from herself, she'd be ready for a real love affair with some appropriately well-established doctor or lawyer who had a whole lot more to offer than Horace Swann, M.D.

Yes, he was only doing this for Anne's own good, Jason mused as he cleaned the counters and sink. And in the meantime, of course, he would serve as her mentor, guiding and protecting the butterfly Anne as she emerged from the cocoon in which she'd hidden for so long.

If the thought of her finding happiness in another man's arms wrenched at his heart in an inexplicable way, well, that was probably the way a parent felt when a child grew up and left home, Jason told himself. It certainly couldn't mean any more than that.

Chapter Four

Jason couldn't have conjured up better weather on Sunday if he'd tried. It was a postcard-perfect Southern California day, without even the morning fog that usually descends in June. The Los Angeles-Orange County basin stretched to the San Bernardino Mountains, which, although usually lost in haze, now were sharply visible, with snow still clinging to the highest peaks.

As the Mustang paced out of Irvine with the top down, a mild breeze ruffled Anne's dark-blond hair. She looked young and adventuresome; it was hard to picture her as a no-nonsense doctor in a white coat. What a complicated woman she was, Jason reflected, remembering how sternly she'd interviewed him for the housekeeping job and then how meekly she'd succumbed when he cooked what appeared to be the first decent meal that she'd eaten in days.

The many sides of Anne intrigued Jason—her underplayed femininity, her intelligence and the dedication it must have taken to become a doctor. He knew some men might be put off by having to measure up to such a highly competent woman, but he'd never felt he had to compete with anyone.

If he had, he decided as they turned onto Pacific Coast Highway, he probably wouldn't create the kind of books he did. There were certainly more prestigious jobs for a photojournalist, not to mention ones that paid a hell of a lot better.

At the beginning of his career, he'd free-lanced for the Associated Press in Europe and had been offered a full-time job based in Paris. He'd turned it down. A photographer for a wire service worked at a dead run, flying to a war zone one day, an athletic competition the next and an economic summit the day after. That wasn't the way Jason wanted to live his life. He wanted to get inside things, to capture on film the essence of people's inner selves.

But today, he was happy just to be driving along the coastal highway with Anne at his side.

They'd left Newport Beach and were heading north through the funkier regions of Huntington Beach. As he paused at a crosswalk for a trio of teenage surfers, Jason glanced sideways at Anne.

She was smiling, watching the youngsters' horseplay as they sauntered across the highway. As he started up the car again, Jason noted the way her eyes traveled to the window of a shop where hand-crocheted sweaters and brightly printed shirts were stretched on wires. From the intensity of her examination, one might conclude that Anne was a visitor from a foreign land who had never seen a beach boutique before.

What went on inside her mind? Jason wondered as they rolled northward. Surely she hadn't always buried herself in her work; when she was younger, she must have spent some time just having fun. Where had that part of her gone? Wherever it was, he intended to find it and bring it out again.

THE TANG OF SALT AIR and the play of sunlight on her cheeks reminded Anne of her college days. Unknowingly, her thoughts paralleled Jason's. When had she stopped going to the beach on impulse? What had happened to the friends who used to call on the spur of the moment to suggest going out for a pizza and beer or taking in a new movie?

I guess we just grew up and drifted apart. The thought saddened her, and she fought to banish it. Today was an island in time, a minivacation that she sorely needed, and she wasn't going to muddy it up with painful nostalgia.

Anne welcomed the distraction as Jason turned off the highway, and then she realized they hadn't reached Santa Monica yet.

To her questioning look, he said, "One of my favorite used-book stores is here in Long Beach. I though you might want to pick up something obscure. Like how to deliver a baby brontosaurus."

Laughter welled up in Anne's throat. "I wouldn't mind digging into an antique medical text—not quite that old, though. Maybe something with leeches and elixir of crushed jewels."

"Sounds terrific." Jason shook his head. "I suppose medicine used to be rather barbaric, didn't it?"

Anne told him about a museum she'd visited in Toronto that displayed wooden forceps and other instruments formerly used in obstetrics. "Some of them look as if they'd be better suited to torturing women than to helping them," she said. "Wood can't even be sterilized."

"Well, I can't promise you'll find a gem of medical history, but there's something about dust and mold that makes dull old books seem fascinating." Jason pulled the car to a halt in front of a rather shabby-looking store fronted by a dusty plate-glass window.

Inside, Anne found, the store rambled from one room to the next, turning out to be much larger than it had appeared at first. Together, she and Jason prowled through the stacks, from time to time selecting a volume and reading aloud from it. Deliberately seeking something far removed from her everyday life, Anne finally selected *The Life and Times of Beau Brummell*.

Jason turned up a few minutes later with a collection of bawdy limericks. "I thought I'd improve my mind by reading poetry," he told the clerk, straight-faced. The man merely nodded as he rang up the sale on an old-fashioned cash register.

For about the dozenth time, Anne found herself wanting to laugh out loud. What was it about Jason that made her spirits feel lighter than they had in a long time?

Or maybe it wasn't Jason at all, just her own natural buoyancy breaking through, she told herself as she paid the huge sum of two dollars for her book. She should have realized that she needed a break from her hard-driving routine.

Still, Anne had to admit as she glanced sideways at Jason, having someone to share her amusement added considerably to the enjoyment.

Back at the car, she tucked the book into her beach bag and settled into the passenger seat. "You seem to know this area rather well. Have you lived in Southern California for long?"

"No." Jason headed back toward the highway. "I make a habit of exploring whatever place I happen to be in, including Southern California. It's amazing how much you can learn from combing the newspapers and guidebooks and then going out and poking around. A newcomer can discover more about an area in a few months than most longtime residents ever know."

"Were you referring to anyone in particular?" Anne murmured, beginning to regret how little exploring she'd done over the past few years.

Jason ducked his head. "Actually, that wasn't meant as a dig. But if the pedal appliance fits . . ."

"Pedal appliance?"

"Well, I don't know the medical term for shoe, but I figured that was close." He grinned and sped away from a signal light.

Oddly enough, his teasing made Anne suddenly uncomfortable. She'd almost forgotten she was a doctor out for a spin with her own housekeeper. The medical reference, even though in jest, brought her back to reality.

How was a person supposed to behave under the circumstances, anyway? she asked herself, and realized there weren't any guidelines. Emily Post never had to deal with this one, she decided.

She fell silent, watching the beach towns roll by. It struck Anne that whenever she'd driven north, she'd always taken the freeway, not the rambling old Coast Highway. It wasn't the sort of road you took when you were in a hurry. And she always seemed to be in a hurry.

By the time they reached Santa Monica, she felt as if she'd traveled through another world, one where time moved at a slower pace than usual. She'd forgotten there were so many children in sunsuits and teenagers in bikinis, so many mom-and-pop coffee shops and daredevil skateboarders and senior citizens on bicycles.

She was jolted from her thoughts as the car stopped alongside a garage in a neat whitewashed alley. A sign on the garage said Park Here and You'll Never See Your Car Again.

"It's okay." Jason opened his door and came around to help her out. "The garage is mine. For the rest of today, anyway."

Anne stretched as she emerged, sniffing the salt air and looking up, her attention drawn by the mewing of seagulls overhead. "I'm surprised you're willing to give it up for Irvine."

"The beach isn't going anywhere." Jason led the way up a narrow outdoor staircase. "If you decide to fire me next month, I can always come back."

Anne bit her lip. She wished that, just for today, she wasn't Jason's employer. Wielding authority was something she did every day at the office and the hospital. Right now, she wanted to be free of all that.

Jason opened the door to the apartment, which sat atop the garage. Anne hesitated for a moment as her eyes adjusted to the dim light.

It was a furnished apartment, impersonal looking now with Jason's own decorations stripped away. The couch was a nondescript brown, the walls a serviceable off-white and the tan carpet an outdated shag.

"The color scheme isn't much, but it hides the sand." Jason opened the curtains, and clear late-morning light flooded in. "Want to change in the bedroom?"

Anne agreed and hurried into the other room. She felt awkward as she pulled off her jeans and blouse and put on the one-piece blue maillot she'd bought two years ago and rarely worn. Dressing in Jason's bedroom made her feel vulnerable somehow, almost as if he could see her.

She returned to find he'd stripped off his own clothes down to rakishly slim gray trunks beneath. As when she'd seen him similarly clad in her own kitchen, Anne was struck by how comfortable Jason seemed with his own body, no more self-conscious than if he were wearing a three-piece suit. Or maybe less so.

"You don't get out in the sun much, do you?" He quirked an eyebrow as he regarded her, and Anne realized how pale she must look beside his bronzed body.

"The lights in the delivery rooms are pretty bright," she shot back. "I'll have to see about getting some adjustments so I can work on my tan while I work on my patients."

"They'd probably appreciate it." He gathered up some towels and a cooler and escorted her out the door, leaving it unlocked. "Why not put in tanning lights? It might take their minds off their labor pains."

"Only a man would think so." Anne led the way down the stairs.

"I have to admit, having babies is one area I don't know much about." Was that a wistful note in his voice? Or was it merely sarcasm?

"Let's get back to suntans." Anne's thong sandals, dug up from the back of her closet, flip-flopped against the pavement as she and Jason turned toward the beach. "Don't you know they're bad for your skin?"

"No worse than eating take-out food," Jason said as they emerged from between two houses onto the sidewalk that ran along the beach.

The Pacific Ocean stretched in front of them, Catalina Island jutting in the distance like a magical retreat. Small waves rippled placidly to shore, and the beach was dotted with bodies, gaily colored towels and squealing children.

Jason found a stretch of sand where they could have a measure of privacy—at least, there wasn't anyone breathing down their necks, Anne reflected. The nearest sunbathers were a young couple lying a few dozen feet away and smooching recklessly on a blanket.

"Ah, youth." Jason spread out their towels and set the cooler to one side. "Want something to drink? I'd offer you a beer, but alcohol is off limits on the beach."

Anne was about to point out that it wasn't a good idea to consume alcohol in direct sunlight anyway, since it could make you more vulnerable to sunburn, but she stopped herself. *Let's forget you're a doctor for the time being, okay?* "I'll take anything low-cal."

They settled down with their soft drinks and began tanning in earnest. Lying there with her eyes closed, Anne found herself tuning in to her other senses. She listened to the beach sounds of voices, surf and gulls and inhaled the smells of the ocean and of sunscreen lotion.

Gradually, she became more aware of Jason's nearness. His leg touched her calf lightly; perhaps he wasn't even aware of it. She could hear his deep breathing and smell the muskiness of the sun against his skin.

Restlessly, she sat up and squinted into the sun.

"Had enough?" Jason sat up beside her. "After all, you've been relaxing for at least ten minutes. We wouldn't want to overdo this. Maybe we could come back next week and try for fifteen."

Anne resisted the urge to throw sand at him. "Smart aleck."

"Am I wrong?"

She couldn't admit that her real motive had been to put a little distance between the two of them. "It's just that I find lying here motionless rather boring. How do you stand it?"

"I think profound thoughts." His eyes glowed amber in the sunlight, and Anne noticed that there was a dimple in his right cheek that flashed whenever he smiled.

"Maybe that's my problem. I have a shallow mind." She took another sip of her cola and found that it had gone flat and warm. Nevertheless, the heat had made her thirsty, and she drank it.

"Want to take a dip in the ocean, or would you find that boring, too?" Without waiting for an answer he stood up, and Anne jumped to her feet, glad for the diversion.

They raced down to the water. It felt surprisingly warm against Anne's ankles as she waded.

As soon as they reached knee depth, Jason dived in and began swimming away from shore with long, sure strokes. Anne continued out to waist depth and lowered herself till the waves tickled her neck, letting the water soothe her body as she watched Jason arc around and swim back toward her.

He belonged here, a free spirit in a place of unfettered souls, she thought. While she—well, she liked to visit the beach area, but the Anne of the old days had gone forever.

"A penny for your thoughts." Jason bobbed up beside her.

"Oh—" Anne shrugged "—I was feeling old and staid."

She looked anything but that, he observed silently. Anne had let her hair down today and it glowed golden against her bare shoulders. Oddly enough, the rather modest swimsuit merely emphasized the long slim line and gentle curves of her body.

"Hardly." He stifled the urge to tell her how lovely she looked; he sensed that compliments would only make Anne uncomfortable. "As a matter of fact, I'd like to take your picture."

"Oh, no, please!" She splashed back onto the beach, then stared in dismay as sand clung to her damp ankles.

"I'll make you a deal. I'll fetch your sandals if you'll let me take a few shots."

Anne considered for a moment. "All right."

He loped over to the towel, scarcely noticing the sand that stuck to his own legs, and brought her shoes back as promised. "You can relax for a minute. I've got to check the light."

"Don't make a big production out of this." Flopping onto the towels, she squirmed a bit—or perhaps it was his imagination—as Jason took the camera from the cooler and adjusted the lens aperture and speed.

Gazing at her through the camera, he recognized the difficulty of his task—to capture her inner womanliness, when the very presence of a camera made her even more tense than usual.

"Why don't you tell me something about yourself," he suggested as he angled around. "Where did you grow up?"

"A lot of places." Anne pushed back a strand of damp hair. "My dad was in the military, so we moved frequently."

"That must have been hard on you." Already, he could see the stiffness easing out of her muscles.

"In some ways." She leaned forward, hugging her knees. "My sister Lori and I got very close, because it was hard to make other friends. And we really valued our extended family, too—we have annual reunions, so that gave us a bit of stability, seeing the same faces every year no matter where we were living."

"Did you go overseas?" She'd almost forgotten about the camera; Jason took a shot and held his breath, hoping the click of the lens wouldn't destroy Anne's thoughtful mood. It had no effect, he noted with relief.

"Yes—Germany, for a while." A faraway look drifted across her face. What was she remembering—some special man, or perhaps a castle on the Rhine? Jason captured the moment on film. "We ended up in Colorado when I was a teenager, and then I came out here to college." Anne stretched with an instinctive grace.

"And then you met your actor friend," Jason prompted.

"Oh, yes." Anne tilted her head to one side. For some reason, recounting her life to Jason was helping her to see how the pieces fit together. "I suppose a part of me wanted excitement—maybe all young people do—and that's part of what Ken represented for me.

"Until you ran into the cockroaches." Jason would have made a good psychologist, she reflected; his voice had just the right impersonal but inviting tone, skillfully drawing forth her memories.

"Oh, I could put up with poverty if I had to—not that I like it." Anne sifted a handful of sand into a small pile. "It was the instability that got to me. So many years of pulling up roots, tearing friendships apart until I stopped bothering to start new ones—well, that made me realize what I really wanted. A home, a community, someplace where I belonged."

"Do you ever regret going into medicine?" He certainly was taking a lot of pictures, she noted, but it was his film and he could waste it if he wanted.

"For about five minutes at a time, mostly when I'm really tired and never want to see a white coat again." She smiled lazily. "But no more than that."

Jason lowered the camera. "You're a terrific model, when you're not thinking about it."

Anne shook her head so her hair fell across one cheek, half-hiding her face. "Just don't ever show me the photographs. Hey! Turnabout's fair play." She reached across and grabbed the camera. "Got any film left?"

"It's a roll of thirty-six—there should be about a dozen shots to go." He didn't seem to mind as she fiddled with the instrument until she got the hang of it. Anne had owned a thirty-five-millimeter camera herself, and this one wasn't too different from the one she'd lost at last summer's family reunion.

"Now, you're the expert on models, so show me how it's done." She peered through the lens. It was easy to see that the man was spectacularly photogenic, with his strong bone structure, lively eyes and well-toned muscles.

Jason lounged back on the towels and grinned. "Shoot away."

Anne clicked the lens. "It's your turn to tell me about yourself."

"Some other time." He seized a handful of sand and tossed it up in the air. "Something about the beach brings out the kid in me." He jumped to his feet. "Follow me!"

Startled, Anne trailed after Jason as he raced down to the strip of wet sand near the waterline and began mounding up what was obviously the foundation for a castle.

Delighted, Anne captured on film the building of what she had to admit was an expert construction, complete with turrets and tiny windows. But the real sight was Jason himself, beaming with enthusiasm as he created his fantasy world.

Soon a circle of children gathered, and Jason put them to work where they would do the least damage. He had a knack for dealing with them, Anne observed. Without talking down, Jason managed to reach the kids at their own level, as if he knew instinctively that one little girl wanted to fetch sand for him in her new red bucket, while an older boy yearned to construct his own tower.

It was almost a relief when the camera refused to advance any farther. Returning it to the cooler, Anne joined the castle-construction crew, shoring up a crumbling wall.

Kneeling in the sand, she scarcely noticed how it clung to her legs. The grittiness that had bothered her when she emerged from the water didn't matter anymore. *After all, no one's going to ask you to scrub yourself for the operating room.*

Finally the castle was complete. Anne was surprised to find they'd attracted quite a crowd.

"It's all yours," Jason told the children. "At least, until the tide comes in."

Anne sighed. "I hate to think that it's only temporary."

"The best thing is just to walk away and not look back." Jason took her arm and drew her to the towels, which they gathered up. "Hungry?"

"Starved." Anne gazed longingly toward a nearby taco stand. "I suppose fast food is out of the question?"

"I make exceptions for special occasions." Jason led the way, and soon they were stuffing themselves on junk food.

Finishing up the last of her diet soft drink, Anne wrinkled her nose. "I'm beginning to feel like I burned a little."

"You're turning red," Jason admitted. "I should have thought about that earlier. Let's go in."

Side by side, they sauntered back to the apartment, where he produced a large bottle of moisturizing lotion. "Let me." He guided her to a seat on the couch. "You can't reach your own back, you know."

Anne sank down and closed her eyes. The couch creaked as Jason sat beside her, his hands strong and cool as they stroked the lotion into her back with a circular motion. She winced as he slid her straps down onto her arms. "I must look like a 'before' ad for Coppertone."

"Something like that." Jason dropped a cold dab of lotion onto her shoulder. It felt wonderful. "You're going to hate me in the morning."

"I hate to think what Ellie will say—she's my receptionist." He was massaging her neck, making her forget about Ellie and the sunburn, about everything but the way his touch shivered down her spine.

"Tell her you were playing tennis with Dr. Intestine. She'll understand." Jason's deep chuckle echoed through Anne's nervous system.

The rich smell of sun rose from both their bodies, mingling in Anne's senses like a rare perfume. She could feel the heat of Jason's body radiating against hers, and his knee brushed sensually against her thigh.

The swimsuit felt clammy on her body, and she found herself wanting to strip it off. The air would be cold, but Jason was here, still warm from the sun....

Slowly he turned her to face him. Anne didn't open her eyes, engulfed in sensations she'd never known before. This feeling wasn't sexual so much as earthy and natural. Skin belonged against skin, not against stretch fibers. Legs ought to entangle with each other, lips ought to touch....

Then his lips did touch hers, very gently. Anne's mouth opened of its own accord. His hands caressed her forearms, and her palms pressed lightly against his chest, feeling the texture of thick hair over broad muscles.

The kiss deepened. Anne's arms twined around his neck and she stretched instinctively, the motion thrusting her breasts forward. Jason's hand at her waist drew her closer.

Anne had felt passion before, or what she'd thought was passion, but not this welling up of desire from deep within, as if she'd discovered a new part of herself.

What's wrong with you? This is Jason. You hardly know him. The unwelcome thought came from a part of her mind that Anne was beginning to dislike intensely. It ruptured the mood, and her eyes flew open.

"I . . ." She didn't know what to say.

Jason released her slowly. "Consider it a natural extension of our day at the beach." Anne was grateful that he refrained from making any disparaging remarks about her inhibitions. Instead, he gave her a wry smile. "I guess we both got carried away."

She stood up and found that her knees were definitely wobbly. "I'll go change. Then we'd better be getting back. I'm on call in a couple of hours." Without waiting for a reply, she darted into the bedroom.

They were both subdued on the drive home. Anne wished she could read Jason's mind. Had their embrace been as special to him as it had to her, or was she merely one in a string of interchangeable women whom he'd held?

She wished they had mutual acquaintances so she could find out more about him. The only thing she knew was that he'd been married once and was still apparently on friendly terms with his ex-wife. But he didn't lack experience when it came to applying lotion to a woman's back. Had he intended their kiss to happen?

His face, as he drove, told her nothing. He looked comfortable, as always. He seemed like the kind of man whom a woman would remain friends with, whether she'd been married to him or not.

Friends. That was good enough, Anne decided firmly. Today she'd let herself go—well, she'd needed a break, hadn't she? That didn't mean she was going to turn into a beach bunny. Surely Jason realized as well as she did that their kiss could never be repeated. They were too different, despite the undeniable physical attraction.

When confronted with a confusing situation, Anne had learned that the best tactic was to analyze things rationally and decide on a course of action. As they whirred home—on the freeway, this time—she did exactly that.

Clearly, she told herself, her own overwork had made her vulnerable to Jason's easygoing charm. She needed to allow herself more time off and spend some of it with attractive men. No doubt her response to his touch was the result of overly restrained impulses....

Boy, do I sound clinical. It's a good thing Jason can't hear what I'm thinking; he'd get a good laugh out of it.

All the same, there was truth in what she'd concluded, Anne mused as they turned off the freeway in Irvine. She'd have to make a point of expanding her love life to include men more appealing than Horace Swann, M.D.

That way, Jason wouldn't dominate her thoughts the way he was doing now. That way, her arms wouldn't ache to hold him again, and her lips wouldn't tingle at the thought of renewing their kiss.

Solutions were easy when you approached a problem sensibly, Anne reflected.

Like hell they were.

Chapter Five

On Monday, Jason developed and printed the roll of film in his bathroom, which he'd turned into a temporary dark-room. Watching the images emerge was, as always, a moment touched with magic. He stared down at the pictures, wishing he could make out more of the details in the red light.

As soon as it was safe, he switched on the overhead light and lifted an eight-by-ten print out of the pan. Anne gazed up at him, her eyes focused somewhere in the distance—or perhaps on a time long past.

Jason examined print after print. As he'd hoped, the camera had caught a range of expressions that together formed a portrait of the woman he was coming to know better than any woman since his divorce.

After the breakup with Jill, Jason had been lonely and had sought out the company of women. But although he'd enjoyed some pleasant relationships, none had really satis-fied him.

Finally the intensity of his yearning had abated, and he'd begun to revel in having his freedom again. Now he could consider future projects without worrying about their ef-fect on someone else. He could travel as much as he wanted, cultivate new acquaintances and not have to worry about how much money he had in the bank, beyond what was needed for his immediate expenses.

He'd thought he was finished with wanting any kind of entanglement. So why was he standing here like a star-struck adolescent, gazing at pictures of Anne and wondering what memories had been floating through her mind when he photographed her?

Jason fished out the last prints, the ones of him building a sand castle. He noted with interest some aspects he hadn't caught at the time: a boy frowning in concentration as he scalloped the edges of a tower, a mother's glowing face as she watched her children play....

Children. That was the reason Jason had wanted to settle down with Jill, to give up his traveling for a few years. Intellectually, he could understand why she'd refused. Children were a big responsibility and a long-term one—and although Jason had never meant to force Jill into any stereotyped roles, he knew that women often found their own interests sidelined when they had little ones to raise. And she'd never wanted a family the way he did.

But emotionally, Jason couldn't see how anyone wouldn't want a couple of those little munchkins toddling along at your side, forcing you to view life through new eyes. It would be well worth making some sacrifices.

How did Anne feel, delivering babies day after day and not having any of her own? Was she so obsessed with her career that everything else took second place?

It was too bad she'd been behind the camera during the sand castle building, Jason reflected as he cleaned up the trays of chemicals. He would have liked to see the expression on her face as she watched the children.

Washing his hands to get rid of the pungent smell of the photo chemicals, he stepped out into the bright light of the kitchen. Monday was grocery-shopping day, according to the schedule Ada had left behind, and he didn't want to slight his housekeeping duties.

Still, it gave him a funny feeling, picking up the envelope of money Anne had left on the counter. Taking a paycheck was one thing; accepting her money, even though it was for expenses, made him feel like a kept man.

Well, what's wrong with that? Jason paused as he tore the grocery list off its pad and folded it into his shirt pocket. He supposed he wouldn't mind, if it was anyone but Anne.

In some ways, he wished he could go back and start over, not as her employee but as, well, a friend and equal. But then, how would he have met her? And what pretext would he have for coming over here day after day, seeing her wander down to breakfast with her hair freshly washed and not yet dried, or watching her stand at the counter fixing a midnight snack, wearing a pair of panda slippers that were especially endearing for being so completely out of character?

No, he couldn't have gotten to know her any other way, so there was no use hassling about it, Jason told himself. What he really needed to do was to get on with his photo project; the sooner he completed it, the sooner he could level with Anne.

Going out the back door, he vaulted over the fence to the house next door and tapped on the rear screen. After a moment, Rosa appeared.

"I was going to the supermarket and wondered if you'd like a ride." Seeing her hesitation, Jason added, "Actually, I don't know my way around the store very well yet. I thought maybe you could give me a few tips."

Rosa nodded. "Okay. You know, you ought to get the newspaper on Thursdays. That's when they advertise the grocery specials. Wait a minute, I'll bring the ad."

A short time later, as they drove to the store through the cool morning fog, Rosa pointed out a sale on corned beef and cabbage and an unusually low price on strawberries.

"Thanks." Jason really meant it; he did love food and cooking, and the strawberries in particular appealed to him.

He could imagine Anne's face as she trudged in from another of her long days. The sight of fresh berries with whipped cream would chase away her weariness. . . .

Oh, Lord, I sound like a television commercial! Next I'll be prattling on about ring around the collar.

The supermarket, like everything else in Irvine, looked discreet, expensive and up-to-the-minute. Tucked into a landscaped shopping center, it came complete with its own bakery, a fresh-fish counter and a bountiful display of cheeses.

Jason and Rosa pushed shopping carts side by side, chatting as they strolled. He'd been here before, to buy food for Anne's dinner date with Horace, but that had been a quick expedition with specific targets. Today there were detergents to choose and a hundred other decisions to make.

It would have helped if he'd drawn up a meal plan for the week, Jason concluded. Well, live and learn.

They were almost finished when Rosa clucked her tongue sharply, drawing Jason's attention to a young Hispanic woman standing beside a cart and looking thoroughly bewildered as she gazed at the brightly lit aisles and stacks of promotional merchandise.

"A lost soul." Rosa heaved a sigh. "She'll probably panic in a minute and run out of here, and there goes her job."

"Why don't we help her?" Jason turned his cart around. "We left the frozen food till last, so nothing's going to melt."

Rosa frowned. "Why are you so concerned? You might get fired, too, if you spend so much time at the supermarket."

"Dr. Eldridge won't know the difference, and neither will your folks." Jason had learned last week that Rosa kept house for a pair of lawyers who worked even longer hours than Anne.

Rosa shrugged. "Okay, I don't mind. You wait here so we don't scare her."

Jason watched as Rosa approached the girl and said a few words in Spanish. The response mirrored on the girl's face at first was fear, then doubt, then relief. Rosa gestured him over.

"Her name is Juanita and she doesn't believe you're a housekeeper, too," Rosa said. Jason turned to the girl and saw a shy smile lighting up her face.

He'd brushed up on his Spanish before undertaking this project, and, begging her pardon for his occasionally fractured verbs, he explained that he liked to take photographs and had chosen the job because it allowed him a lot of free time.

Then he and Rosa read over the list Juanita's employer had written in English and walked through the store with her, pointing out items on the shelves. Fortunately, there weren't many shoppers at that time of day and the aisles were wide, so they were able to manage as a threesome.

Afterward, they paid for their groceries and headed home. Juanita had driven in her employer's car, a large sedan that clearly frightened her, and she admitted she didn't have a driver's license.

"I'm surprised her boss didn't check," Jason muttered.

Rosa clucked. "In Southern California, people take it for granted. You can see, Juanita speaks only a few words of English, but the woman just assumed she could read the list. People don't realize what it's like when you come from another country."

They decided to have Rosa drive Juanita home, while Jason followed in her car. Since Juanita's employer was at the house, Rosa sneaked away unseen with a promise that she and Jason would return the next afternoon, when they could answer more questions for Juanita.

"She's very lonely. You should have heard her talk when we were in the car!" Rosa folded her arms in front of her as she rode back to Anne's house. "She's only been in this country a few months and she was lucky to get this job. Her husband is a migrant worker, and she has two little children who stay with her sister in Santa Ana.''

Jason crossed his fingers on the steering wheel. Juanita sounded as though she might be the subject he was looking for. That didn't necessarily mean she'd be willing for him to photograph her, though. And it bothered him to think that, in a way, he'd be taking advantage of her plight for his own purposes, just as her employer was doing.

Well, that was a concern every journalist and photographer had to deal with, he reflected—that you were exploiting the very people you sought to help.

Anyway, this was no time to lose himself in moral perplexities. As they pulled up in front of the house, he realized the hot June sun had finally burned away the last of the fog. Frozen broccoli and ice cream wait for no man.

THE HOSPITAL CAFETERIA was crowded at noon. Anne debated about skipping lunch but didn't want to take a chance on getting light-headed in the middle of the afternoon.

Standing in line holding her tray, she thought back to yesterday's outing with Jason. Not that she had any problem remembering it—her nose and shoulders smarted from sunburn.

But she didn't mind. In fact, the discomfort was almost welcome. It made her feel that the day wasn't entirely past and that she hadn't completely gone back to being the workhorse she'd become in the last few years.

More than a few years, she reflected ruefully. There'd been medical school, internship, residency, a fellowship at a hospital and then her partnership with John Hernandez—always a reason to work weekends and evenings, to turn down dates and grab a sandwich while she tried to keep up with the latest medical literature.

She'd never paused to ask herself when it was going to end—or, at least, when it was going to slow down a little.

Even now that she was becoming established, Anne felt guilty about taking any time for herself.

She studied a neurologist who was ahead of her in line, a man she'd known for several years. He wasn't much older than she was, but his gray pallor reminded her of her own before yesterday, and he had bags under his eyes.

How come we don't play golf on Wednesdays the way doctors are supposed to? she asked herself. Oh, perhaps some physicians worked so hard because they wanted to make as much money as possible, but she suspected most of them were as stuck on a treadmill as she was.

The problem now was how to get off it without sacrificing her work—and without spending too much time in the dangerously alluring presence of Jason Brant.

Finally reaching the salads, Anne picked out one sprinkled with shrimps and slices of hard-boiled egg. That wasn't enough to hold her all afternoon, she decided, and added a plate of overcooked green beans and mashed potatoes to her tray.

I sure hope Jason never finds out about this. He might start making me come home for lunch.

Unfortunately, she conceded silently, the idea had a lot of appeal. For the first time in ages, she felt as if she actually had a home instead of merely an expensive, empty house.

Rebelliously, Anne took a glass of Cherry Coke. She would have added a slice of apple pie, but better judgment prevailed.

Besides, she might want to wear her swimsuit again this summer.

After paying the cashier, Anne stared around the room, looking for a vacant table. Failing to see one, she searched for an empty chair. Mentally, she eliminated several tables occupied by nonhospital staff—probably relatives of patients—and a long table at which half a dozen nurses were chattering. She wasn't concerned about the unwritten snobbery that separated doctors from nurses, but she knew her presence would make the other women feel restrained.

At that moment, she spotted a couple of hospital volunteers getting up from a table, and she started toward it. Unfortunately, someone else had made the same observation, and he and Anne arrived at the table at the same time.

"I don't mind sharing if you don't." The darkly handsome face and rakish smile belonged to Aldous Raney, M.D., a plastic surgeon with a reputation for playing the field among the nurses.

Anne had been introduced to him once, but they'd never exchanged more than a few words. Now she sank into a chair and said, "Of course not. Please join me."

"Looks like you had a good time this weekend." Aldous was clearly referring to her bright-red nose and cheeks. He flashed white teeth and a dimple at her. "Not used to the beach, eh?"

He himself sported a rich tan. Although many plastic surgeons did excellent rehabilitation work with victims of accidents and birth defects, Aldous was better known for his nose bobs and tummy tucks. As one of the nurses had commented in Anne's presence, he specialized in reconstruction of the rich.

"I suppose I overdid it." How could anyone prepare green beans that had so little flavor? Anne wondered as she ate. And the mashed potatoes would have made the state of Idaho blush with shame.

"So tell me, doctor, what are your hobbies, since you're clearly not accustomed to the great outdoors?" Aldous consumed his meat loaf with flair, holding the fork in his left hand European-style.

"My idea of a really wild Saturday night is to have three patients in labor at the same time." Anne sipped her drink and nearly choked as the bubbles went up her nose. Being with Aldous made her feel adolescent and awkward.

Somehow she managed not to sneeze, cough or tip over the rest of her Coke, but it wasn't easy. Still, she reminded herself, she was almost thirty-four, and she could certainly handle Aldous Raney.

"Sounds like you need some help livening things up." The way Aldous fixed his gaze on Anne conveyed the impression that she was the only other person in the room.

Embarrassed, she wondered what the nurses must think about this little tête-à-tête, then decided it didn't matter. She could handle him, couldn't she? "That sounds like an offer."

"As a matter of fact, it is. I've noticed you for a long time, but you're a hard woman to get near. You always seem to be loping through the halls at a dead run." He sipped his coffee without taking his eyes from her face.

"I guess sunbathing isn't the only thing I overdo." Anne smiled apologetically. "I've been known to run into lab technicians in the corridor without even seeing them."

"How does Saturday night sound?" He certainly didn't beat around the bush.

"I'm on call. How about Friday?" Never let it be said that she lacked boldness, Anne mused.

"Great. I know a little French restaurant in Hollywood, and then we could hit the nightclubs. Or perhaps you'd rather dine at my place? I barbecue a mean steak."

So much for boldness, Anne reflected; she was already having second thoughts at the prospect of being alone with Aldous. *Maybe before I tackled the big time I should have practiced on someone with a little more panache than Horace Swann.*

Without thinking, she blurted out, "Why don't you come over to my place for dinner?"

"Great!" From the masterful way Aldous was working his dimple, she gathered that he expected something special for dessert. "I'll be there about seven."

Anne provided the address and watched with misgivings as Aldous departed, leaving his tray behind despite the signs that urged Please Bus Your Own Dishes.

She wondered what Jason was going to think about this.

"I CAN'T BELIEVE you're actually working for Dr. Eldridge!" Deanie Parker's voice rose to a near squeal over the telephone line.

Jason lifted his ear a little from the receiver. He'd forgotten how enthusiastic—and loud—his cousin could be. "It's just a way to make some money while I work on my next book. Of course, I haven't told her anything about what I really do...."

"No problem! I won't say a word!" Deanie sounded as if she might be jumping up and down with excitement—an alarming thought, since she was eight months pregnant.

Jason had had dinner with his cousin and her husband, Tom, at their house in Newport Beach about six months ago, catching up on old times. Deanie had just learned at the time that she was pregnant and had talked of little else.

It was only this morning, as he was doing the laundry—Tuesday's main chore, according to Ada's schedule—that he remembered her mentioning a Dr. Eldridge. Sure enough, when he'd called a few minutes ago, she'd confirmed that Anne was her doctor.

He'd hoped Deanie knew Anne well enough to fill him in about her background and social circle. In his work as a photojournalist, Jason had learned the value of questioning a third party, and for some reason he found himself wanting to learn all he could about Anne; but his cousin, as it turned out, knew Anne only as the doctor who saw her briefly once a month for prenatal checkups.

Fortunately, Deanie was, as usual, too preoccupied with her own concerns to ask any probing questions about what kind of work he was doing for Anne. She took at face value Jason's remark that he was "just doing some odds and ends around the house," which was understandable, since he had worked as a handyman during the summers when he was in college.

Deanie had a heart of gold, but she just wasn't the type you wanted to confide your deepest secrets to, Jason reflected as his cousin chattered on.

"I mean—the reason I think it's so terrific about you working for Dr. Eldridge—well, you know Tom's company sends him overseas?" Deanie didn't seem to be making much sense, but Jason made appropriate noises of agreement. "Well, he's in Germany right now and I'm afraid he won't get back in time for the delivery."

"That's too bad."

"So I thought maybe you could photograph it, so at least he could see how it went. I mean, since you're working for Dr. Eldridge, that makes it easy, doesn't it? She knows you, so she'll have to say yes, won't she?"

"I think it would be better if you asked her. After all, you're the patient." The idea of photographing a birth appealed to Jason strongly. True, it could be a bit embarrassing when the woman was his own cousin, but Deanie obviously wasn't disturbed by the prospect of having him see her in such intimate circumstances. Childbirth was a miracle, after all, not a time for misplaced prudery.

"Sure! I mean, even if Tom does get back, he'd be too busy helping me to take pictures, wouldn't he?"

"I don't think the doctor will want a roomful of people watching when you give birth, but I'm willing to go along with whatever she approves." Inwardly, Jason winced. He didn't think Anne was going to like this, but once Deanie got hold of an idea, she never let go.

"Okay! Thanks a lot, Jase."

For the rest of the morning, he was busy with the laundry and ironing. Bored with removing creases from blouses and sheets, he flicked on the TV set that Ada had kept near the ironing board and watched a soap opera. It was hard to follow the half dozen plot twists, so Jason tried to make up a story built around the commercials. He came up with something about a rustic family in a log cabin serving powdered lemonade to a jolly green giant, who then staggered through a group of dancing teenagers to buy life insurance from Snoopy.

After he finished folding away the last pillowcase, Jason went next door to pick up Rosa as they'd planned.

"Juanita called and said it's okay to come over." Rosa settled into the passenger seat of his car. "Her lady's gone to the gardening club."

"Gardening?" Jason couldn't suppress a skeptical grin. "In these tiny yards? There isn't room for more than a tub of pansies on the patio."

Rosa shrugged. "Maybe she grows orchids in the bathroom. You never know."

The house where Juanita lived was the largest model in the development, with five bedrooms, and the family that lived there had three teenagers, Jason learned when they arrived. He didn't envy Juanita the job of keeping up with the work.

When they arrived, Juanita was clearly nervous. "Maybe they'll fire me if they learn my friends come here," she explained in Spanish.

"But you live here," Jason pointed out. "Surely you can have a few visitors."

"I don't know. I don't want to ask them." Juanita ushered Jason and Rosa into the utility room, where they sat at a small, scarred table. "It's not that I'm complaining. I was lucky to get the job."

When Jason ventured to ask about her salary, Juanita named a very low figure. Jason tried not to show his dismay. He could understand how her employers might not want her to have visitors in the house and might overestimate Juanita's grasp of English and of American customs, but how could they pay her so little? She was making less than minimum wage and working far more than forty hours a week.

But then, she needed the job so badly she wouldn't dare complain, he reflected angrily.

"Why don't I answer your questions about the house?" Rosa suggested, indicating the computerized washing machine for a start.

Juanita jumped as a car drove by on the street. "Maybe the children will come home from school early. You'd better go."

"But—" Jason started to protest and then cut himself off. The last thing he wanted was to make Juanita any more frightened than she already was. "All right. Maybe we can come back another time."

"Maybe I'll come to your house." Juanita got directions from Rosa.

"When will you come?" the other woman asked.

"Whenever I get a chance. I don't know. I'm supposed to be here all the time, except Sundays." Juanita looked relieved but also rather forlorn as her two guests departed.

As they drove home, Jason said, "Maybe she's exaggerating things in her own mind. Do you really think her employers are such slave drivers?"

"It wouldn't surprise me." Rosa glared out through the windshield. "Last night I talked to my friend who works down the block and she said those people have a bad reputation. They fired the last maid because she had to take a few weeks off to go back to Mexico and take care of her sick mother. And she'd worked for them more than a year."

When he got home, Jason started grating cheese for the lasagna he was making tonight. Anne hadn't gotten home on Monday until nearly ten o'clock and had gone straight to bed, and he was sure she hadn't eaten properly all day. At least tonight she'd be well fed.

You'd think I was her mother! But somebody's got to look after her.

Jason thought about Juanita and about the network of neighborhood domestic workers with whom Rosa kept in touch. In the text that would accompany his photographs, he wanted to make the point that a housing tract was a small world unto itself, with as much intrigue, joy and sorrow in its own way as the larger world.

He finished his advance preparations for dinner by midafternoon and sat down to make some phone calls. He'd already done preliminary research for his book by gathering statistics about domestic workers, but now he wanted some more personalized information.

A woman at a Hispanic-rights group was more than happy to oblige. She knew of families that hired Latino day laborers and cleaning ladies and then intentionally fired them on flimsy pretexts to avoid paying them.

Afterward, as he stirred the sauce for the lasagna, Jason felt his anger begin to subside. In reality, he knew, such abuses were the exception. Rosa, for example, had told him she was happy with her employers, and Anne certainly wasn't exploitive.

Was he being fair in this book? Would a brief disclaimer be enough, or would he be leaving the untrue impression that Irvine was a hotbed of Simon Legrees?

The front door clicked open and Jason heard Anne's familiar footstep in the entrance hall. It surprised him how quickly he'd come to know her habits and even her customary noises—the absentminded way she talked to herself when she was concentrating on a task, the scuff of her shoes when she was tired, the two quick breaths she took as she inhaled the fragrance of good cooking.

"Lasagna?" She leaned wearily in the kitchen doorway. "I'm impressed. And today's laundry day, too. Or did you work out a new schedule?"

Jason laid one hand over his heart. "And abandon Ada's brilliant scheme of things? Never."

It was amazing that a man so masculine could look so good in a kitchen, Anne reflected. Or maybe it was just his talent at the stove that was overwhelming her resistance.

Something red caught her eye, and she looked more closely at the colander sitting on the counter. "Strawberries!"

"With homemade whipped cream." Jason began layering lasagna noodles into a pan. "Now this has to bake for a while. Cocktails and antipasti will be served on the patio in fifteen minutes, so why don't you freshen up?"

Anne nodded and hurried upstairs. Despite the air conditioning in her office and car, the June heat made her tailored suit and white coat nearly unbearable.

Her thoughts returned to the hospital and to her conversation at lunch. Maybe it hadn't been wise to invite Aldous here on Friday, in light of the way Jason had handled Horace.

Or maybe I'm just feeling guilty about letting another man invade Jason's domain.

Jason's domain! Anne shook her head furiously as she slipped on a short-sleeved blouse and a white skirt. He was becoming altogether too cocky. And then there was that phone call she'd received a few hours ago....

It was hard to confront a man who so graciously brought her a daiquiri and an antipasti tray on the patio, but Anne forced herself to look him straight in the eye. "About Deanie Parker..."

"Oh." A sheepish look crossed Jason's face as he sat beside her at the white wrought-iron table. "She gets a little carried away. I agreed to oblige her, but only if it's okay with you."

Anne fought down the urge to refuse this further encroachment of his, this progression from her private to her professional sphere. After all, she did try to accommodate her patients whenever possible, and Deanie had the same rights as anyone else.

Swallowing a gulp of daiquiri, Anne forced herself to say in a calm voice, "My concern is that you not interfere in any way with Deanie's medical needs. Sometimes complications crop up...."

"If that happens, I'll get the hell out of there." Jason wasn't joking this time. His dark eyes bored into Anne's. "Give me credit for a little common sense."

She nodded. "I told Deanie it would be all right, if her husband can't be there. If he's in town, though, I'd rather not have a third party present. Every additional person increases the risk of infection, and frankly, you'd be in the way of the nurses."

"I understand."

Maybe she'd misjudged him. This was probably Deanie's idea entirely. Just because he'd taken over her house before she quite realized what was happening, that was no reason to think Jason wanted to take over the rest of her life, Anne told herself sternly.

"By the way, I'm expecting a dinner guest on Friday." She nibbled at a black olive. "You can take the evening off as soon as dinner is served—I'll clean up. You can use your own judgment as to the menu."

Jason's face was expressionless. "If you tell me a little about your guest, it would help me choose something appropriate."

What would you say if I told you he's the hospital playboy? "I think he has rather cosmopolitan tastes."

Jason nodded gravely. "I can handle that. What time?"

She told him.

"No problem. And I promise to keep my mother's colitis to myself." Before she could respond, Jason vanished into the house to see to the lasagna.

Chapter Six

After vacuuming and dusting on Thursday as per Ada's schedule, Jason flipped through Anne's collection of cookbooks. He enjoyed experimenting with new recipes and could usually tell by reading them whether they'd turn out well. Of course, he wouldn't want to risk giving Anne any unpleasant surprises tomorrow night. Better to stick with one of his old favorites, pork strips stir-fried with peanuts and seasoned with rosemary.

Thoughtfully he drew up a grocery list. They were running low on milk and eggs, as well....

Good Lord. I'm starting to take this housekeeping business seriously! Maybe I should consider it as something to fall back on between books.

But there weren't likely to be many employers like Anne.

Jason lifted his head sharply as he heard noises next door. Women's voices were speaking rapidly in Spanish, one of them near hysteria.

He stuck the shopping list in his pocket and went over the fence, his usual route.

In answer to his rapping, Rosa flung open the back door. "It's Juanita. You heard her wailing all the way over at your house?"

"What's the matter?" His throat tightened. Housekeeping might be a mere diversion for Jason, but Juanita needed her job badly.

Rosa let him inside. At the kitchen table, the younger woman sat sobbing into a tissue.

"Her lady yelled at her for using the wrong kind of bleach with the towels. She ruined a couple of them and she's afraid she's going to be fired if she makes a mistake like that again." Rosa poured three cups from the coffee maker and set them on the table. "I'm trying to convince her to let me come over and show her what to do with all that equipment. They didn't even have flush toilets in her hometown, so how would she know how to use all this fancy stuff?"

It was the longest speech he'd ever heard Rosa make, and Jason couldn't help but be impressed by her concern.

He turned to Juanita and said in halting Spanish, "If no one's at home, why not let us help?"

She stared down into her coffee. "I'm afraid...."

"You see?" Rosa glared at the younger woman in disgust. "She's scared of her own shadow."

There had to be some approach that would work. "Even if your boss saw us, maybe she would think it was funny, meeting a male housekeeper."

Juanita brushed aside a tear. "You weren't joking? That's really what you do?"

"I'm a good cook, too." At least she'd stopped crying; that was a positive sign.

"You aren't ashamed, to do a woman's work?"

"Why? Am I going to turn into a woman if I put on an apron?"

Juanita smiled. "Of course not."

Gradually, Jason drew her out by talking about his own trials and tribulations with housework, including the mess he'd made changing a vacuum-cleaner bag. Rosa helped when his Spanish fell short, and Juanita seemed to enjoy his account.

Finally she agreed to let them both come over and help her out.

He drove them the three blocks to Juanita's house. She went in alone first, to make sure no one else was home, and then invited them in.

Surely her employers couldn't really be such ogres, Jason reflected as he gazed around at the immaculate, tastefully decorated home. But it grated on him to know that they spent so much money on their possessions and yet grossly underpaid their housekeeper.

It took Rosa half an hour to explain to Juanita the intricacies of American laundry and of the computerized washing machine, which, to Jason, was far more elaborate than it needed to be.

Next they tackled the microwave oven, the food processor, the dishwasher and a number of lesser appliances. As time passed, Juanita looked less and less confused, but she jumped every time a car drove by on the street.

Finally, she relaxed enough to fix some coffee and invite them into her small room off the kitchen, where Jason and Rosa sat on the bed while Juanita perched on a small chair.

Under Jason's gentle questioning, she began to talk about her life back in Mexico and her family. Her husband was a farm worker who had to travel to wherever there was planting or a harvest, she explained. Right now he was up in the Salinas area.

Mostly, Juanita admitted, she missed her children, who were two and four years old. They stayed in Santa Ana, about fifteen miles away, with her sister's family, and she was able to see them only on Sundays.

Jason looked around the room. On the wall over the bed was a cross; on the opposite wall hung an inexpensive print of the Madonna. "You don't have any photographs of your children?"

"My sister used to have a camera but one of her children broke it," Juanita said.

"I could take some." Not wanting to trick her, Jason explained about his book and that he wanted to take pictures of her at work, as well. "Of course I wouldn't use your name or show anything that would identify your employers."

"Why do you want to do this?" Rosa asked. "What good will it do?"

It was a fair question. "I'm not sure. Sometimes I think it's important just to show that a situation exists. Maybe someone will pass legislation or organize a union. Maybe some families who exploit women like Juanita will feel guilty and pay them better. Maybe nothing will happen. I can't make any promises."

The women nodded, and Jason was glad he'd answered honestly. Rosa and Juanita might not be very sophisticated in academic terms, but he suspected they could spot a phony a mile away.

"I would like pictures of my children. I will let you take the other photographs, too, if you want. You and Rosa are my friends." Juanita fingered the hem of her embroidered skirt. "Maybe you can show me some of your books."

They set a tentative date for the next morning. Juanita would leave the shade in her room up if it was all right for Jason to come in; if someone else was home, she'd pull the shade down.

"I feel like a character in a spy novel," Jason admitted as he drove Rosa home.

"If someone catches you, you can always say the pictures of her at work are for her children, so they can see what she does," Rosa suggested.

"That's a terrific idea. Thanks."

His plans for the book were working out even better than expected. Jason wished he didn't still have a nagging sense of guilt at the way he was deceiving Anne. He would tell her the truth as soon as he dared risk getting kicked out of her house.

"THE GRAPEVINE SAYS you've got a date with Dr. Raney." It was nearly five and the telephones had finally stopped ringing, giving Ellie a chance to chat with Anne for the first time that day.

"A person certainly can't keep any secrets around here." Anne handed her receptionist a patient's records to file. Her feet ached and her stomach was growling, a reminder that she'd skipped lunch.

"You watch out, Anne." It was John Hernandez, Anne's partner. "Aldous has a terrible reputation and a big mouth to go with it."

"Well, I plan to stuff it full of food, and that's about all I plan to do." Anne really liked her partner, as well as respecting his professional abilities. She wished they could talk more often, but mostly they saw each other for only a few moments a day, like now.

She peered past the reception desk into the waiting room. Two women were leafing through magazines. "Do I have any more appointments?"

Ellie shook her head. "No. One's for Dr. Hernandez and one's having an ultrasound."

In addition to Ellie and a nurse-practitioner, the office employed a part-time ultrasound technician who came in on Tuesdays and Thursdays. Sometimes Anne wondered how doctors had managed without that invaluable tool for diagnosing a wide range of problems.

"Don't change the subject." John broke into her thoughts. "I hope you plan to keep that male housekeeper of yours around to make Aldous behave himself."

"Maybe I should hire a Pinkerton guard. And maybe you should take care of your patient."

John grumbled good-naturedly and moved away.

Although her office duties were over for the day, Anne planned to spend the next hour catching up on medical literature in her office. Science was making rapid advancements in every field, but particularly in obstetrics.

About half an hour later, she heard Ellie moving about, using one of the bathrooms, which she had to do frequently since she'd gotten pregnant. A moment later, the receptionist tapped timidly at Anne's door.

She looked up and was shocked to see that Ellie's face had turned a pasty white. "What's the matter?"

"I'm bleeding." Ellie's voice shook. "I mean—not real heavily but—this hasn't happen to me before."

Anne sprang to her feet. "Has it stopped?"

"I think so."

"Any contractions?"

"No."

"Let's go find out what the problem is. Has the technician left yet?" Anne led the way to the ultrasound room, with Ellie trailing behind.

"I think she's still cleaning up."

Within a few minutes, Ellie was lying on an examining table and Anne and the technician were scrutinizing images on the monitor. The baby, a healthy size for its thirty-two weeks, was moving around and looked fine. There was no sign of a placental abruption, a dangerous condition in which the placenta separated from the uterus before birth and threatened the baby's oxygen supply.

However, the placenta had clearly attached low in the uterus, not quite touching the cervix. That made it vulnerable to bleeding.

After explaining the situation to Ellie, Anne said, "I want you to have your husband come and pick you up. Then I want you to go home and stay in bed through the weekend. Give me a call Sunday night and we'll decide whether you're well enough to come to work on Monday, okay?"

Ellie nodded, looking relieved.

"And I want you to call me immediately if there's any more bleeding or if you feel any contractions."

Ellie's husband, Dennis, arrived twenty minutes later, his face creased with worry. He looked relieved to see his wife smiling, although a bit shakily.

"Try not to worry too much," Anne tried to reassure her friend and co-worker. "It's probably nothing. And you're already at thirty-two weeks, so the baby would most likely be fine if it was born now anyway."

But they both knew that a premature infant would require weeks of hospital care and could suffer from lung immaturity.

That was the problem when medical workers got pregnant—they knew too much, Anne reflected as Ellie departed on the arm of her solicitous husband.

Concerned as she was for Ellie, Anne couldn't repress a twinge of envy. What would it be like to be expecting a child and to have a husband who loved you the way Ellie's husband obviously loved her?

Unexpectedly, Anne caught a mental image of Jason leaning toward her, his eyes alight with tenderness, his hand reaching out to stroke the curve of her belly where their child was growing. What a good father he would make, building sand castles with a toddler, teaching a youngster how to cook....

I must be working too hard, like everybody says. My brain's getting addled.

Wearily, she closed up the office and went home.

Anne noticed something amiss as soon as she walked through the door, but it took her a moment to pinpoint what it was. She didn't smell anything cooking.

"Jason?" She walked into the kitchen.

He was putting groceries away. "Just got back. Things took a little longer than I planned today."

It wouldn't be reasonable to expect him to have dinner ready the instant she got home. For one thing, Anne acknowledged silently, he couldn't have known exactly what time she'd arrive, but she felt disappointed all the same. It wasn't because she was starving, although that was certainly part of it; but the delicious smells of cooking had become a welcome part of her daily homecoming.

"There are probably some TV dinners in the freezer...."

Jason's uplifted hand cut her off. "Nonsense. It's my responsibility to provide dinner. Now look here." He opened a drawer and pulled out a slip of paper.

Leaning against the counter, Anne regarded him warily.

"I bought the newspaper today to clip the food coupons, and I discovered an ad for a new restaurant." Jason read to her from the piece of paper. "Two barbecue-rib dinners for the price of one—seven ninety-five—including corn on the cob and baked beans.' That's a special for four days only."

Anne shook her head. "I don't think ..."

She might as well have been talking to the toaster for all the notice Jason paid. "I went over the grocery list and deleted the stuff I would have bought for tonight's meal, and, along with what I saved by using coupons, I come up with a grand total of twelve dollars and seventy-five cents. Now, I figure that's enough to cover dinner, a glass of wine apiece and a reasonable tip. So, are you going to wear your white coat or would you prefer to change?"

He wasn't leaving her much of a choice, and Anne was too tired to care. Besides, in a peculiar way, what he said made sense. If he'd saved the cost of a restaurant meal out of the grocery money, why not?

Upstairs, as she was changing into slacks and a knit top, the humor of the situation struck her. Jason was acting like an old-fashioned housewife saving nickels in the cookie jar. And she herself felt like an old-fashioned husband, coming home grumpy from the office.

But when she descended the staircase and saw Jason's lean figure silhouetted in the entranceway, he didn't look anything like an old-fashioned housewife. He looked like a very desirable man, and a rather mysterious one, with his face shadowed against the fading daylight.

Who was he really? When she'd asked at the beach about his past, he'd avoided answering, and the only thing she really knew was that his mother had suffered from colitis. Come to think of it, she really didn't know much about what he'd done or where he'd been.

Involuntarily, Anne shivered. During the past week, she'd come to feel comfortable with Jason and to trust him. Yet now she recalled her initial misgivings when she'd seen his résumé.

True, there'd been a reference from a lawyer, but she hadn't even bothered to check whether the man really existed. Anyone could print up letterheads....

The hunger pangs must be addling my senses. What do I think he is, a hit man for the Mafia?

"You know," she said, trying to keep her tone casual as they walked out to the car, "you still haven't told me much about your background."

"If you really want to know, I promise to bore you to death with it over dinner." He held the door for her.

The restaurant looked like a modern version of the Hanging Gardens of Babylon. Inside, plants trailed down from a row of window boxes near ceiling height. Most of the walls and roof were made of glass, revealing the fading pink remains of the sunset against a darkening sky.

"Very scenic," Anne observed as they followed a waitress to their seats.

Jason held her chair, then addressed the waitress. "We won't need a menu—we're having the special." He turned to Anne. "Unless you'd like something else?"

"Oh, no. I wouldn't think of it."

When their glasses of rosé wine had been set in front of them, Jason began, "I promised you my life story, more or less."

"Mmm-hmm." The wine had a pleasant fruity tang.

"I'm from Boston originally."

"You don't have an accent."

"I never did, really—I don't know why. Everyone else in my family has one." His eyes narrowed, remembering. "My dad's an auto mechanic—owns his own shop—and my mother was a secretary. But she was sick a lot when I was young, and being the oldest of five kids, I did a lot of cooking and cleaning."

"Five kids?"

"Three girls and one other boy. They all still live back in Massachusetts. I'm the one who wandered."

"I used to wish I had more than just one sister." Anne rested her chin on the heel of her hand. "And that my family would stay in one place for more than a year at a time."

"And I used to wish I could fly off to some exotic place. My favorite books were *Treasure Island* and *Robinson Crusoe*."

"Did you ever get to travel to places like that?"

"Yes, I did." She hoped he would elaborate, but he merely sipped at his wine for a moment. "That's why I'm still rattling around like a loose wheel at the age of thirty-five. But it was worth it."

Had his wife gotten tired of all that wandering? Anne wondered. Was that why the marriage had broken up? But it was too personal a question to ask.

"You said you were interested in photography. Were you taking travel pictures?"

"Something like that."

Their dinners arrived, and Jason felt as if he'd been saved by the bell. He didn't mind telling Anne about his life—in fact, he wished he could be even more open with her—but it was too soon.

Too soon because of your project? Or because you don't want to risk losing her? The thought startled him. He would have to mull that one over later, when her green eyes weren't focused so intently on his face.

The ribs were tasty but messy. Anne dug in with gusto and didn't seem to mind when she wound up with barbecue sauce on her chin.

Sometimes she could be frustratingly prim and proper, and at other times, like now, a lively, uninhibited side of her shone through. Jason cherished these glimpses of what he considered to be the real Anne, the girl she must have been all those years ago when she battled cockroaches in Hollywood and dreamed of becoming an actress.

"After we finish this, we ought to go jump in the nearest swimming pool." He rinsed his hands in a fingerbowl the waitress had provided.

Anne wiped her chin with the napkin. "Actually, I'm more in the mood for a walk."

Through the broad windows of the restaurant, Jason could see a full moon rising. The night looked clear and inviting.

"I know just the place." He paid the check and helped her up. "One of my discoveries."

"No concrete, I hope?" Anne led the way out of the restaurant. "I feel like getting some exercise, but my feet may give out."

"No concrete. I promise."

He drove up the coast to Newport Beach. Anne didn't appear to be paying much attention to their route; she was gazing through the windshield at the stars.

What was the man like whom she was having over for dinner tomorrow night? Did he mean anything to her? Jason doubted it. There had been no excited ring to her voice when she told him to expect a guest for dinner.

Besides, although Anne would probably rather perform surgery on herself than admit it, the chemistry between her and Jason was too strong to yield to some other, newer attraction.

Chemistry. Maybe that was the wrong word. It was used so often to describe mere sexual attraction, and what he felt for Anne was much more than that.

She intrigued him, true; in many ways they were opposites, and opposites were supposed to attract. But he suspected that at a deeper level they were very much alike.

Still, he might be wrong. He'd misjudged Jill, or perhaps he'd misjudged his own needs within a marriage. He hadn't realized, when the two of them decided to elope on the spur of the moment after graduation, how important having children would become to him later.

His reflections ended as they reached their destination, a quiet side road, where he pulled over onto a dirt shoulder.

"Where are we?" Anne blinked as if she'd just awakened.

To their left across the road stretched a row of standard-issue ranch-style houses. But off to the right, there was merely open space.

"Come on and I'll show you."

Getting out of the car, he sniffed the salt air and listened for a moment to the hushed calls of night birds. Anne joined him, her expression puzzled.

"It feels as if we're out in the wilderness."

"In a sense, we are." He took her arm and led her down a dirt path between tall wild grasses. The air around them even felt different from that in the manicured suburbs; there was an untamed, adventuresome quality to it that he relished.

"The Back Bay!" Her eyes lit up with excitement. "All the years I've lived here I've meant to come down and explore, but I never have."

The Back Bay—whose official name was Upper Newport Bay—was a wildlife preserve despite efforts over the years to turn it into yet another Southern California marina. Silently, Jason thanked the environmentalists who'd fought to save one of the last remaining saltwater estuaries along the West Coast.

A haven for migrating birds, it also was home to many species of fish and small animals, he knew from having taken a tour here one Sunday. Set down into a natural bowl, its serenity shut out the clatter and clutter of nearby housing developments.

They walked for a while without speaking, stepping carefully along the raw pathway. The bay spread before them, scarcely rippling in the moonlight. Its primeval calmness touched them both with magic.

"At times like this I wish I were a poet." Jason helped Anne navigate a treacherous rut in the path. "There's something almost metaphoric about this place."

"Metaphoric?"

"As if it meant something beyond itself. A last wild spot remaining in a tamed land."

Unexpectedly, Anne felt tears prickle in her eyes. Jason might as well have been describing himself. She sensed the restlessness within him, the wanderlust that could never be stilled. This man who had turned her suburban dwelling into a home would never be happy living there permanently; he was too much like her father, eager to see what lay beyond the horizon.

But then, she'd never expected Jason to stay with her permanently, had she?

It must be the moonlight that's making me maudlin. She swallowed hard, glad for the darkness that hid her expression.

They stopped at the edge of a low cliff, looking down over the water. Far off, Anne could hear the murmur of cars across the bay bridge on Pacific Coast Highway. Beyond lay Lower Newport Bay, which over the decades had been dredged and turned into a major pleasure-boat harbor.

That wasn't so bad, either, she reflected. She'd gone sailing with friends once on the bay and had been entranced by the row upon row of tethered boats of all sizes.

Although the day had been hot, the air was turning chilly now, and Anne shivered. Jason slipped his arm around her, and Anne relaxed into the warmth.

Her head rested against his shoulder and she could feel the pulsing of his heart even through the soft fabric of his jacket.

How strange it was that they'd come to be here, that they'd met at all, she mused.

It felt like the most natural thing in the world when he turned her toward him and his lips grazed her forehead, then touched the tip of her nose and moved down to her mouth.

For a moment Anne couldn't breathe. The reality of Jason blotted out everything else around them. She wanted to stroke his cheek, to explore the contours of his bones and the sinuousness of his muscles beneath the jacket.

Slowly she responded to his kiss, her tongue flicking lightly against his teeth. Jason's mouth opened wider and his arms tightened around her waist.

Her entire body responded, silvery sensations flickering through her. How good it would feel to entwine her legs with his, to run her hands along his back, to nuzzle the soft shock of hair on his forehead....

Reluctantly, Anne drew back. *Too dangerous.* "We'd better go."

A glimmer of moonlight touched Jason's eyes as he nodded slowly.

They walked back to the car together, not touching, but Anne felt as if her entire body were being caressed. She'd never responded to a man this way before. What was it about Jason that affected her so strangely?

At home, alone in her room upstairs, she undressed in front of the mirror, wondering how she looked to him and what he thought of her.

She tried not to think about how she would feel when, like a wild bird, he took wing from his temporary perch and resumed his migrations through the world.

Chapter Seven

Juanita's face filled with wonder as she gently polished an antique vase and traced the intricate figure of a Greek goddess. The morning light, filtering through lacy curtains, emphasized her broad cheekbones and dark eyes as she studied the beautiful vase, giving an ethereal, timeless air to the photograph Jason was taking.

Friday morning had been a time of revelation to him. The house where she worked might be a symbol of materialism and exploitation to Jason, but to Juanita—now that her initial fears were fading—it was a storehouse of wonders and, in a way, a promise of what she might achieve someday here in America.

"You should see the village where I grew up," she observed half an hour later as he took pictures of her mopping the redwood deck, with a hot tub in the background. "The streets are dirt. The houses are made of adobe; sometimes a man gets drunk on Saturday night and puts his fist right through a wall."

"I'd like to see it." Jason was coming to realize he would have to visit Mexico in order to complete his book. "Would it be all right if I went to see your parents and told them I was your friend?"

"Of course." She gave him the name of the village and the province. "They would be so glad to meet someone from America who knows me."

"And I'd be delighted to meet them."

She also agreed that a week from Sunday would be a good day to photograph the children.

Afterward, over a cup of coffee, he produced copies of both of his books and autographed them for Juanita. They were sitting in Juanita's small room, drinking from two chipped cups that obviously didn't belong to her employers.

She leafed through *The Private Life of a Revolutionary*, examining the pictures of a dusty Middle Eastern training camp, the grim-faced young men and women in fatigues, the piles of weapons. "Why are they so angry? Why do they want to make war?"

Jason wished he could find the words to explain in Spanish. Or maybe the problem wasn't words; it was that he himself found it hard to understand why mankind seemed so intent on blowing itself up.

"Sometimes when people suffer, they learn to hate." She nodded in understanding at his words. "We have a saying in English—two wrongs don't make a right. But some people don't believe that."

"We suffer, too, where I come from, but there is also much joy."

"I'm sure there is." He checked his watch. "I'd better be going. Your lady is due back soon from her gardening club, isn't she?"

"Yes. Thank you for coming. You and Rosa have helped me very much. And I look forward to having pictures of my children."

There was always more to a story once you got involved with it than you'd expected, Jason mused as he strolled the three blocks back to Anne's house. In his study of the politician, he'd been intrigued by the man's wife, a real old-

fashioned Southern lady who epitomized the image of an
iron fist in a velvet glove.

Now, working on this story, the vague ideas he'd had of
an oppressed woman had given way, bit by bit, to a portrait
of a real, three-dimensional person. Juanita was intelligent
and sensitive. In addition, he sensed an undercurrent of
strength in her; it was a trait that reminded him of Anne.

Well, he'd better not forget that he had a job to do, in
addition to taking pictures of Juanita.

Friday was, according to Ada's schedule, the day for
scrubbing the bathrooms and kitchen. Ignoring her supply
of plastic gloves, Jason went to work with a whistle, running through his favorite tunes by Rodgers and Hammerstein.

Within an hour, both his musicality and his skin were
fading fast. Reluctantly, he pulled on a pair of the gloves—
fortunately, Ada had had large hands for a woman—and
resumed work with renewed respect for the term "dishpan
hands."

By three o'clock his back ached, and he soaked in a bath
for half an hour before beginning preparations for Anne's
dinner date.

He'd decided to make sauteed pork strips with peanuts,
saffron rice and a *niçoise* salad, served with a Chablis from
his favorite small winery, Glen Ellen. Then, for dessert,
there would be a rich crème caramel.

This guy had better be worth all the trouble.

SEVERAL OF THE NURSES in the obstetrics-gynecology wing
shot knowing looks at Anne. Damn the hospital grapevine,
and damn Aldous's big mouth.

She was beginning to wish she'd never accepted his invitation. Did he really think she'd believed that old line about
him wanting to get to know her better?

Really, she'd much rather just slump home in her usual Friday-night fog and let Jason perk her up with a tasty meal and his easygoing comradeship.

Well, she couldn't back out of it now. Besides, it would be interesting to find out what Aldous really had in mind and how he operated. Maybe he'd surprise her, Anne told herself without much conviction as she drove home. Maybe he'd actually prove to be an interesting, likable fellow.

Coming in the front door, she could smell something delicious in the air—was that saffron and rosemary?—and hear Jason moving about in the kitchen, stirring something in a pan and whistling under his breath.

She tried to identify the song and then wished she hadn't. It was "People Will Say We're in Love" from *Oklahoma!* Was that a satiric reference to her date or a comment on last night? Her stomach fluttered in midair, remembering the taste of his lips on hers.

Nonsense. He's probably not even aware of what song he's whistling.

She went upstairs to get ready.

Anne's instinct was to put on the highest-necked, longest-sleeved dress in the closet. But she refused to make herself look like a stereotypical prim old maid. No, she would wear a floating lavender crepe dress with a somewhat daring scoop neck.

When she came downstairs, Jason was whistling "I Cain't Say No."

Smart aleck, she commented silently.

It was a quarter past seven when the doorbell rang. Standing outside, Aldous sported a smooth grin and a dozen roses wrapped in green paper, the kind vendors sold at freeway off-ramps.

"They're beautiful." Anne sniffed the flowers as she took them, but there was no fragrance. "I'll put them in a vase."

She rattled around in her china cabinet before realizing that Jason must have already put some flowers in her favorite vase. Sure enough, she spotted it on the mantel in the living room, full of yellow and purple tulips.

How did he know that's the vase I like best?

Finally the roses were ensconced in another vase on the coffee table, and Aldous was reclining on the couch, guzzling Anne's Scotch.

"Boy, did I have a rough time today!" He proceeded to regale her—rather amusingly, she had to admit—with the story of his run-ins at the hospital. It was only half an hour later, as Jason announced dinner, that she realized Aldous hadn't once asked how *her* day had gone.

Not that she particularly wanted to tell him.

The food was delicious, but Anne scarcely tasted it. Aldous apparently believed food was the perfect vehicle for lovemaking. He fed her morsels from his plate—a tactic that disgusted her, but she was at a loss for a way to refuse without insulting him—and pursed his lips at her as he downed an anchovy from his salad.

Behind her, Anne heard Jason cough discreetly as he brought out a second bottle of wine. Subtle as the signal was, Anne knew Jason well enough to deduce from one cough that he found Aldous's posturing every bit as repulsive as she did.

Well, she wasn't going to admit it, not in front of Jason. Resolutely, Anne smiled at her guest.

His eyes gleamed wolflike in the light from the chandelier.

Oh, good heavens.

When Jason served the crème caramel and a bottle of brandy to go with it, she feared for a moment that he was going to spill something on Aldous. When she could do so unobserved, she shot Jason what she hoped was a quelling look.

He blinked in pretended innocence. But at least he didn't spill anything.

Finally, Aldous had romanced the last of the dessert and suggested they retreat to the living room. Restraining an impulse to pitch him out on the seat of his too-tight slacks, Anne agreed, if only to show Jason that she knew what she was doing.

But did she?

Aldous cut off her attempts to sink into an armchair by seizing her arm and guiding her to the couch, where he slid down beside her with his leg touching hers.

So much for subtlety.

"There's something I've been wanting to tell you," Aldous murmured in her ear.

"There is?"

"Yes. You know, as a plastic surgeon, I am an expert in bone structure."

That wasn't what she'd expected to hear. "I'm aware of that."

"But I've never seen a face like yours." He ran his fingers along the line of her jaw and tipped her face toward his. "Such classic perfection."

Such classic garbage!

Anne was about to pull away when she heard footsteps approaching through the dining room.

"Don't mind me." Jason knelt by the fireplace and lowered an armful of firewood to the hearth with a clatter. "I just thought you two might enjoy a nice fire."

"In June?" Aldous snapped. "It must have been eighty degrees out today."

"But it gets cold at night." Jason wedged a log into the fireplace and began stuffing kindling around it.

Anne glared at him. "Thank you, Jason, but we can do without the fire."

"Oh, well—if you insist." With a shrug, he stood up, brushed his hands off noisily and ambled away.

"Are you sure hiring a male housekeeper was such a good idea?" Aldous looked distinctly displeased at the interruption.

"It's just an experiment—for a month."

It didn't take Aldous long to get back to his attempted seduction. "You know, some men would be intimidated by you. But I like liberated women."

"You do?"

"I could see at once that you don't believe in old-fashioned inhibitions, that you take what you want when you see it. I'm the same way."

"Oh?" Anne was curious to hear what came next, but she didn't get the chance.

Jason bustled into the room carrying a plate of chocolate-covered wafers. "I thought you folks might like some after-dinner mints."

An inarticulate noise issued from Aldous's lips.

"No, we would not." Anne's tone was crisp.

"I'll leave them, in case you get hungry." Jason set the plate on the coffee table. "Boy, I really made a mess with that kindling, didn't I?" He pulled a small brush from beside the fireplace and began sweeping up the shavings. "Just pretend I'm not here."

"Out!" Anne's temper snapped. "And don't come back! Even if the house burns down!"

Jason shrugged. "Anything you say, Dr. Eldridge." He finished a last bit of sweeping and departed.

"The man is insufferable." Aldous shifted uncomfortably on the couch. "How can anyone feel the least bit romantic with him around?"

"Exactly." Anne seized the opportunity to pull away. "I should never have suggested we have dinner here. But it was a lovely evening, wasn't it?"

Aldous ignored the hint for him to depart. "I'm glad you got rid of him. Now, at last, we're alone."

Before Anne could think of an appropriate rejoinder, she found herself seized in Aldous's arms as he rained kisses on her neck, heading lower and lower toward the cleavage revealed by her low-cut dress.

"Hey, wait a minute!" She braced herself against him. "Just cut that out!"

"You've been giving me signals all night." Aldous pressed her down onto the couch. "It's not unusual for a woman to get cold feet. Let me show you how wonderful lovemaking can be. You need a real man to arouse the woman in you."

"I need—" Before she could get the words out, his lips closed over hers.

Anne found herself struggling in earnest. She couldn't believe Aldous actually meant to assault her, but obviously his idea of a romantic evening and hers were not even in the same universe.

All she could get out was a series of unintelligible grunts as she fought to free herself.

What was it they taught you in self-defense class? Grab his little finger and bend it backward until it breaks. No, that was when someone was choking you. Knee him in the groin—that was it! But how was she supposed to do that when her legs were pinned underneath him?

Then, suddenly, Aldous's unwelcome weight lifted off her. Anne gasped for breath and then saw with amazement what had happened.

Jason had a lock-grip on Aldous's throat and was marching the plastic surgeon across the living room toward the front door. Aldous's protests were stifled by the firm grasp across his throat, and Anne felt a moment of intense satisfaction at seeing the tables turned.

Somehow Jason managed to open the door without losing his grip on Aldous and tossed the gasping physician out onto the doorstep.

Without a word, Jason slammed the door. He turned to face Anne. "Are you all right?"

Embarrassed, she nodded. "I—he really jumped me. I wasn't expecting that."

"Neither was I." Jason came to sit beside her. "Frankly, I thought his technique would be a bit smoother than that. But those noises you were making didn't sound like you were having a good time."

Relief washed over her as she leaned against Jason's sturdy shoulder. He smelled fresh and good, of spicy after-shave lotion and a hint of saffron.

"Where did you learn to do that? You handled Aldous like a real commando."

Jason coughed. "I, uh, included a little military training in my travels. Just to see what it was like."

"Thank goodness."

He slipped an arm around her waist. How different it felt from Aldous's selfish gropings, Anne reflected as she heard a car start on the street and listened to Aldous drive away. This would be one encounter he wouldn't gab about to his pals at the hospital.

For a time, Jason sat there holding her, comfortingly. He seemed to sense that Anne didn't want to be fondled or kissed, not so soon after Aldous's attack.

The phone rang.

"Are you on call?" he asked.

She shook her head. "But I'd better get it. You never know."

Reluctantly, he released her, and she went to get the phone.

It was Ellie. "I know you're not on call but—I've started having contractions." Her voice sounded shaky. "They're about fifteen minutes apart."

"I'll meet you at the hospital. Come right in through the emergency room and have them take you up to Labor and Delivery. I'll call to let them know you're coming."

The crisp commands seemed to relieve Ellie. "Thanks. I—we'll be there in a few minutes."

Anne hung up and quickly explained the situation to Jason.

"Do you want me to drive you?"

"No." She managed a weak smile. "I can handle it." But it felt good, knowing Jason was there if she needed him.

There was no more time that night to think about Jason or about her close encounter with Aldous Raney.

Ellie's contractions were only ten minutes apart by the time Anne examined her. She had already instructed the nurses by phone to start giving Ellie medication intravenously. The question now was whether it would take effect before her labor progressed too far to be stopped.

It wasn't the first time Anne had dealt with premature labor, but never before had she been dealing with someone she felt close to. Of course, she cared about all her patients—but she knew Ellie's hopes and dreams for this child, and that made the danger all the more real to her.

While Ellie's husband held his wife's hand, Anne made arrangements for a staff neonatalogist—a specialist in dealing with newborn babies—to stand by in case he was needed. There was no time to test for the baby's lung maturity, so they would have to assume it might need extra care.

When she went back to check on Ellie, Anne saw the relief on her friend's face at once.

"They're slowing down."

Anne checked the printout on the monitor, which showed both the baby's heartbeat and the mother's contractions. Sure enough, the contractions were spacing out, coming about twenty minutes apart and slowing down.

"The baby looks fine." Anne smiled for the first time in hours. "The heartbeat's strong and reactive—it speeds up during the contractions, which means he's getting plenty of oxygen."

Under other circumstances, Anne would have gone home now and let the nurses keep in touch by phone, but instead she waited until the contractions had stopped.

It was close to four o'clock in the morning when she took her leave. "I'll have them transfer you over to a semiprivate room in a couple of hours," she told Ellie. "I think you'd better stay in the hospital for a few days."

Her friend nodded. "Thank you."

The exhaustion didn't hit until Anne was halfway home. Then, all at once, she found herself yearning to sleep for a month.

Yet, despite the weariness, she felt a sense of satisfaction, too. At this stage in a pregnancy, every day inside the mother meant the baby had a stronger chance of surviving in good health. Maybe Ellie would go full-term, or maybe she'd deliver early, but if they gained a few weeks or even a few days, that could make a tremendous difference.

This is what I studied so hard for. This is why I gave up weekends at the beach and going to the movies with my friends.

It was worth it.

At the same time, as she staggered out of the car and up the front walk, Anne was glad she wasn't coming home to an empty house. Even though he was probably sound asleep, Jason was there.

Trying to make as little noise as possible, she fit her key into the lock and opened the door. A lamp glowed in the living room, and she went in to turn it off. That was when she saw Jason asleep on the couch, where he'd obviously been trying to wait up for her.

Anne smiled. How young he appeared in repose, his face unlined, his dark eyelashes pressed against his cheek. She could imagine how he must have looked as a young boy—rather angelic, but no doubt with a devilish glint in his eyes.

Perhaps he sensed her presence even in his sleep, for at that moment he woke up. "What time is it?"

She checked her watch. "Almost four-thirty."

"You must be wiped out." He sat up.

"I'm okay. You should have seen me when I was an intern—once I worked for forty-eight hours straight. This is nothing by comparison."

But she hadn't been thirty-three years old then, either, had she? Anne thought as she tried to make her weary muscles carry her toward the stairs. Instead, she staggered and had to grab onto a chair for support.

Jason caught her arm. "First of all, you need some nourishment. I prescribe hot chocolate with real milk, none of that instant stuff." How could he be so wide awake at a time like this? "You're not due anywhere first thing in the morning, are you?"

"Not on Saturday."

"Good." He escorted her into the kitchen, where Anne collapsed into a chair while Jason bustled around at the stove.

"You would have made someone a good mother."

An unreadable expression crossed his face—almost regret, she thought, but was too dazed to try to figure it out.

The hot chocolate tasted wonderful, but by the time she finished Anne was nodding over the table.

"Time for bed." Jason helped her up.

It wasn't until they'd reached the bedroom that it occurred to Anne she ought to shoo him away. She tried to find the words, but nothing came out.

Calmly, he retrieved one of her nightgowns from the closet.

"You—you shouldn't . . ."

"Hey. You're talking to the man who does your laundry every week, remember? I washed this, ironed it and hung it up. Let's just say that putting it on you is merely an extension of my duties."

In her befuddled state, what Jason was saying almost made sense.

Vaguely, Anne was aware of her outer clothing being removed and the gown being slipped over her head. She thought about protesting and dismissed the idea as far too strenuous.

A rustling noise told her Jason was turning down the bedcovers, and then Anne found herself being lifted into bed.

Her body ached all over, but it was a pleasant ache as she relaxed against the sheets. Strong hands moved over her back, finding the tense muscles and soothing them into submission. His sturdy, probing fingers took on a life of their own; Anne yielded with a sigh.

A stray wisp of hair was brushed away from her cheek, and someone touched a kiss to her temple. She was a child again, trusting and dreamy.

The mattress sagged beside her, and she felt a warm breath across her neck. Then the massage resumed, moving from her shoulders down her spine to the small of her back.

Gradually the movements slowed. Anne slept, and Jason slept beside her.

Chapter Eight

Anne came awake all at once, a habit she'd picked up during years of responding to medical emergencies. Sunny morning light flooded the bedroom, and someone was snoring quietly beside her.

Oh, my God.

She rolled over slowly. Despite her alertness, last night had blurred in her memory. She knew where she was, but not who this was.

Aldous? It couldn't be....

Then she nearly laughed. Of course, it was Jason, his head thrown back on the pillow, his well-shaped nose pointing skyward and a faint but unmistakable snore emanating from his nasal passages.

Anne's mirth died quickly. They hadn't made love, had they? Surely she would remember. But he was here beside her, and she was wearing a nightgown.

He, however, was still clad in the slacks and shirt he'd worn the night before. It was hardly likely he would have put them back on after making love to her.

She ought to be relieved. So why did she feel a pinch of disappointment?

Quietly, Anne slipped out of bed. In the bathroom, she changed into jeans and a blouse, then tiptoed downstairs. Trying not to bang the pots, she began fixing cheese omelets and bacon, with fresh-brewed coffee. Activity always helped to clear her head, and right now she needed to think.

As she popped the bacon into the microwave oven and the cheese into the food processor for grating, Anne tried to assess what was troubling her.

Without realizing it, she'd grown closer to Jason than she ever had to a man before—even to Ken back in her college days. Jason belonged here, in Anne's house.

But he didn't belong in her life. Like Ken, he appealed to the wild side of her, the part of herself that she'd left behind when she went to medical school. Sure, for a while Anne might be happy living in a more carefree way, throwing aside the routine that sometimes chafed at her, traveling with Jason and spending long lazy days at the beach.

But not permanently. And she couldn't see him living here permanently, either. There was a restlessness about Jason beneath the deceptively domesticated exterior. He was only playing at being a housekeeper until he saved up enough money to take off again.

And how would she feel when he did?

Anne turned, the omelet pan in her hand, as Jason sauntered in. "A heavenly smell wafted upward and roused me from the arms of Morpheus. And to think, I didn't believe you could cook."

"Only when necessary to avoid starvation." Anne transferred the food onto plates she'd warmed in the oven. "Or when I owe somebody a favor. Thanks for waiting up for me last night, Jason."

"My pleasure." He poured two cups of coffee.

"But . . ."

He cocked an eyebrow at her.

"This isn't working."

"What isn't?"

"Our experiment. Having you as my housekeeper." Anne took a deep breath as she sat beside him at the breakfast table. "Things have gotten out of hand."

He was silent for a moment. Anne would have given a month's income to be able to read his mind.

Finally the stillness became unbearable, and she blundered on. "It's...too intimate, living in the same house, seeing each other constantly. I'm asking you to leave as soon as you can find another place to stay. I'll pay you for the whole month; that was our deal."

Jason continued to stare down at his black coffee.

"You do understand, don't you?" Darn him, why didn't he say something!

"I suppose I do." He spoke slowly, his face more serious than she'd ever seen it before. "But I think we could work this out."

"I don't."

They finished their breakfast without another word. Jason collected the dishes, and Anne sat at the table feeling as though she'd just lost her best friend.

Glumly, she put in a call to the hospital. Chatting with Ellie cheered her up a little; her friend was feeling much better and was even talking about coming back to work on Monday, but Anne wouldn't hear of it. When Ellie was well enough to leave the hospital, she was going home on strict bed rest for at least two weeks.

The rest of the day dragged by. Jason gathered up his swimsuit and took off for the beach before noon, but his presence continued to fill the house. Everywhere Anne looked, she saw some reminder—the tulips blossoming in her favorite vase, a rumpled cushion where he'd fallen asleep on the couch, a recipe for spaghetti *alla carbonara* set out on the kitchen counter in readiness for tonight.

The house took on an empty, hollow feel, like a model home in a new development. Anne tried to read a medical journal, but she found the articles intensely boring and finally switched on a television documentary about wild geese, which turned out to be a sure cure for insomnia.

Although she was on call, the phone rang only twice, and both times it was a patient with questions that didn't require any immediate action. Just when Anne could have used a good emergency to keep her mind off Jason!

He returned about four o'clock, his bronze skin smelling of suntan lotion but his expression still sober. After a brief hello, he retreated to his room, and a moment later Anne heard his shower running.

That night, she went out to a movie by herself. It was a light comedy, and several times during it she noted that Jason would have enjoyed a particular line, or she wondered what he would have said about a character's actions.

When she came back, he was sitting in the living room with his feet up, watching an old Cary Grant movie on TV with a big bowl of popcorn at his side. It would have been a lot more fun spending the evening here than going out, Anne thought, and to her disgust found herself wanting to cry.

It would be a good thing after all when he left, she told herself as she went upstairs. She was acting like a lovesick teenager.

WHY WAS IT BOTHERING him so much?

Of course, it would be inconvenient, having to move out so soon. And of course he'd miss Anne's companionship—but they could stay friends, couldn't they?

Staring at the comics on Sunday morning without really seeing them, Jason listened to the sounds of Anne getting dressed upstairs. He would have recognized her noises anywhere—the way she scuffed her panda slippers across the floor, her habit of leaving the water running while she brushed her teeth, the scrape of hangers as she considered and rejected several outfits before deciding what to wear.

He would tell her today why he'd really come to work here. There wasn't much more she could do than to throw him out, and she was already doing that.

Upstairs, Anne finally decided on a pair of white cotton slacks and a red-and-blue-print blouse. Not that it mattered what she wore; she was just going to be sitting home reading her journals and perhaps skimming the newspaper. But Jason would be living here for only a few more days, and it did seem reasonable for her to dress up a little.

The phone rang. Since she wasn't on call, Anne's first thought was that something had gone wrong with Ellie.

She grabbed the phone off the night table. "Yes?"

"Anne? Am I interrupting something?" The connection was as clear as if the call came from next door, but Anne immediately recognized her sister's voice, all the way from Oregon.

"Oh—no, Lori. I thought it might be some bad news about one of my patients."

They chatted for a moment as Lori caught Anne up on the doings of her husband and two sons. Then there was a brief but awkward pause, and Anne knew her sister was about to ask for a favor.

Lori never intended to get into a fix, but she always had, even when they were children. She just couldn't seem to plan ahead, to weigh the consequences of her actions, and as a result she frequently bit off more than she could chew. Anne, the well-organized one, usually ended up stepping into the breach. In fact, she sometimes reflected, maybe that's why she'd become so well organized, because one of them had to be.

So she wasn't surprised when her sister said, "Actually, I have a request to make."

"Oh?" Anne pretended innocence.

"I, uh, I have kind of a problem."

"Gee, Lori, I hope it isn't anything serious." She knew perfectly well that it wasn't, or Lori would have gotten to the point immediately.

"No, no, but..." A child shouted in the background, and Anne could hear Lori turn away from the phone to make peace between her youngsters. "Sorry about that."

"I always enjoy hearing my nephews' voices, even when they're fighting." Anne sat down on the bed, wishing she could see the boys. They must have grown a lot since last summer.

"It's...well, you know I'm hosting the family reunion this year." Lori plunged ahead. "Anne, I just can't do it. We're adding a playroom onto the back of the house and the contractor is way behind schedule. Jeb and Sammy both had chicken pox, so the carpenter had to wait, and then it rained... The house is a mess and the reunion's only three weeks away. I'll never make it!"

Anne groaned aloud. This *was* serious! Since childhood, she'd looked forward every year to these annual gatherings, the one stable event in their peripatetic existence. Now that she was grown, it remained important, a chance to see her extended family and to watch the children grow.

"Everyone looks forward to it. You knew what was involved when you took it on."

"Yes, but..." Lori's voice quavered. "Oh, Anne, I know I'm always asking you to get me out of scrapes, but I'll never do it again, I promise! I can't ask Mom and Dad, not after Dad's ulcer attack last month. If you can't host it, I'll have to cancel."

"You wouldn't!" It would mean not only a severe disappointment to Anne but an even greater one to her parents and some of the older members of the family.

Furthermore, their branch of the family hadn't hosted the reunion in several years. Even if one of the cousins took on the project at the last minute, it wouldn't be fair—and Anne knew that her own embarrassment would dampen the fun of attending.

"Anne, there's no way we can have the house ready in three weeks! Please, please, please. If you say yes, I'll call everyone myself, today, and make the arrangements. I'll even mail out little maps so people can find you! The only thing you'll have to do is actually host the event. Your house is big enough, and it always looks perfect...."

I'll have to keep Jason until then. I wouldn't be able to manage by myself.

He would do a splendid job. Anne could picture him, whipping up mammoth breakfasts for the whole gang, swapping jokes with the kids....

"Well, I don't suppose I have much choice." There was no point in letting Lori get off too easily; one of these days, she'd have to learn her lesson. "But it's really inconvenient."

"I know! Oh, Anne, thank you!" Lori renewed her promise to call everyone, and finally they said goodbye.

Well, she should have expected it, Anne told herself as she hung up. But she'd thought that this time, finally, Lori would come through.

Still, her sister was delightful, and she could be wonderful in a pinch. Once, when Anne had come down with the flu during medical school, Lori had moved into her apartment for a week to ply her with chicken soup and aspirin while Anne studied for exams.

Her spirits surprisingly light, Anne went downstairs to tell Jason.

He was sprawled on the sofa reading the comics, looking as comfortable and unselfconscious as a cat. When she entered the room, he glanced up and they both spoke at once.

"Anne, there's something—"

"Jason, I've got a—"

They both stopped.

"You go ahead," Anne said.

"No, you."

She took a deep breath and explained about Lori and the family reunion. "There's no way I can manage it myself. Would you consider staying on for another three weeks?"

He nodded. "Sure. I'm not the one who wanted to leave. How many people can we expect?"

"Usually about thirty. Most of them stay in hotels or in their motor homes. But my parents and Lori's family will be staying here—that's six people altogether. We usually eat buffet-style, with everybody bringing something. Thank goodness for kitchens in motor homes!" As she spoke, Anne dropped into an armchair. How easy it was to work things out with Jason; even Ada would have squawked about taking on such a chore on short notice.

"Nothing I can't handle." He appeared to be doing some mental calculations. "You'll have to give me a list of how many meals we'll be having and when everyone will be hitting town."

"Sure." It wouldn't hurt to have him stay the extra few weeks; in fact, now that Anne thought about it, it made perfect sense. He'd have more time to find another place to live, and she'd have time to locate another housekeeper. "What were you going to say?"

"I beg your pardon?" His eyes had a faraway expression, as if he were already planning the menus.

"When I came into the room, you started to say something."

"Oh." He looked down at his hands. "Have you ever noticed how newsprint turns your fingers black? You'd think modern technology could come up with a better kind of ink."

"Is that what you were going to say?"

"Actually, no." He tossed the comics aside. "Mmm—are you busy next Sunday?"

She reflected for a moment. "I don't think so."

"Maybe you could come with me to Santa Ana." He told her that he'd offered to take photographs of some children for their mother, a live-in housekeeper whom he'd met at the supermarket. "They don't live all that far away, but it's a different world from Irvine. I thought you might be interested in coming along."

"Well—sure." Anne's curiosity was aroused. It was certainly generous of Jason to do the mother a favor, but she sensed there was more to it than that. "Are you taking on some special project? Some kind of charitable work?"

"This isn't charity." The sharpness of his tone surprised her. "Juanita wouldn't accept charity unless she was desperate. These people may be poor, but they have their pride."

"That wasn't what I meant. It was the way you sounded, as if you were on some kind of mission. When I hired you, you said you wanted to pursue your own photography interests. Is this part of it?"

"In a way." He jumped up. "I'm going to get a cup of coffee. Want some?"

"Sure." Now what was he being so secretive about? But she didn't have a right to pry, Anne told herself. Jason was entitled to his private life, one that didn't include her. After all, he would only be working here for three more weeks.

THE APARTMENT BUILDING in Santa Ana had obviously seen better days. A ramshackle one-story structure, it had peeling paint, a dirt yard pierced only by a few bedraggled weeds and walls defaced by graffiti.

Anne inhaled the cooking smells of chilli powder and hot peppers as she slid out of Jason's car. A dirty-faced little girl ran past her, not more than three years old but playing with the other children without adult supervision.

And there certainly were a lot of children. The yard was full of them, kids of all ages, most with lovely dark hair and olive skin but also some with blond hair and blue eyes. Despite the shabbiness of their clothing, they looked as if they were having a good time as they shrieked and sprayed each other with a hose.

Juanita had insisted on coming down earlier in the day by bus so she could go to church with her family. Now, Anne and Jason threaded their way along a cracked walkway littered with toys as they searched for the right apartment.

Most of the numbers had crumbled away, and finally Jason had to knock on an apartment door to ask directions.

The woman who answered couldn't have been more than Anne's age, but habitual weariness had creased the skin around her eyes and mouth. She carried a baby on one hip and in the apartment behind her Anne could hear a toddler banging on pots and pans.

I wonder what she does about medical care?

The thought troubled Anne as they thanked the woman for her help and proceeded on to Juanita's sister's flat. A lot of women right here in Southern California never got medical care, Anne knew; they gave birth at home, with an unlicensed midwife in attendance. Minor problems went untreated and often became serious as a result.

The number of low-cost health clinics had shrunk in recent years. For a long while she'd been meaning to do something to help, but she'd never been able to find the time. But she would. One of these days.

When they reached the right apartment, Juanita answered the door. Anne liked her at once. There was a calm strength about Juanita that was extremely appealing, as well as an aura of happiness at being with her children.

The two youngsters, Carlos and Lourdes, were neatly clad in their Sunday best, with shining clean faces brimming with curiosity. Jason immediately scooped them up, one on each knee, and sat on the worn sofa joking with them.

"This is my sister." Juanita spoke in English as much as she could, and Anne guessed that the woman was trying to improve her skills. She was grateful, since her own Spanish was limited to the few phrases needed to tell a laboring woman when to push and when not to.

The sister, Maria, had a distracted air, and it was easy to see why. Three young children dashed about, and, Juanita informed them, Maria's two older ones were playing outside.

"Seven children in one apartment?" Anne glanced down the corridor and could see there were only two bedrooms and one bathroom.

"And her husband and his brother." Juanita shrugged. "What can we do?"

Anne turned to Jason and saw that his expression was grim. She shared his dismay.

Maria offered them something to drink, but they declined, not wanting to impose. Anne had to suppress her instinct to run out to buy the family a couple of bags of groceries. Jason was right—these people had pride. But there had to be something she could do to help.

The apartment was dark even though there was bright sunlight outside, so Jason suggested they walk to a nearby park to take the pictures, and Juanita agreed.

Her children proved to be well behaved, especially considering they were only two and four years old. They clung to their mother's hand and kept quiet as they walked, but their big eyes stared around with fascination.

The park was only two blocks away, but Anne guessed from the children's delight that they didn't get to visit it often.

The park was well tended, with thick grass and luxurious cypress trees. On the far side, some booths had been erected and decorated with balloons and banners. From the number of people gathering there, Anne surmised a local carnival was in progress.

"Let's take them to the playground." Jason pointed the way to an area far from the booths. "I'd like to shoot them in action, without a lot of people around."

The two were shy at first, but with their mother's encouragement they tentatively began exploring the jungle gym and then the slide. Soon the air filled with their laughter.

Anne studied Jason as he moved intently from one position to another, taking photographs of the children and their mother. Clearly he'd closed off awareness of everything but what he was seeing through the lens.

He certainly had talent; she knew that from the pictures on his wall and from the shots he'd taken at the beach. She'd never been photogenic, so it had amazed her to see how much of her inner self was revealed in those prints.

If he wanted to, she was sure Jason could make a good living as a studio photographer, but it was easy to understand that he'd get bored shooting weddings and graduation pictures. Or perhaps he could work for a newspaper. But apparently he'd rather have the freedom to choose his own subjects, even if it meant working as a housekeeper to cover his expenses.

You had to admire him for that, Anne reflected as she sat on a bench to watch.

Jason didn't appear to be in any hurry, nor did he seem concerned about how much film he was using as he shot roll after roll.

Soon Juanita and the youngsters had all but forgotten he was there. Watching the joy in the other woman's face as she played with her children, Anne couldn't help envying her. Juanita was rich in her own way, even if she only got to enjoy it one day a week.

Finally the children began to tire, and Juanita scooped little Lourdes up in her arms. "You go to the carnival," she commanded Jason. "It will show you something of our life here, not just crowded apartments."

It surprised Anne that Juanita would be so concerned about Jason's impressions, but she supposed she'd feel the same way in Juanita's place.

Jason agreed, and they said goodbye to the mother and children.

"They're really delightful." Anne strolled beside Jason across the grass. Ahead, a mariachi band began to play its cheerfully enticing music. "I'd like to do something to help, but I don't want to seem like I'm playing Lady Bountiful. You were right; I can see that Juanita wouldn't take charity."

"What she needs is a job that pays enough for her to have her own apartment or that provides live-in arrangements for the children." Jason seemed to be speaking to himself as much as to her. "And her husband is a migrant farm worker, so it would be nice if he could stay with them, too, when he's in town."

At the moment, Anne hadn't a clue where to find such a job, but she tucked the idea away in the back of her mind.

The carnival, they soon found, made up in exuberance what it lacked in grandeur. Around them, young couples and large families shopped for food and souvenirs at unimposing booths and danced to the music of the band. The bright colors of clothing added to the festivity of balloons and banners.

Unobtrusively, Jason began taking photographs. Some included Anne, but most focused on the events around them. She could see that he zeroed in on faces: a youngster's, smeared with ice cream; an old woman's, creased by a Mona Lisa smile; a young man's as he gazed lovingly at his wife. Through close-ups, she could tell, he was capturing the spirit of the festival.

Finally Jason tucked his camera away in his shoulder bag and caught Anne's arm. "Wanna dance, lady?"

"I'm not sure I know the steps."

"Neither do I, but I'll bet we can fake it."

At first, Anne felt stiffly self-conscious amid the whirling crowd of uninhibited merrymakers. But Jason had the knack of blending in wherever he was; he hooted and cheered, clapped and kicked up a storm with the best of them, and Anne's laughter quickly dissolved her restraint.

Breathlessly, she caught Jason's arm and let him swing her around. Energy welled up in her, and she threw her head back, joining in the general noisemaking.

Jason caught Anne's waist and swung her off her feet, around and around.

Her green eyes sparkled in the sunlight, and her dark-blond hair had come loose from its bun and floated around her shoulders. He'd never seen her let go this freely, and he never wanted the afternoon to end.

When the band finished, she leaned against him, catching her breath. Jason felt as if he held a wild creature in his arms, one that had begun to trust him at long last.

Afterward, they munched on tacos and wandered through the crowd. Anne tried on a straw sombrero, pulling it low over her eyes. "Hi, amigo." She faked a low voice. "You want to come and cook at my cantina? I hear you make a mean enchilada."

"Try this." Jason selected a green-and-gold woven serape and tossed it over Anne's shoulder. "Not your usual style, but the colors look vibrant on you."

"You think so?" Anne took off the sombrero and examined the serape. "It looks nice and warm for evening walks along the Back Bay."

Jason handed a bill to the booth owner. "My treat."

"I wouldn't hear of it!" Anne started to reach for her purse.

"Consider it a souvenir of the day."

"Yes, but ..." She hesitated. "Jason, I don't feel right somehow."

"Because I work for you?" He accepted his change and waved away the offer of a paper bag to wrap the purchase in. "My money's still as good as the next man's."

"I didn't mean that." Anne pressed her cheek against the soft wool of the serape. "Thanks, Jason. I really like it."

The crowd was beginning to disperse, and the two of them headed back toward the car.

Anne certainly needed a man who was worthy of her, not some jerk like the two doctors she'd brought home for dinner, Jason mused as he watched the play of sunlight and leaf shadows across Anne's face.

She needed someone who would bring out the spirited woman inside her, someone who would put her needs on a par with his own, someone whose life meshed with hers....

What she needed was someone like him.

Jason had to fight the impulse to stop dead. How could he have failed to see it before? He didn't want to bring out Anne's sensuous inner self and then hand her over to another man. He wanted her for himself.

And he was going to get her. But it was a task that called for tremendous delicacy, skill and gentleness.

And he had only three weeks to do it.

Chapter Nine

Juanita's problem remained in Anne's thoughts for the nex
few days, but she didn't come up with any brilliant solu
tions. She was also troubled by her memory of the othe
woman they'd seen in the complex, haggard looking as sh
answered the door to give directions.

Anne had read enough articles and attended enough lec
tures to know that babies were dying or becoming ill unnec
essarily here in Orange County, one of the wealthiest place
in the world. And women were going without proper med
ical treatment. Anne wanted to help.

Her partner, John Hernandez, had always taken an in
terest in the needs of the community, so she asked him fo
suggestions.

He paused in the hallway of their office, brushing a lock
of graying hair off his forehead.

"Well—" John stared off into space, in the genera
direction of the temporary receptionist filling in for Elli
"—I did hear something about a new clinic opening in Sant
Ana. If you like, I could check into it."

"I'd really appreciate it." Anne pulled a folder from it
wall holder to check the medical records of her next pa
tient. "It may be hard to find the time, but I promise ou
practice won't suffer."

"Don't worry. I only gave up volunteering myself until I put my kids through college. We'll make the time—it's important."

What a good man, she reflected as she read over the chart. Like Jason. Caring about others was high on both their lists of priorities.

Her thoughts were interrupted by the receptionist. "Dr. Eldridge? It's the hospital. One of your patients is in labor. Deanie Parker."

"Fine. Pull her records for me, will you?" As she went in to see the waiting patient, Anne mulled over the name. Deanie Parker. Deanie Parker. Which one was she? Why did her name ring a bell?

A few minutes later, pausing for a red light on her way to the hospital, Anne finished reading over Deanie's records and was still puzzled. Her pregnancy had been uncomplicated, so there was no reason for her to stick in Anne's memory.

It wasn't until Anne arrived in Labor and Delivery and saw Jason waiting, scrubbed and wearing a blue gown and mask, that she remembered.

Deanie was his cousin. And he was planning to photograph the birth.

Well, Anne had given her consent, hadn't she? But it was unnerving to see him in her professional setting, in this other part of her life.

She gave him a curt nod. "You'd better wait out here. Does Deanie have a coach?"

"Not as far as I know. She's kind of scatterbrained. I doubt if she took classes."

"I'll get one of the nurses to stay with her."

Unfortunately, as it turned out, Deanie lived up to Jason's description of her. She hadn't participated in childbirth classes, so she was unprepared to deal with the waves of pain. One of the nurses had to sit with her and conduct

on-the-spot training, teaching Deanie breathing patterns t
cope with the contractions.

Fortunately, nurses in Labor and Delivery tended to b
very patient and sympathetic, Anne reflected. She'd ofte
been impressed with how calmly they dealt with their pa
tients during the difficult transition stage.

Deanie was close to that phase of labor, but it was prc
gressing slowly, in part because this was her first child. A
ter checking the patient and the monitors and making sur
everything was normal, Anne went out to get a cup of co
fee at the nurses' station.

"How's it going?" Jason was putting film in his camera
leaning against the counter. The secretary eyed him wit
considerable interest, Anne noted.

"She's coming along." Anne poured the coffee into
Styrofoam cup. "It would have helped if she'd been pre
pared."

As if to validate Anne's words, a moan emanated fror
Deanie's room. Anne turned to one of the nurses. "Hov
long has Mrs. Parker been in labor?"

"About twelve hours."

"Twelve hours!" Jason stared at her in shock. "Dea
nie's been going through this for twelve hours?"

"I'm sure it wasn't this intense in the beginning." Ann
had seen dozens of women—or was it hundreds by now?-
go through labor. Suddenly it struck her that someday sh
might experience it herself.

What would it be like for Anne? Would she be one of th
lucky ones who had a relatively easy time of it, or woul
complications set in? Well, she'd deal with that when th
time came, she supposed. It was too bad a medical degre
didn't make you any more immune to pain than anyone els

"Yes, but—shouldn't you do something? I mean, give he
something to kill the pain?" Jason's whole body radiate
tension, as if he were identifying with his cousin, which h
probably was.

"Not until the end, or the labor will stop. And we don't want to give any more anesthetic than necessary, for the baby's sake." Anne drained her cup. "Jason, twelve hours isn't long. Some women go through this for twenty or thirty hours."

As another moan sounded from the room, he shook his head in disbelief. "How do they bear it?"

"Most of them at least have practiced breathing techniques and have someone to coach them. But I'm sure it's never easy."

"You don't just let it go on and on? That can't be good for the baby, either."

"Of course not. If the labor doesn't progress normally, we have to do a cesarean section. But we'd rather not. Surgery has certain risks, too." She had to smile at his anxiety. "If you're this upset about your cousin, I can't imagine what you'll be like when it's your own baby."

The expression that crossed his face was so complex Anne wished she could photograph it and study it at length. Wonder; alarm; yearning; or was she reading all that in? Maybe it was just plain fright at the prospect of settling down someday.

"I'll tell you one thing—the first thing I'd do is read every book I could find on the subject, so I'd know what to expect." He scratched the back of his neck. "The TV shows make it look like a glorious experience. I should have known better."

A nurse came to tell Anne that Deanie was fully dilated. After that, things happened fast. The patient, moaning all the way, was wheeled into the delivery room, while Jason adjusted the settings on his camera.

Anne watched to be sure Deanie hadn't changed her mind about having the birth photographed, but the young woman didn't even seem to notice Jason's presence.

After confirming that Deanie was ready, Anne instructed her to push. The moans grew more frequent, and a nurse whose hand Deanie was holding winced in pain.

Although she'd delivered many babies, Anne never lost her wonder at the miracle. There was nothing else in life that could match the thrill of pulling a tiny baby into the world, watching its little face scrunch up and its mouth open and hearing the resounding wail that brought air into its lungs.

Quickly, a nurse took the baby boy and began suctioning his mouth to clear away the mucus. Within minutes, the infant was swaddled and placed in his mother's arms.

"Oh, my God." Deanie, her face bathed in sweat, stared in amazement at the perfect little features. "I mean, it's really a baby, isn't it? He's really mine?"

Keeping her in the center of his viewfinder, Jason snapped the shutter. He knew he'd caught that moment of intimacy of bonding between mother and child. He would never forget the look of joy on Deanie's face, so swiftly replacing the discomfort of moments before.

I can't imagine what you'll be like when it's your own baby. He couldn't get Anne's words out of his head.

It would tear his heart out to see the woman he loved go through any pain. To see Anne suffering that way, to hear her cry out. But now he could picture what she'd look like afterward, how exhilarated she'd feel and how incredibly miraculous the whole experience would seem in retrospect.

He couldn't wait.

Jason's eyes met Anne's, and he saw that she was smiling. But she couldn't possibly guess what he was thinking. If she did, she'd probably run right out of here this minute, toss his possessions out of her house and bolt the door, family reunion or no family reunion.

He turned to Deanie. "Have you got a name picked out?"

"Alexander James Parker." She didn't even hesitate.

Anne glanced up at the clock overhead, and Jason realized it was after 6:00 p.m. "Congratulations, Mrs. Parker."

A few minutes later, they met outside in the hallway. A hint of weariness showed at the corners of Anne's eyes. "What would you like for dinner?" Jason asked. "Tacos? Burgers? Pizza?"

"Pizza, with lots of cheese and mushrooms and pepperoni."

"Done. I'll meet you at the old homestead."

He ordered ahead, calling from a nearby bank of pay phones. Next to him, a young man was eagerly pouring quarters into the phone, calling relative after relative to announce, "It's a girl!"

Jason felt a squeeze in the vicinity of his heart as he strode out to the parking structure. Would it ever be him at the phones?

Until now, he'd thought of children rather vaguely, in terms of the youngsters at the beach and other kids he saw on the street. The reality of what it would mean to have a baby had never come home before. Now, driving to the pizza parlor, he mulled over the sight of Deanie's son emerging into the light and letting out that life-giving squall. He could still see his cousin cradling the infant in her arms.

As he parked at the pizza parlor, Jason noticed a discount mart next door. Impulsively, he went inside, making his way to the baby department.

What a lot of equipment it took for such a tiny person! There were strollers and high chairs, playpens and bassinets, and rack after rack of clothes, crib sheets, bibs, bottles and quite a few things he'd never even heard of before— receiving blankets, nursing pads, activity centers.

Finally he selected a musical crib mobile, along with a book on infant care, since he suspected Deanie wasn't prepared in that department, either.

The purchases tucked under his arm, Jason picked up the pizza and headed home.

He found Anne in the living room, a scrapbook spread in front of her. When he came in, she lifted dreamy eyes that widened as she inhaled the rich aroma of pizza.

"What are you doing?" He couldn't help smiling at the picture she made, reclining on the carpet with her head resting against the armchair. There was something young and vulnerable about her and very, very sensuous.

"Looking at pictures of my nephews when they were little." Anne flipped the scrapbook shut. "Would you believe my sister delivered both her kids at home? My reputation would have been ruined if anyone had found out! Lori's as scatterbrained as Deanie. But fortunately everything turned out okay. And the pictures are great—kind of fuzzy, but the wonder shines through."

"That's one scene it would be hard not to photograph well." Jason was reluctant to risk breaking the mood by leaving the room, but he was also near starvation, so he went into the kitchen to fetch plates and tall glasses of iced tea.

They ate sitting on the rug in the living room, thumbing through family photo albums. Anne turned out to be quite a packrat. She'd amassed pictures going all the way back to her great-grandparents, along with dozens of shots of herself and Lori as children.

"I'm surprised you pried these away from your parents." Jason finished off his second slice of pizza.

"Actually, it wasn't hard. The last time my parents moved, they decided on a small apartment, and my mother was delighted to give me her boxes of photographs. She pointed out that I certainly had room for them." Anne paused in the middle of reaching for her iced tea. "I suppose it is rather strange that I bought such a big house just for one person, isn't it?"

"Not at all." Jason stretched out his long legs. "You were giving yourself what you always wanted as a child."

She turned to look at him. "How come you figure out things like that? You're really perceptive."

He couldn't resist teasing her. "Oh, some of us manage to figure out a few things even though we don't have advanced degrees."

"That wasn't what I meant." She punched his arm playfully. "To tell you the truth, I've met psychiatrists who didn't have as much insight as you do; at least, not in everyday life."

"I'll send you my bill in the morning."

"Do you take Monopoly money?"

"I can see what you think my brilliant perceptions are worth." He decided four pieces of pizza really were enough, although the remaining two slices were staring up at him enticingly.

"You know, it works both ways." Anne reclined next to him on the carpet. "By traveling around the world, you've been filling in what you needed in childhood, too."

He reached over and casually traced a finger along the curve of her jaw. "Since I've grown up, I've been giving myself a lot of things I missed as a child."

"Are we talking about childhood or adolescence?" But she didn't push his hand away.

He decided the wisest course was to overlook her remark. "I certainly saw a different side of you today."

"Oh?"

"Anne in action. Anne the doctor. Of course, you were rather stiff and stern the day you interviewed me, but I'd never seen you with nurses leaping at your command."

"I try not to make them leap. It's tough on their feet, and they work hard enough as it is."

Jason gave her a gentle poke in the side. "You know what I mean. It's one thing for me to be aware, intellectually, that you're a professional; it's something else to see you actually in charge of a delivery room, pulling that baby out of Deanie."

"Does it bother you?" She rolled over to face him, her expression serious.

"Bother me?"

"To see me in charge of things. It makes some men really uncomfortable. I made the mistake a few years ago of dating one of my fellow residents. Then one night we were both on duty at the same time. The next day he muttered something about how much he respected my professionalism, and that was the end of our relationship."

"What a donkey." Jason teased a strand of her hair down from its topknot. "Frankly, I find competence in a woman highly appealing."

"Kind of a turn-on?"

"You might say." He hadn't meant to caress her, but his hand couldn't resist the inviting curve of her cheek. "You were exciting in the delivery room, Anne."

She ducked her head. "Isn't that carrying things a bit far?"

"I like people when they're most themselves, when there aren't a lot of conventions and anxieties blocking their emotions. And you weren't holding anything back when you looked at that baby. It's nothing to be embarrassed about."

His comments and the way he was stroking her combined to arouse Anne in a way she'd never experienced before. It wasn't exactly sexual; it was far more complex and far deeper.

She wanted to lie here forever next to Jason, to let their words drift into murmurs, to let their bodies slide closer and closer until there was no distance between them at all. It felt safe being with him, as if she need never fear that anything she did would offend or displease him, not as long as she was honest and open.

Her entire body tingled. She was keenly aware of the coolness of the room and of the tangy spice smell of Jason's skin.

Gradually, her arms found their way around Jason's neck, and their bodies touched, hip against hip, her breasts grazing his chest. Anne nestled her nose against his throat, closing her eyes, at peace.

Languorously, his lips found hers. The touch of his mouth was whisper light and tantalizing. Anne pressed closer, wanting to experience him more fully. Her tongue explored the edges of his teeth, then the firmness inside his mouth, and gradually he responded.

Strong arms encircled her. Every movement of his muscles resounded through her sensibilities, so keenly was she tuned to his being.

His lips found the corners of her mouth, then the tip of her nose, then the delicate contours of her temples. His warm breath sighed against her skin deliciously.

With one hand, Anne traced the shape of his shoulder blade, probing around it to find and release a small knot in the muscle. Then she explored the vertebrae of his spine, one by one.

He in turn massaged the small of her back, his touch sending quivers along her hip bones and into her core. Some long-frozen pond inside Anne turned liquid.

By mutual understanding, their mouths met again, more fiercely this time, and his grip on her tightened. The shape of his body seemed to imprint itself against hers, and Anne pressed closer, wanting to eliminate even the faintest hint of space between them.

The phone rang.

"Ignore it," Jason murmured.

Anne started to agree, then pulled away. "Oh, hell. I'm on call."

The answering service relayed a message that another patient had been admitted to the hospital in the early stages of labor. It would be several hours before Anne would be needed, but she'd have to keep checking in by phone.

As she hung up, she shook away the last remnants of the daze that had come over her in Jason's arms. She must have been crazy. Plain old crazy. There was no denying the chemistry between them, but that wasn't enough.

You can't make the same mistake again, the way you did with Ken. You're not nineteen anymore.

Slowly, Anne walked back to the living room. "I'm going upstairs before we both do something stupid."

Jason was sitting on the carpet, calmly finishing up the last of the pizza. "This tastes pretty good cold."

"Did you hear me?"

"Yes." He licked his fingers. "I'm not going to get into an argument, Anne. I knew perfectly well that once we were interrupted, your intellect was going to start working again and sound off all the alarms."

She waited, expecting him to say more, but he just sat there looking infuriatingly smug, as if he knew her better than she knew herself.

The possibility that he might be right was something she didn't want to deal with. And she didn't want to consider how he might be planning to circumvent her intellect, since he obviously had rejected the direct approach.

"Well—I'll see you in the morning." She started toward the stairs.

"Sleep well."

But she didn't, not for more than an hour, while she listened to the sounds of Jason moving around downstairs: the shower running, the refrigerator door opening and closing, the TV muttering. She knew he was probably watching another old movie—he loved the films of the thirties and forties and Rodgers and Hammerstein musicals—and wondered if it was one she'd seen.

So many of them had bittersweet endings. Well, that was life, wasn't it? she thought, and finally fell asleep.

THE NEXT DAY Anne decided to give Ellie a break from hospital food and had a catered lunch brought in from a nearby Chinese restaurant.

The other bed in the semiprivate room was vacant, so they had the luxury of talking freely as they consumed Mongolian beef and *moo shu* pork.

The contractions had stopped, and Ellie was already planning how she'd manage once she got home, since she would be allowed to get up only to go to the bathroom.

"Dennis can fix breakfast and leave a cold lunch for me in the refrigerator," she itemized, sitting up in bed and eating on the freestanding tray table that Anne had swung into position. "My mother's already offered to bring dinner over several times a week, and Dennis can pick up takeout food the other nights. My sister's offered to loan me her cleaning lady. Say, I could get used to this!"

Anne chuckled. "Don't get too spoiled. Babies have a way of turning households upside-down."

"I won't mind." Ellie settled back against the pillows. "Oh, Anne, do you really think the baby's going to be all right?"

"Of course it is." Anne handed her a fortune cookie. "Here's everything you ever wanted to know about your future. Read it to me."

Ellie broke it open and unfolded the slip of paper. "It says, 'You are headed in the right direction.'"

"What did I tell you?"

"Go on. Read me yours."

Anne retrieved her own fortune. "'The other person in your life is the right one for you.'"

"What other person?" Ellie perked up. There was nothing she loved better than gossip. "Not Dr. Raney!"

Anne laughed and told her how Jason had thrown him out of the house. "I don't think he'll be coming back."

"I can't wait to meet Jason. He sounds more like a jealous husband than a housekeeper."

Her remarks caught Anne off guard, and she swallowed her tea the wrong way. The fit of coughing did nothing to throw Ellie off the scent.

"There's something going on between you two, isn't there? Come on, you can't fool me."

Anne shifted uncomfortably in the straight chair at Ellie's bedside. She glanced at the open door to make sure none of the nurses was close enough to overhear. "It's more of a brother-sister thing."

"Uh-huh." Ellie sounded totally unconvinced.

"No, really." Anne pressed on, talking more to herself than to her friend. "Although I'll admit, having him around has helped me realize a few things."

"Like what?"

"How much I want children, for instance." Anne saw Ellie's expression soften. "There hasn't really been time to think about it until now, or maybe I haven't wanted to. But now I've sort of gotten used to having another person in the house, and that got me thinking about what it would be like to have a family. And then yesterday..." She described how Jason had photographed his cousin's delivery.

"You sound like a changed woman." Ellie sipped at her tea. "Up to now, all you've talked about were what conferences you planned to attend and what new techniques you'd learned. Suddenly, I'm hearing about men, and now it's babies. I'd say you were ready for a new phase in your life."

"Thanks, Confucius." Anne ducked her head, not wanting Ellie to see the heat rising to her cheeks. "I didn't realize I'd been so fixated on my work before. I must have been a real bore."

"Not at all. I find your dedication inspiring. In fact, when the baby's older, I've been thinking of going back to school and getting a nursing degree so I could work in obstetrics." Ellie hurried on before Anne could respond. "But don't think I'm going to change the subject. What you need is a husband, and if you'd like any help..."

Anne smiled. Ellie loved helping people out and solving their problems. "No, thanks. I'd prefer to find my own man."

"Maybe you already have."

She shook her head firmly. "Absolutely not. I need stability, and he's, well, a free spirit."

"Sounds like just what you need."

"You're impossible."

"I do my best." Ellie stacked the empty Chinese-food cartons neatly to one side. "Honestly, I've never seen you look as happy as you have since you hired that man. He's the best medicine you ever took."

At Ellie's words, Anne's thoughts flew to the special times she'd shared with Jason: that day at the beach, their walk in the Back Bay at twilight, the festival in the park. She *had* felt more energetic than usual these last few weeks, hadn't she?

But her own practical side intruded. "Ellie, I'm not about to pick up and travel around the world with him. That's no way to raise children."

"Maybe he wouldn't expect you to travel all the time. You could work something out." Ellie tended to believe there was a solution to any problem. If only she were right!

"Even so, he doesn't earn enough to let me take a few years off or even for me to work part-time. And I don't want my children to grow up in day-care centers. I know some mothers have no choice about going back to work, but I think it's best if kids can stay home with a parent for the first few years." Anne wished she didn't sound as if she were delivering a lecture. No doubt Jason would say it was her intellect speaking.

"Well, I haven't met Jason, so I can't say for sure he's the right man for you." Ellie's eyelids were beginning to drift down, but she fought to stay awake. "Dennis has a good friend I think you might like...."

"No, thanks. Now I'm going to let you get some sleep." Anne stood up. "You'll need it after the baby comes, believe me."

But the conversation wouldn't stop resounding through her mind. Talking with Ellie had crystallized some thoughts that had been troubling Anne for the last few weeks. Driving back to her office, she decided it was time to consider the situation objectively.

She was thirty-three years old. Even if she met Mr. Right now, it would be a year or so before they'd be ready to get married and have a baby. By then she'd be at least thirty-five. And since she'd really like to have two children...

There was no time to waste.

The problem wasn't meeting men; Anne met quite a few in her line of work. And she knew that when she bothered to take the time with her hair and makeup, she could be reasonably attractive.

But her last two dates had been disasters, and her attraction to Jason proved how easily she could be led astray. How was she going to zero in on the right man so she didn't waste any more time?

As usual when confronting a problem, Anne proceeded to analyze it. She'd always felt that getting one's priorities organized was half the battle.

She needed a list of criteria, something she could check off mentally to eliminate men who simply weren't right for her. Well, that ought to be easy.

First of all, he had to be dependable and settled, financially as well as emotionally. That eliminated Jason.

He had to be honest and fair-minded, someone she could respect. That eliminated Aldous Raney.

And of course he should be someone she found attractive. So much for Horace Swann.

Furthermore, he would have to want children and be a good father.

That seemed like a reasonable list, Anne decided as she pulled into her reserved parking space. She had the feeling there was something missing, something she'd overlooked, but she was sure it would come to mind sooner or later. In the meantime, at least she'd reached a starting point.

Chapter Ten

During the next few days, Anne made a point of keeping busy and out of the house. In only a couple of weeks Jason would be gone, and she didn't trust herself to spend too much time with him in the interim.

Unfortunately, crowding her schedule with seminars and consultations did little to ease the sense of emptiness inside Anne. Grabbing a quick dinner in the hospital cafeteria, the way she used to do, now struck her as a lonely way to cap off the day. And on Sunday afternoon, lecturing to a group of nurses on new developments in obstetrics, she had to chase away the mental image of Jason sprawled on the living-room carpet reading the comics, and the strong desire to be lying there next to him.

When she came home late that evening, he merely whistled his way around her, inquiring politely about her lecture without a hint of possessiveness. But she knew him well enough to be sure that his disinterest was a sham. What was he up to?

Jason could see that he had her puzzled. Frankly, he reflected as he fixed her a late-night snack of graham crackers and milk, he was a little puzzled himself. He knew what he wanted to accomplish, but he was still figuring out exactly what tactics to use.

Anne's long absences from the house didn't surprise him. Each time her emotional inner self broke through, he'd observed during their time together, it was followed by a period of denial and intellectualizing. That was the way Anne was, and he loved her in spite of it.

Patience, Jason sighed to himself as he handed the tray to Anne at the foot of the steps and watched her vanish into her sanctum upstairs. He'd learned patience as a photographer, waiting for the right light, the right moment. But it never came easily.

Still, her busy schedule had given him time to work on his book undisturbed. He'd taken more photographs of Juanita and gone through hundreds of negatives selecting the ones to print for his publisher. In addition, he'd printed up several dozen for Juanita herself.

The one step remaining was a trip to Juanita's village in Mexico. Actually, the timing with Anne had worked out well; he'd have to be leaving here soon anyway, even if she hadn't fired him.

But he planned on coming back.

And this time things would be on a different footing, Jason mused as he wiped crumbs off the kitchen counter and switched off the lights. When he returned, he'd tell her the truth. She'd probably be angry, but gradually she would come to see that he was a more responsible man than he'd seemed, that he was someone she could rely on when it came to raising a family.

And he intended to be the one she raised a family with. Whether she liked the idea or not.

ANNE CHOSE A SEAT near the front of the hospital auditorium. She was tired from a long day's work and didn't feel like craning her neck to see over the heads of the rest of the audience.

Under other circumstances, she probably would have skipped the talk on "Legal Aspects of Medical Care" and gone straight home to take a hot bath. But she suspected that if she did, Jason would be waiting outside the bathroom door, probably with a towel draped over one arm and a tray of perfumed soaps in his hand.

The irreverent image made her smile.

At that moment, she glanced up and saw a man smiling back at her, apparently thinking she'd meant to be friendly.

Well, what was wrong with that? He wasn't bad looking—not as tall or distinctive as Jason, but he had well-groomed brown hair touched with gray, and pleasant crinkles around the eyes.

She'd never seen the man before. Surreptitiously, Anne took in his expensive tailored suit and general air of confidence. He was chatting with the hospital director, so he must be someone important.

The guest speaker! Quickly Anne glanced down at the flier she was holding. Mitch Hamilton, attorney at law. According to the photocopied information sheet, he was a prominent civil lawyer who had represented several doctors in malpractice cases.

She peeked at his left hand. No ring.

Glancing up, she felt herself flush with embarrassment. He'd seen her examining his ring finger. But he looked pleasantly amused rather than scornful, and she answered with a playful shrug.

Flirting with a man across a room was something Anne hadn't done since her college days, and she hoped she wasn't being awkward. What complicated everything was that she didn't feel entirely sincere. She kept mentally comparing the man to Jason and finding him less intriguing, more ordinary.

But from what she could see so far, he was right in line with her list of criteria.

The lecture turned out to be well organized and informative, but afterward Anne didn't remember a thing Mitch Hamilton had said. She was too busy wondering if she should stick around and find an excuse to talk to him or if she was simply going to make a fool of herself.

As it turned out, once the question-and-answer session was over and the attorney stepped down, he saved Anne the trouble by coming over to her.

"Dr. Eldridge." He'd apparently managed to read her name badge. "I believe I know your partner, John Hernandez."

Anne perked up. "How do you know John?" Any friend of her partner's was likely to be worth knowing.

"We've been involved in some fund raising together." He didn't specify for what cause. "You know, obstetrics is a particularly vulnerable field for lawsuits. I understand some doctors have entirely stopped delivering babies."

"There's a lot that can go wrong," Anne agreed. "Of course, since we deal with many high-risk cases, we practice very aggressive medicine. And we keep our patients fully informed of what we're doing and why."

She had the feeling neither of them really cared about this conversation. It was just a ploy to introduce themselves. That would be all right, but where were the sparks that should be flying between them?

Forget sparks. They aren't on the list.

They chatted for a few more minutes, during which time she learned that he was amicably divorced but had no children, that he liked to play tennis and was a connoisseur of fine wines.

The only thing that struck her as a bit odd was that his former wife had been a nurse. Was he particularly attracted to women in the medical field? Perhaps it was because that was his area of specialization and he enjoyed having a knowledgeable wife; she couldn't fault him for that.

Unlike Aldous, Mitch showed a reasonable interest in Anne's activities, too, although she found herself rattling off facts rather than divulging her feelings. Well, the hospital auditorium was hardly a place conducive to heart-to-heart revelations.

When they'd finished with the amenities, Mitch asked her to dinner Saturday night, and Anne agreed. She was relieved when he suggested an elegant restaurant in Newport Beach; after her last two dates, she had no intention of inviting Mitch home for a meal.

For some reason, Anne found it hard to tell Jason that she wouldn't be home for dinner Saturday night and why. Over the next few days, she found herself reviewing her phrasing and imagining his responses.

Anne, breezily: "Oh, by the way, I'm going out for dinner Saturday night."

Jason: "Great, I'll come too."

Anne: "I've got a date."

Jason: "After the last two you've brought home, I'd say you need a bodyguard."

Better to take a different tack.

Anne, distantly: "I'm going out for dinner Saturday night, so you can have the evening off."

Jason: "Fine. Maybe I'll try one of the local restaurants. Where are you eating?"

No. She'd have to put her foot down.

Anne, sternly: "I have a dinner date Saturday night and I don't want you interfering."

Jason: "I wouldn't dream of it. I'll just watch quietly."

In the end, Anne said nothing until Saturday morning, when she noticed Jason's fettucine recipe set out in its plastic holder. She couldn't let him go to all the trouble of fixing it and then discover she wouldn't be there.

Anne found him in the dining room, cheerfully polishing her best silver. "Jason, about tonight, I'm—"

"Going out to dinner?" He buffed a serving spoon to a bright shine. "Okay. I was planning to wander around the swap meet this afternoon, and flea markets always wear me out. I could use a break from cooking."

Lack of interest was one response she hadn't anticipated. "Well, good." Anne waited for him to say something further, but he merely turned his attention to a salad fork.

Going back to her bedroom, she felt rather deflated. Perhaps she'd misjudged Jason's possessiveness toward her.

Laying several dresses out on the bed, she wondered why she couldn't work up much enthusiasm for selecting an outfit for tonight. Mitch did seem to have the qualities she was seeking, although it was too soon to know how he felt about children.

Well, there was no hurry in deciding what to wear. It wasn't even noon yet. She had plenty of time to do something relaxing today—like pay the bills that had piled up on her desk.

It was her own fault for keeping so busy, Anne admonished herself as she trudged downstairs to her office.

A few minutes later, she heard Jason whistling "Oh, What a Beautiful Mornin'" as he went out the door. Was he meeting someone or going alone? It was none of her business, of course. But it would be fun, wandering through the swap meet, picking through tables of everything from junk to antiques.

The afternoon dragged by. Anne actually found herself with a free day, and she didn't know what to do. If Jason had been home, they could have played Scrabble, or gone for a walk, or just talked.

Anne called the hospital and made sure Ellie had been discharged as scheduled. Yes, the nurse told her, Ellie's husband had picked her up that morning. It was easy to picture him escorting her solicitously out to the car, tucking her into the front seat, gazing at her lovingly....

I'll have to get her a gift, Anne decided. There was still time to run out to the bookstore today.

But as she was getting ready to go, the phone rang.

"Anne? Mitch."

Her first thought was, *he's canceling the date. Oh, terrific.*

"Hi. What's up?" She was pleased at the casual sound of her voice, although she was ready to strangle the man if he disappointed her.

"Listen, I've been playing tennis this afternoon and I hurt my back." He uttered a convincing groan. "I really hate to postpone our date, but I'm not going to be able to sit up straight for a couple of days, so I don't think I can handle a restaurant."

Anne thought rapidly. Jason was gone for the afternoon and didn't want to cook, so he'd probably eat out. Maybe things had worked out better than she could have hoped.

"I'll tell you what," she said. "If you can handle reclining on my couch, I could cook dinner for us. I've got a lap tray you can use."

"If it wouldn't be too much trouble." He sounded relieved. "That's really kind of you. I'd like that."

Anne felt rather pleased with herself as she hung up.

She decided to use Jason's fettucine recipe, since the ingredients were already on hand. Although she felt somewhat as if she were stealing something of his, she reminded herself that it was her money that had paid for the groceries.

By six o'clock, half an hour before Mitch was to arrive, Anne was dressed and had covered herself with one of Ada's oversize aprons. Carefully, she put water on to boil and measured butter into a large pan.

The phone rang. Surely Mitch wouldn't change his mind at this late hour....

It was Ellie. "I wanted to let you know that I'm home and I feel fine. Are you sure I can't get up? Some of our friends from church are having a barbecue, and I promise I'll stay on the chaise longue...."

"Bed rest means bed rest!" Anne delivered a quick lecture on the need to stay flat.

Ellie conceded gracefully. "I just thought I'd ask."

"I'll come and visit you as soon as I get a chance. Meanwhile, if I catch you misbehaving, it's back to the hospital!"

As she hung up, Anne smelled something burning. Oh, no! She'd left the pan on the burner!

The butter was hopelessly scorched, and the pan was going to need a tough scouring. Jason would kill her, Anne reflected miserably as she ran water onto the mess. And here she was with a kitchen full of smoke and Mitch scheduled to arrive any minute.

What would he think if she sent out for pizza? Somehow, she couldn't picture Mitch digging into pepperoni and cheese with gusto.

It was with mixed emotions that she heard a key turn in the back-door lock and someone whistling "Some Enchanted Evening."

She wondered briefly if Jason chose his tunes sarcastically. But then, how could he know she was still home?

He lifted an eyebrow as he came in. "I thought you were going out. Mmm. What a wonderful smell. But you're supposed to char-broil things outside on the grill, Anne, not in the kitchen."

"Cute. Very cute." She glared at him. "As you can see, I'm not much of a cook." She explained about Mitch's back. "Don't worry, I'm not going to ask you to work tonight. I'll run out for Chinese food or something."

Jason lowered a canvas tote bag to the floor, and Anne heard something clank. He must have picked up some interesting stuff at the swap meet. "I've got to eat anyway, so I'll cook enough for three. And don't worry. I don't plan on interfering with your date, unless he jumps you like the last one."

"Thanks. You're a good sport." The doorbell rang. "And just in time. I owe you a favor for this, Jason!" She disappeared out the kitchen door.

Wearily, Jason stretched his sore muscles and pushed the tote bag out of the way. He couldn't even muster much pleasure at the thought of his purchase, a lightweight folding tripod. Shopping at the flea market would have been more fun with some interesting companionship. Like Anne's.

Well, he'd volunteered to cook, so he'd better get on with it.

As he pulled out a clean pan and began to melt butter, Jason listened to voices in the other room. He couldn't help hoping this Mitch would turn out to be as big a loser as the other two men.

Unfortunately, that wasn't true.

Jason had to admit, after delivering plates of fettucine and salad, that the man seemed reasonably presentable. Not bad looking, polite and even affable, considering the pain he must be in as he reclined on the sofa.

It would be just like Anne to let her intellect talk her into marrying the guy simply because he wasn't a jerk. Even though, of course, her heart belonged to Jason.

The problem was that she didn't know that. Or wouldn't admit it.

The best Jason could do, he decided, was to make sure she and Mitch didn't have a chance to get too well acquainted that evening.

After considering various alternatives, he settled on the tender-loving-care approach. No use trying the fireplace bit again; Anne would have a fit the moment she saw him approaching with an armful of firewood.

Instead, Jason dug out a heating pad that Ada had left behind in her closet. He filled it with warm water, making sure it wasn't too hot; you didn't want to burn a lawyer, not with the way liability suits were going these days, he reflected mockingly.

He ignored Anne's wary glance as he entered and offered the heating pad.

"Hey, that looks terrific." Mitch sat up straighter so the pad could be slipped behind his back.

"Nothing hurts like a back injury." Jason made a point of fluffing up the cushions that supported Mitch. "Can I get you anything else? Some aspirin?"

"Well, yes, if you don't mind." The guy settled back with a murmur of relief.

"Right." Avoiding Anne's glare, Jason vanished into the bathroom and found a bottle of aspirin, then poked through the medicine cabinet. What else could he use to distract the man? Did he dare suggest a massage? Well, what the hell.

To his surprise—and Anne's disgust—Mitch agreed immediately, after Jason explained that he'd once studied massage with an expert from Sweden, which was not entirely untrue. He omitted mentioning that she'd been a Swedish actress whom he'd dated briefly and that the massages had been preludes to more intimate encounters.

Anne sat back, her arms folded stiffly, as Jason administered the massage. He quirked an eyebrow at her, as if to ask whether she'd like to do the honors herself, but she ignored him.

He knew she was angry. But he was saving her from herself, after all.

"Boy, that's terrific," Mitch said as Jason finished. "My ex-wife was a nurse, and she could give a great back rub, too. That's one of the things I missed most after the divorce."

Jason refrained from asking what the other things were and, instead, stayed on the subject of Mitch's back. "Has it bothered you before?"

"Oh, quite a bit." The attorney relaxed against the heating pad. "But you know what really bothers me? My feet. You can't imagine how sore they get. I have a terrible time finding shoes that fit. My wife used to buy those foam innersoles and cut them specially."

Jason didn't dare glance at Anne. "I guess it helps to marry a nurse."

"It sure does." The man appeared to have forgotten where he was and whom he was talking to. "I can't tell you how nice it is to come home after a hard day in court and have a hot bath waiting...."

Jason let him ramble on for a while before excusing himself to go and clean up the kitchen. He had a feeling Mitch had cooked his own goose with Anne.

Sure enough, it wasn't more than ten minutes later that he heard the front door closing and light footsteps approaching. Quickly Jason poured some detergent into the burned pan and began scouring it mightily.

Anne stood watching him for a full minute without saying anything. Finally Jason couldn't stand the suspense.

"Well? Are you going to kill me?" He looked up and was startled to see her smiling.

"No, you goofball." Anne was somewhat surprised herself. She'd been angry at first at the way Jason was interfering, but gradually she'd become more and more annoyed with Mitch for allowing it. Then, as she realized what a hypochrondriac Mitch was, she'd found herself fighting back a chuckle at Jason's masterful performance. "I did wonder if it was a coincidence that he seemed attracted to women in the medical profession."

"Can you blame him?" Jason set the pan aside to soak overnight. "What man wouldn't want to come home to a hot bath and a woman who cut foam innersoles for his aching feet? She probably rubbed his corns with baby oil, too, and applied leeches to his throbbing back...."

Laughter burst from Anne. She didn't know why she felt so lighthearted. After all, Mitch had seemed like the perfect man for her, and she ought to be severely disappointed. "You rascal."

"I was only trying to help." Despite his earnest expression, Jason couldn't suppress a chuckle. "You don't mind

that I used some of your perfumed oil for the massage? The
man must smell like a flower shop.''

"Thanks a lot!"

"Hey, don't take that the wrong way. What smells good
on a woman doesn't necessarily sit right on a man.''

Standing here laughing with Jason, Anne felt right and
natural and completely at home. She didn't want to question that feeling just now. "We didn't even get to dessert.''

"What did you have in mind?''

"Chocolate mousse will do.''

Jason peered into the freezer. "How about vanilla ice
cream topped with Grand Marnier and fresh cherries?''

"Sold.''

They sat across from each other at the kitchen table,
spooning up the delicious sundae. Despite her elegant silk
dress, Anne curled her legs up, hooking her feet on the chair
supports. She felt like a 1950s bobby-soxer on a soda date.

Every time she dared look at Jason, he would say something like, "Gee, my feet hurt, Anne. Would you mind...?''
and they'd both be off in gales of laughter.

It was only after they'd finished, as she was getting ready
to go upstairs, that Anne felt serious again. "Why do you
suppose I have such lousy luck with men?''

"Because you're picking the wrong ones." Jason downed
the last of the cherries.

"And where do I find the right ones?''

"Try the kitchen.''

Her heart thudded loudly in her throat. He was bringing
it out in the open, the attraction they felt for each other.
"Jason...''

"Wait a minute." He leaned forward, elbows on the table. "Anne, you crazy woman, do you think I don't know
what's going on in your head? You've intellectualized this
whole thing, sorted it out and analyzed it and decided you
need a particular type of man, and I don't fit the description.''

"It's not that simple." Wasn't it? She ignored the question as soon as it popped up. "I know myself, despite what you think. I know what I need."

"And I'm not it?"

"In some ways, you probably are. But this wouldn't be the first time I'd be leading myself astray...."

"Forget what happened in college." He swung to his feet and advanced toward her, his eyes hungry and demanding. Anne's knees threatened to buckle, and she leaned against the door frame. Her mind told her to run away, and her heart told her to fall into his arms.

Then Jason reached her, and her heart won the skirmish. Strong arms encircled her and drew her close, and his lips claimed her with kisses that started on her mouth and blazed down her throat.

Her blood turning to liquid silver, Anne melted into his embrace. Her fingers found the buttons to his shirt and opened them, then pressed into the thick mat of hair on his chest.

His breathing quickened, matching hers, as his thumbs stroked upward from her waist, brushing the edges of her breasts. Anne felt herself come alive in a new way, as if she'd just been born into an unexplored world of flame and brightness and incredible desire.

A radiance enveloped her as she yielded to him, sought him, caressed him and felt his answering caresses draw passion from its hiding place in her soul.

"I'll never let you go," Jason murmured. "Anne, can't you see that we belong together?"

His words broke through the spell he'd woven. Anne's mind kicked into gear again. Belong together? That was just the problem. For tonight, for a few weeks or even months, she and Jason could blaze together like a shooting star, but they would never belong together. They were too different, in their goals, their life-styles—even their passions.

Wrenchingly, she pulled back. "No. No, Jason, I'm sorry. It was wrong to ... to let this happen tonight, between us. I should never ..."

"Would you cut that out?" Anger flared across his face. "This has nothing to do with what you 'should' do. Damn it, Anne ... !"

"I'm going upstairs before we both say something we'll regret." She wished her words didn't sound so prissy and trite, but she had to get away from him somehow, before she gave in to the fire still raging through her body. "Good night, Jason."

His hands clenched into fists as he watched her go. A few minutes ago, he'd broken through that protective armor she always wore, and then it had snapped shut again. Damn it! Jason glared at the dirty ice-cream bowls, as if they were somehow to blame.

Well, he wasn't going to throw them, so he might as well rinse them. He carried the dishes to the sink, working off his fury on the dinnerware.

Gradually, as his frustration cooled, Jason had to admit that he was partly at fault. If he told Anne the truth about himself, that he wasn't just a happy-go-lucky wanderer but a serious photographer, surely she could see that they did suit each other, that they could work out their differences.

He thought about going upstairs after her. But this wasn't the time, not while they were both upset. It was important that he explain things to her calmly and at length, that he be able to soothe her resentment at having been deceived and bring her to see that he, as much as she, had been caught off guard by the love blossoming between them.

Tomorrow was Sunday, an easygoing day and the perfect time to have a heart-to-heart talk. His mind made up, Jason went to bed in good spirits.

ANNE HAD TROUBLE FALLING ASLEEP until the early hours of the morning, and as a result she slept until nearly noon.

Waking to see the sunlight streaming through the window, she groaned to herself.

By now, Jason would be ensconced in the living room. It would be difficult to avoid another confrontation.

At least she wasn't on call today. Maybe she could sneak out of the house and have breakfast somewhere else.

The muscles in her neck and back ached as Anne crawled out of bed, and she knew she must have been tensing them in her sleep. She could use one of Jason's massages right now....

No. She wouldn't even think about it.

Groggily, she washed up and slipped on slacks and a blouse. Then, feeling like Daniel venturing into the lion's den, she went downstairs.

A quick glance into the living room showed her newspapers strewn about, but no Jason. From the kitchen wafted the whistled notes of "Oklahoma!"

Feeling like a thief, Anne scurried out the front door, scarcely daring to breathe until she was in her car and had taken off.

Well, great. Now she was in exile from her own house.

But only until she could sort out her thoughts, she reminded herself. Still, she had to go somewhere, so Anne headed for the Fashion Island shopping center. There was a good bookstore where she could find something to help Ellie pass the time.

Jason. What was it that made her forget all her careful reasoning when he took her into his arms? And how was she going to steel herself against him?

Anne hadn't reached any momentous conclusions by the time she arrived at the bookstore. Well, after she bought Ellie a gift, she'd have breakfast at some coffee shop and mull over the whole mess thoroughly.

The bookstore was bright and modern, with eye-catching displays of the latest releases. Anne browsed through the bestsellers, wishing she had time to read some of them herself.

Ellie liked travel books, Anne recalled. Nearby was a selection of oversize photography books, and she wandered over to it.

A pictorial of Ireland looked interesting, but there wasn't enough reading material to keep Ellie occupied. Anne took her time, sorting through the books carefully. Perhaps she should be more practical and get something on child care instead....

As she turned away, Anne glimpsed a book out of the corner of her eye, something about a politician on the campaign trail.

It wasn't the sort of book she had in mind, and yet it drew her. After taking a closer look, she realized why.

The author's name was Jason Brant.

Now, there was a coincidence. She smiled, wondering if she should buy it for Jason, or if it would bother him to learn that there was another, more successful photographer with the same name.

Curious, she leafed through the book. The photographs were striking, and the accompanying text looked intriguing.

Then she stopped, aghast. One of the photographs was all too familiar. A print of it hung on the wall in Jason's room.

Her throat tightening, Anne flipped to the back. There on the inside flap of the cover was a photograph of Jason.

With a numb feeling of betrayal, she read the brief summary of his life. A former wire-service photographer in Europe...author of a previous book...

And what was his current project? The private life of a California obstetrician?

Moving in a fog, Anne picked out a child-care book for Ellie and took it to the register along with Jason's book.

And then she went home, to face the man whom she'd trusted and who had been playing her for a fool.

Chapter Eleven

A light turned red ahead of her, and Anne slammed on the brakes. She'd been so preoccupied with her anger that she hadn't been paying attention and could easily have had an accident.

I've got to calm down before I see him.

Impulsively she headed for Ellie's house a few blocks from the beach in nearby Corona del Mar.

For a moment after the car halted, Anne sat there unmoving, inhaling the salty breeze and wondering whether to tell Ellie what she'd discovered. No, the wound was too fresh to share with anyone. But the visit would give her time to collect herself.

The child-care book in hand, Anne went inside.

She was pleased to find Ellie, as per instructions, tucked in bed. The remains of a lunch sat on a tray atop the bedside table.

"See? I've only been up to go to the bathroom. Honest, doc!" Her friend grinned at her.

Anne managed a smile. "Glad to see it. Here's something to help while away the hours."

Ellie examined the book with delight as Anne pulled up a chair. "Hey, this looks terrific. I've bought quite a few books, but I don't have this one."

"It, um, seemed to have a lot of practical tips and also some good pointers on child development." Actually, Anne wasn't quite sure what had led her to select that book; she'd been too upset about Jason to pay much attention. "So—everything's going along smoothly with your housekeeping arrangement?"

"Mmm-hmm." Ellie studied her, head cocked to one side. "Okay, out with it."

"Out with what?"

"You've got something on your mind. Come on, fess up. You know I can read expressions—it's my speciality." Hands folded in her lap, Ellie wore an air of patient waiting.

I should have known better than to come here. Anne searched for a credible explanation. "Well, I'm concerned about a Hispanic woman who works down the street from me. She has to be away from her children...."

The story of Juanita spilled out, bringing an expression of concern from Ellie.

"So what she needs is a job where her children could live with her," Anne concluded. "I wish I could hire her myself, but..."

"You wouldn't want to fire Jason," Ellie finished for her with a wink.

Swallowing hard, Anne nodded vaguely. "Besides, I don't have enough room."

"I can't imagine having to live apart from your children." Ellie tapped her fingers against the quilt. "You know, I think I'll ask around in our church. There might be someone who needs a maid—it's a large congregation. The minister will be visiting me this week, and I could talk to him."

"Would you? I'd appreciate it." Anne decided to depart before her friend's all-too-keen intuition impaled her again. "Give me a call if you find anything. And stay in bed!"

"I promise."

It would certainly be nice if Ellie could come up with a solution for Juanita, Anne reflected as she drove home. But neither Ellie nor anyone else could come up with a solution for Anne.

Jason. How could he have done this? He'd used her, plain and simple. She didn't yet know why. Surely he didn't plan to publish those photographs he'd taken of her at the beach? Heat stung Anne's cheeks as she recalled how open she'd been with him.

When she came through the front door, Jason was lying amid the newspaper sections, reading the entertainment pages. A look of surprise flashed across his face as he saw her.

"I thought you were still asleep upstairs."

Wordlessly, she held out the copy of his book.

Jason frowned. "Where did you get that?"

She ignored the question. "What an interesting book. Can you imagine, the author has the same name you do. And he looks like you, too."

Damn it. Jason had to fight down the impulse to take her in his arms. That was obviously the last thing she wanted. "I intended to tell you about it today."

"Oh, sure."

"It's the truth. I've been trying to figure out how to explain things for quite some time. I'll admit, I've been something of a coward." His words were inadequate; he could see that from the pain in her eyes. Lord, he'd never meant to hurt her! "Anne..."

"Would you mind telling me exactly what you're doing here?" Her whole body quivered with anger. "You can skip the apologies. Just get to the point."

"I'm working on a book about housekeepers. Exploited ones, like Juanita. That's how I got involved with her, why I was taking pictures of her kids." There was a lot more he wanted to say, but Anne cut him off.

"And am I one of the exploiting employers? Is that the idea? You can show me frisking about the beach, having a good time while—"

"Those pictures weren't for my book!" Outraged, he strode across the room and gripped her arms. "Anne, how could you even think that? My working for you was just a way to make contacts. And I really did need the money. Books of photography don't exactly earn millions, you know."

"I want you out of here!" She knew she was losing her grip on her emotions, that the tears were going to stream out any second.

"I'm not going to leave you in the lurch, with your family coming next week." He kept his tone level, trying to calm her. Thank heaven for the reunion; it would give him time to reason with her, time for her to calm down and listen to him rationally.

"Don't bother, Jason. I'll hire someone, get a caterer—I don't care." She took a step backward, fists clenched.

"Maybe you could send out for pizza." He did his best to sound bland and helpful. "Or bring in Chinese food. Your aunts and uncles and cousins could all sit around digging into little white cartons with chopsticks. That would be a family reunion to remember, wouldn't it?"

Anne would have been all right if it weren't for Great-aunt Myra.

As Jason spoke, she could picture Great-aunt Myra's thin face twisting as she confronted a pair of chopsticks and a carton of cashew chicken. Great-aunt Myra was outraged by finding anything foreign on her plate. Served a taco at a picnic once, she had wrinkled her nose, regarded it as if it were a roach caught sneaking into her house and pushed the plate away with a snort of disgust.

At the image of Great-aunt Myra eating takeout Chinese food, Anne felt the corners of her mouth start to twitch. Darn it, she wasn't going to let Jason see her smile!

She turned away sharply. "Very well. But the day after the reunion—out!" Without waiting for a response, Anne mounted the stairs to her room.

Safely inside, she realized that she hadn't eaten breakfast yet. But it would be too humiliating to go down again now, after her dramatic exit.

Then she heard the front door shut and the sound of Jason's car starting on the street.

Where was he going? In spite of herself, Anne hurried to the window in time to glimpse the Mustang disappearing around a corner.

She knew he hadn't gone for good; for one thing, there hadn't been time to pack. And she ought to be glad that he'd gone out and left her some privacy.

The trouble was that she loved him.

The realization hit Anne hard. For a moment, she couldn't breathe. It was true. In spite of everything, she'd fallen in love with Jason, so much that it hurt to see him drive away without a word, even though she herself had ordered him out. So much that she wanted to know where he was going for consolation and when he would be back and what he was thinking.

A hard lump formed in her chest as she went downstairs to the kitchen. Getting over Jason was going to take all her strength. But it had to be done.

She had one more week to enjoy his madcap smile and the teasing sound of his voice. And then, Anne told herself, she would never see him again.

Chapter Twelve

Deanie Parker's house looked as though a tornado had blown through it, Jason observed as he stepped inside. Although it was afternoon, his cousin still wore her bathrobe, and he'd never seen her hair in such a mess.

From a back bedroom came the persistent, angry wailing of a baby.

It didn't take a genius to figure out that Deanie hadn't slept much last night. And, as she blearily informed Jason, her husband was still overseas, so Deanie was trying to cope with a colicky infant alone.

"I had no idea it would be like this." She led the way back to the nursery. "In all the TV shows, the babies coo and smile, and the mothers look radiant."

The tiny face of Alexander James Parker was scrunched into a mask of indignation as he shrieked, pausing only briefly to suck in air before launching into another tirade.

Maybe it was because he hadn't been kept awake all night, but Jason found himself intrigued rather than dismayed. For one thing, it was a relief to deal with a straightforward problem rather than replaying the scene with Anne one more time, trying to figure out what he might have said to get through to her.

"I've fed him, diapered him, rocked him—I just can't take any more." Tears streaked down Deanie's face. "I'm not cut out to be a mother, Jason. I don't know what to do with him.''

He assessed the situation quickly. ''You need a few hours of uninterrupted sleep. Go on, Deanie. I'll make sure Alexander doesn't take the house apart.''

She looked dubious but finally went off to bed.

Left alone with the baby, Jason began to doubt his own sanity. He'd changed a few diapers for friends' babies over the years, but that hardly made him an expert in child care.

Gingerly, he reached down to pick up the squalling infant. Alexander's cries intensified. Oh, great. At this rate, poor Deanie would never get to sleep.

More firmly, Jason lifted the baby, supporting the little head. ''Now look here,'' he said. ''We've got to get this figured out, okay?''

The baby paused, perhaps at the sound of an unfamiliar voice. Then his face started to wrinkle again, preparing for another round of wails.

''Oh, no, you don't!'' Jason scooted through the house, clutching the wriggling child. ''Uh—how about a rattle?'' He found one in the living room, but Alexander ignored it and began screaming full tilt.

He'd have to take the baby outside to give Deanie some peace, Jason concluded. And, he discovered, the rocking motion as he walked seemed to calm Alexander, at least briefly.

For the next hour, Jason walked around the block, talking to the baby all the while and cringing when fresh cries burst forth. But gradually they diminished until the tiny head rested against Jason's chest and the little eyes closed.

Strolling back to Deanie's house, Jason gazed down at the now angelic face. Tenderness and wonder tugged at his heart. How trusting the little guy was, and how vulnerable.

Raising a child wasn't going to be easy, Jason reflected as he sat down on the front-porch steps, cuddling Alexander. He could imagine how tired Anne would be after a long night of breast-feeding and soothing a baby. But then he would take over and let her go to bed for a long snooze.

Well, maybe it wouldn't always be so idyllic. But gazing down at the baby, Jason knew for certain that it would be worth it.

He was going to win Anne back. There wasn't much time left, but somehow he was going to break through that intellectual barrier she'd raised around herself and introduce her to her own heart.

JASON DIDN'T COME HOME until Sunday night, and Anne was too proud to ask where he'd been. Besides, she told herself sternly, it was none of her business.

There was some kind of stain on his shoulder, she noted as she walked past him that evening to fetch herself some graham crackers from the kitchen. And he smelled of something familiar....

Baby powder.

She smiled to herself. He must have gone to visit his cousin. It was just like Jason to plunge right in and play with the baby and not to care if he ended up with a stain on his shirt.

It was hard, staying away from him all evening and then hurrying off to work on Monday morning without a word. There was so little time left before he would be gone forever. But Anne had to be honest about her own weakness. If she gave in now, she might never be able to bring herself to send him away.

Monday night, going over medical charts in her office after John and the staff had left, Anne was surprised when the phone rang. Who would call on her private line at this hour?

It was Ellie. "I called your house and Jason said you were still at work. Listen, I've got good news! My minister has some elderly cousins who've been looking for a live-in housekeeper, and they've got an apartment over their garage. I just called them...."

The couple was willing to hire Juanita right away, based on Anne's recommendation. The wife had recently broken a hip, and she and her husband needed a housekeeper urgently.

"I already told Jason about it," Ellie added. "You know, he's very interesting. We talked for quite a while. You ought to hold on to him."

"I'll be the judge of that." Anne immediately regretted her sharp tone. "Look, Ellie, I really appreciate what you've done for Juanita."

"I'm just glad I could help."

By the time Anne got home, Jason had already informed Juanita and called the new employers to make arrangements for her to move in Wednesday evening. "I offered to provide transportation."

"We'd better use my car." Anne dropped her purse on a table in the front hall. "It's got a bigger trunk."

"Good idea." There was something tender in the way Jason was looking at her. "Anne, I didn't expect you to solve Juanita's problem. Rosa and I had been talking to people around the neighborhood, hoping to come up with something. It was really kind of you."

Maybe it was her weariness, but Anne resented the implication. "Just because I live in a nice house doesn't mean I don't care about other people!"

"I never thought that."

"Didn't you?" She looked directly into his eyes for the first time since Saturday night. "Tell me the truth, Jason. When you began this project, when you took this job, didn't you expect me and everyone else who lives around here to be insensitive and selfish?"

He was about to argue when he remembered his thoughts that first day, imagining a male Dr. Eldridge who spent his time raking in money and running around with women. "I suppose I did have some prejudices, Anne."

"Well, that's quite an admission." His words had deflated her anger, but she didn't want to let him get too close. "Score one for the citizens of Irvine."

"Anne, I can't blame you for getting the wrong idea about me." He wasn't about to let this opportunity slide by. "I know I got off on the wrong foot with you."

She lifted a hand in warning. "I don't want to talk about it, Jason. It's been a long day and I'm in no mood for an argument."

Jason took a deep breath to stop himself from pressing her further. Were there any words, no matter how carefully selected, that could make Anne see the truth, that they loved each other and belonged together?

There were only a few days left until the reunion, and yet to pressure her would only backfire. "Okay. Go and get comfortable and I'll get your graham crackers and milk ready."

He could see the tension ebbing from her shoulders and neck. "Thanks, Jason."

But I'm not giving up. He watched until she was out of sight upstairs before heading for the kitchen. He'd have to give matters a rest for the time being.

On Tuesday, Anne worked late again—intentionally, Jason knew—so he had no chance to talk to her until dinner on Wednesday, for which he prepared one of his specialties, lamb chops flambé.

Anne hardly spoke until they reached dessert, which was homemade apple pie. Then she said, "By the way, I figured Juanita didn't have much in the way of furniture or kitchen equipment, so I made a few phone calls. Several people I know said they'd be glad to help."

"Have some whipped cream." Jason handed her the bowl and watched as she plopped a spoonful onto her pie.

"My partner's loaning us his pickup—that's what I drove home in, in case you hadn't noticed." He hadn't. "You can take Juanita and her kids tonight, and I'll drive around and pick up the equipment."

Jason had to think fast. It was important to get Juanita's family settled, but he didn't want to be apart from Anne. There was only a day and a half left until her relatives began to arrive.

"You can't lift furniture yourself." He kept his tone matter-of-fact. "Hold on a minute." Before she could object, he dashed out the door, leaped over the fence and went to confer with Rosa. She gladly agreed to drive Juanita and her children in Jason's car.

He returned and told Anne about the arrangement. "So I'm free to provide manual labor. Okay?"

For a moment, as she stared at him without speaking, his heart sank. Then she shrugged. "Sure. I suppose it makes sense."

Dinner over, they set out in the pickup. As Anne drove through the fading daylight, Jason observed her from the corner of his eye. She looked tired, and he felt a pang of guilt. If it weren't for him, Anne wouldn't have made such a point of working late this week.

If only he had another month! They needed a chance to cool off and spend some relaxing time together. One more day at the beach, perhaps. He'd even settle for an evening spent tossing out another unsuitable boyfriend.

The first house they arrived at was only a few shades this side of a mansion, on a cliff overlooking Newport Harbor. The owners had set out a refrigerator and a box of dishes in the driveway.

Jason reached down to the floor of the truck for his camera.

"You're going to take pictures?" Anne frowned. "I'm not sure..."

"Look." He slung the camera over his shoulder and came around to help her down. "Obviously, I had some stereotypes about the rich people of Irvine. Well, it's only fair to show their generous side, too, don't you think?"

She nodded slowly. "I suppose it is."

During the next two hours, they collected a convertible sofa, twin beds, an assortment of pots and pans, towels and flatware and even several framed reproductions of Van Gogh paintings.

"I'm impressed," Jason admitted as they headed through the twilight to the address Ellie had given them. "Your friends aren't even getting a tax deduction."

"They were delighted to help." Anne had relinquished the wheel and was curled sleepily in the passenger seat. With her hair falling across one cheek, she looked remarkably childlike. "Jason, just because people settle down and buy comfortable homes doesn't mean they're Scrooges."

"I didn't think that. Well, not exactly." The last thing he wanted was an argument, especially when she was in such a mellow mood. "I suppose the problem here is the system. The maids like Juanita don't have anyone to go to bat for them, and they need the work so badly they'll take almost anything."

"So you're not really attacking the employers?"

"I suppose not." He had intended to, he conceded silently, but he was certainly getting a different perspective on things. "Of course, some people are exploitive. But mostly the Hispanic immigrants here are victims of economics." He started to explain about his plans to go to Mexico and visit Juanita's family, but they'd reached their destination, a charming California bungalow in a middle-class neighborhood of Costa Mesa, one of the towns bordering Irvine.

The two children came out running ahead of their mother. "Jason! Jason!"

Juanita followed, smiling. "So many things. All for us?"

"You can thank Anne and her friends." Jason began unloading the truck. "Where do we put them?"

It took another hour to drag everything up the stairs to the
apartment above the garage. Then Jason and Anne paid
their respects to Juanita's new employers: a hearty white-
haired man and his wife, who welcomed them warmly from
her wheelchair. With their permission, Jason took photographs for his book, using the soft illumination of the porch
light.

Watching the happiness shining on the two deeply etched
faces, Anne felt a pang of envy. She was sure it would be
obvious even in a photograph that the lives of these two
people had intertwined over the years, like morning-glory
vines on a picket fence.

And if anyone could capture that inner joy with a camera, she knew it was Jason.

In spite of herself, Anne looked forward to seeing his
book when it came out. She wished she could compare the
final product to the way Jason had envisioned it initially.
After the pictures he'd taken tonight, she suspected his out-
look had undergone considerable revision.

Her attention snapped back to the present as Jason put his
camera away and Juanita wheeled their hostess into the
house.

"We were so glad to find Juanita," the husband explained as he walked them to the truck. "I don't mind
helping my wife around the house, but she knows how much
I love playing golf, and she gets upset when I stay home all
the time. She's crazy about kids, too. Our grandchildren live
in Oregon, so we don't get to see them as much as we'd like,
and Juanita's pair are real cute."

Waving goodbye as they pulled away, Anne felt a squeeze
in her heart. This was what she wanted in her own life—an
old-fashioned marriage, an old-fashioned home. But to have
that, she needed an old-fashioned man, not a muckraking,
world-wandering photographer.

The truck rattled down a slope and turned onto Coast Highway, headed for Irvine.

Jason began to speak as if addressing himself. "Now, there are two schools of thought on the subject of graham crackers."

"I beg your pardon?"

"There are those who maintain that they're basically a form of cracker and therefore not unhealthful, perhaps even virtuous."

"A virtuous graham cracker?" She wasn't sure what he was getting at, but weariness had made her so light-headed that it didn't seem to matter.

"On the other hand, some people assert that the graham cracker is merely a cookie in disguise and that its sole merit is that it is usually consumed with milk."

"Are you out of graham crackers?" she guessed. "Is that why you're telling me this?"

"I was merely trying to ascertain your point of view." Jason steered around a slow-moving van. "Because if you happen to believe that a graham cracker is a cookie at heart, then you might be willing to consider hitting a cookie boutique on the way home."

Anne could almost taste the richness of a thick, gooey chocolate-chip cookie. "Twist my arm."

But it was after nine o'clock, and they soon discovered that cookie boutiques didn't keep late hours.

Now that their appetites had been whetted, finding those rich cookies became an irresistible challenge. By ten o'clock, they had covered half a dozen neighboring towns, only to be taunted by the sight of luscious nut-studded cookies locked away behind glass.

"There's one last place I want to try." Jason guided the truck through an intersection.

"I'm afraid to ask. Do we need another tank of gas first?"

"I promise, it's not far." Sure enough, a minute later he pulled into the parking lot of a supermarket. "Coming in?"

The store had its own bakery, Anne was surprised to find. And then she realized that she hadn't been inside a supermarket in months. She was impressed by the array of coffee cakes and homemade pies, although the bakery itself was closed now.

On the counter stood a glass-covered rack of the thickest, richest-looking chocolate-chip cookies Anne had ever seen.

"Those aren't chips, they're chunks," she murmured.

"Would I steer you wrong?" Jason lifted the glass covering and transferred a dozen cookies into a white paper bag.

"That's a lot of cookies." Anne stared at them, feeling like a child at Christmas. "On the other hand, are you sure you took enough?"

He added six more.

They were hardly through the quick-check stand when Jason fished a cookie out of the bag and wolfed it down.

"Hey!" Anne grabbed playfully at the bag. "That's cheating! You have to wait until we get home."

"Who says?" He began munching on a second cookie before handing her the bag.

"Well, you could be arrested for driving under the influence of cookies."

"I'll take it slow. They'll never suspect."

She couldn't resist. Anne chomped down one. It was entirely worth the effort they'd expended to find them.

At home, they scarcely paused to pour two glasses of milk before attacking the remaining cookies. Anne had never felt so happily piggish. After the long hours she'd worked all week and the physical labor of helping load and unload the truck today, the treat seemed like a fair reward.

"I ought to find a recipe for these." Jason gestured at her with half a cookie. "They're not all the same, did you notice? This one has macadamia nuts."

"If you can make cookies like this, I'll follow you anywhere."

"Is that a promise?"

She felt light spirited and reckless. "Yes, but only as long as the chocolate chips last."

"I'll take my chances." He reached across the table and flicked a crumb from her lips. Instinctively, Anne nibbled at his finger. "Still hungry, eh?" He picked up the last cookie and waved it in front of her tauntingly. "What's it worth to you?"

"May I remind you who your employer is?"

"Ah, but I'm a short-timer, remember?" Jason dangled the cookie above his mouth. "Say bye-bye to the chocolate chips."

"Don't you dare!" Anne lunged at him, nearly knocking over the table in the process.

Jason leaped up from his chair and dashed into the living room, with Anne in hot pursuit. She caught him near the fireplace and wrestled him down onto the carpet, finally catching the edge of the cookie and breaking it free.

With one swift motion, he pinned her to the rug. Her breath coming rapidly, Anne found herself suddenly, intensely aware of his body pressed against hers, their legs tangled together and her hip nestled against his waist.

In that instant of immobility, he snatched the cookie back and brushed it across her mouth. Anne took a bite, and then his lips closed over hers and the sweetness of the cookie blended into the sweetness of his kiss.

She hardly dared breathe. After all her protestations, and her rational reasons for sending him away, she could no longer deny that at least for this moment she wanted him.

His fingers fanned her hair out on the carpet, stroking from the scalp. Anne closed her eyes, feeling him massage

ner temples and the bridge of her nose, until he leaned down
o kiss her again.

Jason. She knew his scent, the masculine tang spiced now
with chocolate; but she'd never known his body this way,
never traced it before with such loving hands. Slowly she
explored the strong line of his cheekbones, the curve in his
collarbone and the broad power of his shoulders.

Velvet kisses traced her throat and made a V on her chest.
She offered no protest when he slipped off her blouse and
caressed the soft swell of her breasts.

"Anne." He spoke her name as if it were a jeweled thing,
bright and timeless. "My love."

She couldn't say the word aloud, but it echoed through
her mind. Love. Love. She loved him.

They didn't need a fire on the hearth as their last reservations melted away. Anne shed her clothing with a sense of
relief, of becoming at last the self who had been locked away
for so long.

Tonight, time lost its meaning as Jason caressed her,
pausing to gaze into her eyes, then unexpectedly finding
some sensuous curve of flesh to arouse, from the arch of her
foot to the back of her earlobe.

Mind fused with body for the first time in Anne's life. She
relished the gentle friction of her bare skin against his and
took pleasure in stroking him until his moans mingled with
hers.

Long before the act of union, they were united. Over the
past few weeks, without her realizing it, Jason had become
a part of Anne. Now, floating her hair across his stomach
tantalizingly, she had a sense of coming home.

But when he drew his hands to the most private regions of
her being and roused her expertly, the waves of desire caught
Anne unaware. There was no gentleness in this, but a raging fire she'd never guessed lay hidden within her.

Eagerly, Anne caught his shoulders, but Jason would no be hurried. Deliberately, he brought her again and again t the edge of an inferno.

And then he plunged them into it. Gasping, Anne clun to him, writhing with him through the flames. Jason. He arms would never let him go, her body never survive with out this joyful thrusting.

They blazed together, hotter and hotter, until a tide o pleasure washed over them, momentarily heightening th flames and then soothing them away, leaving behind a quie pool of contentment.

Sleepily, she felt herself lifted and carried up the stairs. *ought to walk. I'm too heavy for him to lift. He shouldn't..* But the sensible voice within her muttered away into si lence. For one night, it had lost its grip on Anne.

Chapter Thirteen

The alarm clock woke Anne much too early, to hazy morning sunlight. Outside, birds hooted, chirruped and babbled. She had never noticed before how loud they were or how insistent in their varied calls.

Beside her, Jason stirred, groaned and went back to sleep. The sheet was thrown at an angle across his chest, baring his shoulders. Anne fought back the urge to run her hand over his skin and caress him into wakefulness.

She had to go to work.

For the first time, Anne found herself strongly resenting the demands of her job. There were rounds to make at the hospital, nurses waiting for prescriptions, patients restless to be visited and examined; and then the waiting room at the office would fill up with women needing her attention.

This one day, Anne wanted to keep all her attention here at home. For a rebellious moment, she thought of calling in sick.

Instantly, her rational mind filled with the consequences. Ellie's substitute would have to try to reach all the patients by phone; John would have to rearrange his plans to make her hospital visits....

She couldn't be that selfish. Damn it.

Regretfully, Anne rolled out of bed. Jason uttered a vague *whumphing* noise and went back to sleep.

Maybe he had the right idea. Take life as it came, and to hell with responsibility.

Almost by instinct, Anne went through her morning ritual of showering, dressing and eating breakfast. She felt as if she were pretending to be someone else, another Anne from another world.

Her daze filtered away slowly during the drive to the hospital. It vanished entirely when she reached the obstetrical ward and learned that Ellie had been admitted, in labor and already four centimeters dilated, too far to be stopped.

Panic knotted Anne's throat for a moment, and she had to force herself to breathe calmly. Ellie's pregnancy was in its thirty-sixth week; a week later, and it would have been considered full term. There was no reason the baby shouldn't be just fine.

For the rest of the day, Anne went through her duties with half her mind attuned to the continuing reports from labor and delivery. Ellie's labor was progressing normally; monitors indicated the baby was receiving plenty of oxygen. But she couldn't shake the feeling something would go wrong.

Maybe it was because of Ellie's previous episode of bleeding, followed by premature labor. But such things weren't uncommon with a low-lying placenta, and ninety-five percent of the time everything turned out okay.

It was the remaining five percent that had Anne worried.

She had just finished a routine examination in her office when one of the nurses called to say that Ellie was dilating rapidly and would soon be in transition, the stage just before delivery.

"I'll be right there." Calling to John—who'd been warned in advance—to take over the rest of her patients, Anne raced for her car.

She arrived to find Ellie's husband, Dennis, pacing worriedly in the corridor. "She's started bleeding," he blurted out as soon as he saw Anne. "Is that normal?"

Without a word, Anne rushed into the room. Yes, Ellie was bleeding—a lot. "We're going to do an emergency C-section," she called to the nurses. It took all her self-control to sound calm as she turned to her friend, whose hair was matted with perspiration and whose eyes widened with fear. "Don't worry. Everything's going to be all right."

But was it?

A placental abruption was one of the complications of pregnancy that doctors feared most. More than three weeks ago, the ultrasound had shown that the placenta was still in place. And the bleeding could mean other things, but Anne wasn't about to take any chances.

Within minutes, an anesthesiologist was preparing Ellie for surgery. A neonatalogist and a team of nurses were summoned to take care of the baby in case it had trouble breathing when it arrived.

The next hour was the tensest of Anne's life. She'd worked on emergency cases before, but never had it been a friend. Damn it, she should have referred Ellie's case to John or to another colleague. It was too difficult emotionally to take life-or-death responsibility for the child of someone who meant so much to her.

Well, it was too late to worry about that now.

Anxious moments ticked by as she made the incision. The doctor assisting her said little, seeming to pick up Anne's spring-coiled intensity.

For one terrifying instant, as she lifted the baby girl from its mother's womb, Anne thought it wasn't going to start breathing. And then that life-giving cry burst through the operating room, and the tension wheezed out of her like air from a balloon.

The placenta was still adhering to the wall of the uterus by a patch. Had Anne been less concerned, had she waited even a few more minutes to operate, the baby might have been lost.

Instead, Ellie had a healthy little girl who weighed in at five pounds four ounces, a good size for a preemie. She'd probably be able to go home from the hospital when Ellie did.

Afterward, congratulating Dennis and watching the infant being wheeled to the nursery, where she would be observed closely for the next few hours, Anne realized for the first time that it was almost seven o'clock in the evening and she was bone tired.

Jason would be worried. No, he'd probably called the office already and found out where she was.

As she washed up, Anne realized that she hadn't thought about him for hours. Already their night together seemed like a dream, like someone else's dream.

What if I'd called in sick this morning, as I wanted to?

The possibility sent a chill shuddering through her.

Driving home, Anne faced a grim truth. There was another person who lived inside her, a younger, wilder Anne who was ready to throw everything aside for love. But that wasn't the person she'd become, the person she had to live with for the rest of her days.

This morning, she'd gotten everything backward. The stranger hadn't been Anne Eldridge, M.D., it had been Anne, Jason's lover.

Under other circumstances, perhaps the two could have merged. If only she'd fallen in love with a man who fit in with the life she had to lead!

But Jason... She respected his talent and his role as an outsider and critic of society. But travel and risk taking were vital to his career. It would be as unfair to expect him to give up his work as for him to demand that she abandon the trust her patients had placed in her.

Painful as it was, Anne at least felt on familiar ground as her intellect returned to its accustomed place, ruling over her emotions.

She'd read enough about marriages to know that love rarely survived the daily toll of conflicts between two fundamentally incompatible people. And there had probably never been two souls more different than she and Jason.

Even if he agreed to stay here in Irvine, there was the problem of children. She didn't want them raised by a housekeeper or a day-care center. It might be possible for her to work part-time for a while, but Jason would have to give up the work he loved and accept some spirit-grinding job as a studio photographer to support them. Eventually, he'd come to hate it—and her.

Marriage would destroy the love between them. The result would be two miserable adults and, eventually, children growing up in a broken home.

The time to stop things was now, before they went any farther, Anne told herself firmly. Their night together would remain a moment of bliss stolen from the locked treasury of her heart.

She tried to ignore the knife twisting in her chest. Anne knew she would be doing the right thing, to send him away after this weekend.

IT TOOK ALL of Jason's self-control not to slam shut the door to his room as he headed into the bathroom-turned-darkroom.

Blast Anne's intellectual rubbish! He'd known there would be repercussions, recriminations, uncertainties after last night. But this cold dismissal of him was infuriating!

She'd had her speech all rehearsed the moment she came through the door, before he could even greet her with a glass of sherry and the tempting hors d'oeuvres he'd prepared.

What nonsense! Career conflicts, finances, children. Those things could be worked out. Those things meant nothing compared to the love blazing between the two of them. Why couldn't she see it?

As usual, his words had bounced off her like play darts against armor. The impulse to sweep her into his arms and force out the passionate side of her had been restrained only by the conviction that such tactics would backfire. In the end, he would have to win her brain as well as her heart, and Anne's intellect was a formidable enemy.

As usual when he was upset, Jason found relief in the absorbing magic of printing photographs. Images blossomed up at him from the tray of chemicals: Juanita moving into her new home; the elderly couple with their arms around each other; the pickup truck filling with donated furniture and supplies.

As he calmed down, Jason began to assess the situation rationally.

There were two phases left to complete his book: traveling to Mexico and putting the finishing touches on the text. Then he'd need to deliver the manuscript and prints to his publisher. Of course, they could be mailed, but Jason felt safer presenting the entire precious package in person.

He didn't want to leave Anne, but there was no time to bring her to her senses. The relatives would start arriving tomorrow, and he suspected there wouldn't be a quiet moment all weekend. And then he was under orders to leave, unless she changed her mind. Which wasn't likely to happen, in view of the mood she was in tonight.

Maybe some time apart would be good for them. It might finally give her stubborn brain a chance to work itself around to the truth, that they belonged together.

And there was something else nagging at him, Jason conceded as he finished his printing and turned on the overhead light.

Money had never been important to him before, except to have enough to pay his current expenses. But now he wanted to become a family man. He didn't mind sharing the earning power with his wife, and he wasn't chauvinistic enough to insist that he had to earn more than she did.

But there was a matter of pride here. He wanted this book to do well. He wanted to show Anne that he wasn't the ne'er-do-well drifter he might have seemed at first.

He would need to concentrate on making this book the best it could possibly be. For that, he'd need some time alone, holed up somewhere—perhaps in New York, near his publisher—to concentrate on selecting the right pictures from the stacks that he'd taken and making sure the text was the most evocative he could create.

So for the time being, he had no choice but to go along with Anne's edict that he leave.

But he would be coming back. Whether it took weeks or even months, he would be coming back to Anne.

Chapter Fourteen

The Eldridges didn't so much arrive at Anne's house as they invaded, swarming into the neighborhood in a bevy of vehicles that ranged from the elegant to the barely operating.

At first it seemed to Jason that there must be Eldridges from every state in the union. He noted the long-jawed accent of Oklahoma, the lively tang of Tennessee, the nasal enthusiasm of New York.... And children! They ranged from a three-week-old infant, to supercilious preteens, all the way up to a young man about to enter Stanford.

Without realizing it, he now saw that he had envisioned dozens of people very much like Anne: self-controlled, highly educated, with a sense of fun bubbling beneath the surface but usually kept in check.

Instead, he found that family occupations ranged from farming to pharmaceuticals, that there was a prim Great-aunt Myra and a bluff joke-cracking Uncle Gary who used to be a rodeo rider; that, in short, most of them were nothing like Anne.

It was all he could do to suppress the temptation to photograph them. What a rich assortment of portraits they would make, from the bright eyes of the baby to Uncle Gary's weathered face! But he knew that if he so much as removed a lens cap where she could see him, Anne would take drastic steps. And he didn't want to spoil the reunion by finding out exactly what those drastic steps would be. Still, he might manage to sneak in a few shots here and there.

As the babble of the first day subsided, Jason began to sort out the players. Loving Anne as he did, he wanted to get to know the people most important to her.

Matters were simplified by the fact that only her immediate family was actually staying at the house. After the last plate of ham and baked beans had been cleared away—he'd decided to keep the fare simple—and the last game of Uno had been played, the uncles and aunts and cousins retired to their hotels and motor homes. Only Anne's parents and her sister's family were left behind.

From his careful observations that day, Jason knew that Anne's father, Sutter Eldridge, was the center around which the others revolved. So he wasn't surprised when the older man, whose straight back and proud bearing bore testimony to his military experience, cornered Jason in the kitchen.

"My daughter says you're her housekeeper." Sutter poured himself a glass of milk, regarded it with distaste and then downed it in a gulp. "Now, exactly how does that work?"

Jason had no intention of beating around the bush. "Sir, I'm in love with your daughter and I intend to marry her."

Even Sutter hadn't been prepared for that much directness. He nearly choked on his milk but recovered quickly. "And what does Anne say about this?"

"In a word, 'No.'" Jason went on to explain how he'd come to work here and why Anne was throwing him out as of Monday. "But I'll be back."

Sutter wasn't a man to belabor a point. Apparently satisfied that Jason was neither a bum nor an opportunist, he changed the subject. "Tell me about this photographic work of yours."

After showing polite interest in the book about the politician, Sutter perked up when Jason described the paramilitary camp he'd visited in the Middle East. An hour later, they were firmly ensconced at the kitchen table, Jason on his second beer and Sutter on this third glass of milk.

From the living room they could hear the soft voices of the three Eldridge women, but not what they were talking about. An occasional giggle wafted from upstairs as Lori's husband, Bob, read their sons a bedtime story.

"Damn stuff," Sutter observed as he regarded his milk. "Take it from me, son, never get ulcers. So tell me, what's your next project?"

"I haven't quite decided." Jason leaned back in his chair. "There are several ideas I've been toying with."

"Such as?"

"One of these days I'd like to photograph the private lives of three factory workers." Sutter was proving to be a splendid audience, and Jason allowed his imagination free rein as he described how he'd like to examine one worker in Japan, one in the United States and another in the U.S.S.R. "It would tell us more about our values and economic systems than all the doctoral dissertations ever written."

"I'll drink to that."

A rustling noise in the doorway made Jason look up. Anne was leaning there, a slight frown puckering her forehead. How long had she been listening?

"Either of you want to make a fourth for bridge?" Neither her tone nor her expression revealed anything.

"Sure, I'm game." Sutter scraped his chair back. "You're a fine young man, Jason. Good luck with all your projects."

It was hard to keep a straight face, but he managed. "Thank you, sir."

Well, at least he had her father's blessing, Jason reflected as he went to work on his menu for tomorrow.

SATURDAY'S HIGHLIGHT was a picnic in a nearby park. The weather was perfect, everyone's spirits were high.... So why did Anne feel restless, she wondered as she spread a checkered tablecloth across a wooden picnic table.

She took a deep breath and willed herself to relax. Gradually some of the tautness eased from her shoulders and back, but a reservoir of it remained.

There was no reason in the world not to share everyone else's good cheer. She'd called Ellie this morning, even though John was officially in charge this weekend, and had been delighted to learn that mother and baby were both doing well. Nothing to worry about on that score.

And no one in the family seemed upset by the last-minute change of location. Even Great-aunt Myra had cocked a knowing eye at Anne last night and said, "I didn't expect we'd actually end up at Lori's house. The age of miracles is long past."

As others began loading up the table with buckets of fried chicken, corn on the cob and potato salad, Anne's attention turned to Jason.

Having worked since early morning to coordinate the feast, he was taking a few well-deserved hours off. But instead of heading for the beach, he'd chosen to stay with her family. At the moment he was trotting toward the playground, each hand clasped by one of her nephews, with a handful of other children swarming around them.

There was something about Jason that drew children like a magnet, Anne admitted to herself with a touch of envy. He knew just how to wiggle his fingers at a baby and tickle a toddler, how to address a high-school student with suitable dignity and, a moment later, one-up a preteen with lines like "What tells jokes and changes colors? A stand-up chameleon!"

"He's some guy." Lori finished setting out napkins and came to stand beside Anne. They didn't plan to eat for another half hour, until the children had raced off some of their energy, and the other adults were drifting over to the inviting shade of benches around a manicured duck pond. "Are you sure he's just the housekeeper?"

Thinking of the night Jason had spent in her arms, Anne blushed guiltily and ducked her head so her sister wouldn't see. "He'd like to be more than that, but it just wouldn't work."

"If you say so." Lori plopped onto the bench. "Hey, thanks a lot for stepping in for me this weekend. You saved my life."

"Lori, you've got to start planning ahead." Relieved to change the subject, Anne delivered a short but pointed lecture about the need for responsibility.

"You're absolutely right." Lori met her gaze squarely. "Bob and I both tend to leap before we look. But you know what, Anne? People can be happy even when they're not perfect."

"Exactly what does that mean?"

"You're always so hard on yourself." Lori's freckled face wore an unaccustomedly serious expression. "You expect so much. Anne, I know that Bob and I have had a lot of ups and downs. Maybe you remember that minimarket we invested in that went broke. And then he hurt his back skiing right after we bought our house and I had to go to work while the kids were still small. But things have worked out."

"You and I have always been very different, Lori." Anne closed her eyes, letting the sun warm her face.

"What I'm trying to say..." Her sister paused, searching for words. "Anne, it's not in spite of the foul-ups that we've been happy. In a way, they've actually strengthened our marriage. We've had to pull together, make adjustments."

"I wouldn't argue with that." With her eyes shut, Anne was intensely aware of the shouts of laughter emanating from the playground, of Jason's deep bass counterpointing the sweet sopranos of the children. "But, Lori, you and Bob are fundamentally compatible. You have the same values. What you both wanted most was a home and children.''

"Don't you?"

It wasn't like Lori to be so probing. Anne opened her eyes reluctantly and turned to face her sister. "What are you getting at?"

"I can't help notice certain, well, vibrations between you and Jason.

"And you're trying to save me from myself?"

"Just because I goof up when it comes to practical things doesn't mean I'm completely lacking in sense. Anne, sometimes I think you're so organized you haven't left room for love.''

Lori's words hit much too close to home. But her sister couldn't possibly understand what Anne's life was like. "I know what I'm doing. Trust me."

The younger woman sighed. "You're so self-assured. I've always kind of envied you, Anne. But...well, I guess I've said enough."

Touched by the remorse in her sister's voice, Anne cupped her hand over Lori's. "I appreciate your concern. Believe me, I've gone over those same thoughts more than once. But I know myself, and I have to choose what's right for me. Now, I'm starving. How about you?"

Without waiting for an answer, Anne rang the large dinner bell, and they were promptly inundated with hungry relatives.

The rest of the day sailed by smoothly. Part of the family made an outing to Disneyland, while the others assaulted a nearby beach. Jason was kept busy preparing dinner, to Anne's relief, and that evening he played poker with Bob and some of the other young men.

If she could only get through the rest of the weekend without finding herself alone with him....

That hope dwindled the next morning. Used to getting up early during the week, Anne woke at six-thirty and an hour later abandoned hope of falling asleep again, even though visitors weren't expected until ten.

Making her way downstairs, she heard her nephews playing quietly in their room. Despite Lori's scatterbrained approach to life, she'd raised two contented, well-behaved little boys, Anne had to admit.

It was in the front hall that Anne ran into Jason. Wearing a light jacket against the coolness of the morning, he had one hand on the front doorknob when he spotted her.

"I'm going out for doughnuts." He grinned engagingly. "Can I talk you into coming? Otherwise, I might not get enough chocolate ones. Or is it peanuts you like?"

"Chocolate with peanuts on top." Suddenly Anne was starving. And she knew the doughnuts tasted best right at the bakery. The prospect of waiting here for a half hour or so until he returned was pure agony. "I suppose you might need help carrying them...."

He held the door for her.

Already regretting her impulsiveness, Anne headed down the sidewalk. How was she going to get out of this one? It was too much to hope that Jason wouldn't take advantage of the opportunity.

Rescue arrived in the form of a taxi pulling up in front of her house. As Anne watched, mystified, Great-aunt Myra paid the driver and climbed out.

"Thought I'd leave the hotel early and get a head start on the rest of the family," she informed Anne and Jason as she came up the walk. "Figured you could use some help with breakfast."

"How thoughtful." Anne took her great-aunt's arm. "As a matter of fact, we're going out for doughnuts, and we'd love to have you come and help pick the varieties."

"Well." Great-aunt Myra regarded the two of them sharply. She might be eighty-six years old but there was nothing wrong with her powers of perception. "I wouldn't want to be in the way."

"Not in the least," Anne said heartily, and Jason was forced to agree.

On the way to the doughnut shop, Anne pointed out places of interest to distract Great-aunt Myra. Unfortunately, there weren't many, so the conversation finally died away.

"The two of you getting married?" the older woman inquired out of the blue.

Anne coughed. "I beg your pardon?"

"Getting married? With the two of you living together, a person can't be blamed for wondering."

"You don't understand." She refused to meet Jason's eyes. "Jason works for me. He's my housekeeper. He has his own quarters downstairs."

"I can see that." Great-aunt Myra's voice conveyed barely restrained impatience. "And I can see a great deal more than that. So can anyone else who's got eyes."

Only their arrival at the doughnut shop saved Anne from trying to answer the unanswerable.

Among the three of them, they made a large selection of fragrant doughnuts—maple covered and cream filled and sugarcoated and chocolate and frosted with multicolored sprinkles.

Jason consulted his watch and turned to Great-aunt Myra. "We've got another hour before people start arriving. Now, I personally think doughnuts taste best when they're fresh, don't you? And I'm sure Anne would agree."

"The tea here is probably that terrible instant stuff," the older woman observed. "However, I suppose that can be tolerated."

And so the three of them sat at a booth and consumed far more doughnuts than Anne was willing to count. As they ate, Jason regaled Great-aunt Myra with tales of his housekeeping mishaps, and she responded with an openness Anne had never seen in her great-aunt before.

"My fiancé sent me a beautiful sweater from England during the Great War," Myra recalled. "The softest wool you ever saw, and a fine shade of lavender. Well, first time I wore it, wouldn't you know I spilled something on it. So I got out my washboard and I soaked that thing in the hottest water I could find, and then I scrubbed it and scrubbed it. By the time I was done, there wasn't enough left to use as a postage stamp."

"That must have broken your heart," Anne sympathized.

Her great-aunt impaled her with a look. "Broken my heart? I should say not. What broke my heart was when my fiancé was killed in action six months later. Oh, I had my share of suitors later on, but none of them was good enough for me. Damn fool I was."

This speech left Anne too startled to reply.

"People ought to take love where they find it, wouldn't you say?" Jason, of course, never ran short of words.

"I would indeed." The older woman stared straight at Anne. "Some people have too much pride for their own good."

"I think we'd better be getting back." Anne stood up, brushing away the crumbs that had evaded her skimpy paper napkin.

Without a word, Jason rose and offered each lady an arm. The three of them remained silent on the trip back, but the air vibrated with Great-aunt Myra's final words.

It isn't pride, Anne told herself, wondering why the remark stung. *It's common sense.*

Is it possible a person can have too much of that for their own good, too?

She was grateful for the hullabaloo that greeted their arrival. Her nephews, Jeb and Sammy, came running out to help carry in the doughnuts, and for the rest of the day there was no more need to be alone with Jason—or with Great-aunt Myra.

That evening, Anne had arranged a special treat: she'd chartered a yacht. Since it came with its own crew, including a cook, Jason was free to mingle on the deck with the rest of the family, and a group of children quickly gathered around him.

"Now, that's a sloop." Jason pointed to the boats in Newport Harbor as the yacht glided past. "And that one with the colorful sails is a catamaran."

"Why's it called that?" one of the girls asked. "Does it have something to do with cats?"

"Nope." Jason hoisted her up so she could see better. "It's because there are two separate hulls. Originally, a catamaran was made by lashing two logs together. The name comes from the Tamil language that's spoken in the country of Sri Lanka, in Asia. *Kattu* means to tie and *maram* means tree."

"Wow." The little girl's eyes widened. "Have you been to that place?"

Even before Jason nodded, Anne knew the answer. Of course he had, she reflected with a pang. And if he hadn't, it was probably on his list of places to visit next.

She thought back to the conversation she'd overheard between Jason and her father. So Jason's next project was going to involve traveling to Japan and Russia. Terrific. And what was she supposed to do while he spent his days photographing factory workers?

A crew member called out that dinner was served, and she wandered in, feeling lost and apart even as she stood elbow to elbow with her laughing relatives.

The swordfish was superbly prepared; Jason freely admitted he couldn't do better. But Anne hardly tasted it. She was too busy trying not to look at him as he amused Jeb and Sammy with stories of the exotic foods he'd eaten in China and India.

After dinner, one of the crew members appeared on deck with a guitar and launched a sing-along.

Anne's first thought was, *doesn't the salt air warp the guitar?* And her second was, *maybe I really have forgotten how to have fun. The condition of his guitar is none of my business.* The reunion was almost over, and she was letting her own anxieties spoil it. Shaking away her mantle of worry, Anne joined the circle of relatives singing "If I Had a Hammer."

Then her spine tingled like a tuning fork. Not far behind her, someone was whistling the melody. Jason. Nobody could whistle like that but Jason.

And then he was standing by her side, his arm linked through hers as the group finished mangling the melody and began dismantling "Lemon Tree."

She could feel the heat of his body in the cool night air. Every sensory detail of their night together rushed back into Anne's veins like an infusion of wine. Weakly she leaned against Jason, and his arm encircled her waist.

To one side, Great-aunt Myra was smiling.

All too soon, the yacht returned to the dock, and the family trooped off reluctantly. Children yawned and drooped in their parents' arms as goodbyes were said.

Except for Anne's immediate family, she wouldn't see the others for a full year. Hugging Great-aunt Myra, she wondered how much longer the feisty older lady would be around, and she was grateful she'd had a chance to get to know her better—in spite of the unwelcome advice.

Jeb and Sammy rode home with Anne and Jason. At the house, after a late-night snack of doughnuts that Jason had managed to secrete that morning, the family trooped up to bed.

But sleep didn't come easily for Anne. Trained by her years as an intern and resident, she usually dropped off immediately. But tonight, staring out the window at a mariner's sky brilliant with stars, she couldn't stop thinking about the fact that she would be saying goodbye tomorrow to more than her family.

Jason. There was no more reason to keep him around—except for that near-fatal temptation she was determined to resist.

It was hard to imagine the house without him. No more whistling when she came down in the morning; no more cooking smells when she arrived home at night; no more newspapers scattered around the living room; no more having someone here to talk things over with at the end of the day; no more strong arms clasping her....

Restlessly, Anne got out of bed and began to pace. A floorboard squeaked beneath the carpet. Darn, he'd hear her downstairs; besides, she knew her father had ears like a fox.

Drawing a flannel robe around her and sticking her feet into the panda slippers, Anne made her way quietly downstairs. Through the side door by her office, she padded out onto the patio.

The night was quiet. Far off, Anne could hear the occasional murmur of a passing car, and somewhere a bird mumbled in its sleep. There was no wind.

Love. When she was younger, she used to dream of finding it, magically, perhaps at a glittering ball, or accidentally, while browsing through a bookstore. Always the handsome stranger and she would recognize the truth at first sight; obstacles would melt away before them, and after that...well, she'd never worried about what came next.

Smiling to herself, Anne thought back to the day Jason had first come to this house. She'd been startled to see him sitting in the living room with the other applicants. An attractive man, she'd noticed immediately, but unsuitable for the job, of course.

Of course.

How had he talked her into hiring him? Looking back, it was hard to remember. Vaguely, she recalled that he'd taken over the kitchen and that she'd been dying of hunger. Even then, he'd known instinctively how to bypass her defenses.

When had she fallen in love with him? Maybe it had been when he routed Horace Swann with those ridiculous questions about his mother's colitis. Or when he tossed Aldous Raney bodily out the door. Or when he showed Mitch Hamilton up for the hypochondriac he was.

Or had she fallen in love that night when they walked by the Back Bay and she realized the freshness Jason brought to her everyday world?

It was impossible to say. More likely she'd fallen a little bit at a time, day by day, living here with Jason. He was charming, admirable and caring, she admitted. If there had been no question of having to plan a future, of taking care of children, of conflict with Anne's own needs and goals...

"Can't sleep?" It didn't surprise her to find Jason standing in front of the sliding glass doors that led out from the kitchen. He'd probably known instinctively that she was here.

"Overexcited, I guess." Anne sat on one of the patio chairs. "I'd been looking forward to the reunion for so long, it's hard to believe it's over."

Jason sat across from her, leaning across the wrought-iron table. "Anne, I have to say this...."

"Please don't."

"You don't know what I was going to say."

"I think I do."

The silence of the night sifted between them. Anne caught a whiff of poignant sweetness from the neighbors' lemon tree. Jason, sitting there regarding her, seemed to fill the whole world.

"I'm going away," he said.

Anne caught her breath sharply. She'd expected him to argue. Deep inside, she realized with sudden and painful insight, she'd expected a fairy godmother to wave a magic wand and somehow resolve the differences so that Jason could stay. But it wasn't going to happen.

"I . . . I know." Surely he could hear how breathless she was, how stunned.

"There are a lot of things I want to tell you, but maybe it's better if I don't." He looked away. "We had fun tonight, didn't we?"

"Yes." She ached to lean across and smooth the sadness from his face. "This whole weekend went beautifully. Thank you, Jason." The words sounded stiff and distant, not at all what she meant, but she didn't know how to explain without letting him know how much she yearned to keep him here forever.

"I kept thinking you would change your mind." He inhaled deeply. "I love you, Anne."

She hadn't expected her own tears, so sudden and overwhelming. Could he see them in the darkness? If she sat here for one more instant, she'd lose the will to resist. With a low moan, Anne wrenched herself away from the table and ran down the path to the side door.

Jason didn't try to follow her. He was too angry to confront her now; angry not with the Anne he loved but with that damn interfering brain of hers, the one that told her things that simply weren't true.

Several times this weekend, he'd thought she might waver. He'd noticed the heart-to-heart talk with Lori; and then there'd been Great-aunt Myra's pointed remarks; and it had been obvious tonight on the boat that everyone in the family thought the two of them belonged together. They'd been accepted as a unit, by everyone except Anne.

Yes, it was best that he go away tomorrow and finish his book. But he'd wanted to discuss his absence with her, to assure her that he'd be coming back.

Chapter Fifteen

"Here's the information you wanted." John Hernandez handed Anne a jiffy-printed brochure with the name of a clinic on it. "They just opened in Santa Ana and they're desperately in need of doctors to volunteer a few hours a week."

She stared at him blankly. This morning, saying goodbye to her parents and sister and trying to avoid Jason's eyes as they ate breakfast, she'd scarcely thought about work.

Arriving at the office had been a bit of a shock to her nervous system. Everything looked smaller than she'd remembered, more confining. It had been hard to concentrate on her cases, and now...

"Oh. Right. I'm sorry, John." She tucked the brochure into her pocket. "I'm kind of distracted this morning."

"I noticed. Must have been a busy weekend with the family. Everything go okay?"

"Terrific." Forcing herself to smile, she turned to go about her work.

An hour later, at lunchtime, Anne drew the brochure out of her pocket as she consumed a sandwich in her office. The clinic, it said, had been started by a coalition of nonprofit community groups concerned about the lack of adequate medical care for the poor.

Several doctors, dentists and nurses were listed on the brochure as having agreed to donate services. But there was no obstetrician, Anne noticed immediately.

This was exactly what she needed to take her mind off Jason. And, at the same time, she could fulfill one of her goals in pursuing a medical career—to help women who really needed it.

As the afternoon went by, Anne resolutely pushed the thought of Jason's departure from her mind. Instead, she called the clinic and set up an appointment for later in the week to meet with the director. The woman who answered her call sounded excited when she learned of Anne's credentials.

"We can really use your help. There was a girl in here today—nineteen years old and pregnant, and she doesn't know where to turn for medical help. We get them all the time. They're afraid to venture out of the area, and they're confused by paperwork, so they don't even get what treatment's available. The director will be thrilled when he hears."

As soon as she hung up, Anne got a call from the hospital about a patient ready to deliver, and she was busy for the rest of the afternoon. By six o'clock she was bone weary and ready to go home.

Pulling up in front of the house, she felt her spirits lift automatically. Coming home was always something to look forward to. What would Jason be cooking tonight?

As soon as she opened the door and sniffed the air in vain, the realization hit her.

He was gone. He'd really left.

Anne stiffened. It was what she'd wanted, wasn't it?

No, but it was the right thing. Regardless of what anyone else thinks.

Still, her first impulse was to turn right around and march out the door, away from this cold and empty house that echoed with his memory. She could go out and get a pizza.

No; pizza was one of Jason's favorite foods, and she'd think of him with every bite. How about chicken? Or Mexican food? Or Chinese?

If she left this house now, she might never find the nerve to come back again.

Rationally, Anne knew she wasn't just going to walk away from her house. But she didn't see how she could face coming back to it again tonight. No, she'd better stay right here and raid the refrigerator. There were, she knew, plenty of leftovers from the weekend.

Almost too tired to propel herself forward, she forced herself into the kitchen, the room which most reverberated with Jason's absence. And stopped in the doorway, shocked.

The entire wall adjacent to his room was covered with a mosaic of photographs.

Slowly, as if in a dream, Anne walked along the wall, retracing the weeks she and Jason had spent together. Here was that precious day at the beach—the sand castle, her introspective mood, Jason's high spirits. And there were Juanita and her children at the playground, one of the youngsters laughing as he swooped down the slide into his mother's arms.

And of course the fiesta afterward, with its gaiety and wealth of interesting faces. Oh, and moving day— Anne stood for a long time gazing at the picture of Juanita's new employers, their arms around each other, their eyes reflecting a serenity she might never know.

The last photographs were a surprise. Jason must have returned alone to the Back Bay to capture its spirit: the wildness contrasting with the silhouette of houses in the background; the balletic movements of a flock of migrating birds settling onto the water; the enchanting play of light over the high grasses. She could almost see movement in the still photographs.

Then there was the family reunion. Anne had to smile at the man's audacity. Somehow he'd managed to snap pictures of Jeb's and Sammy's dirt-smeared faces at the picnic; where had he hidden the camera when she was around? He'd even composed a portrait of Great-aunt Myra sitting on Anne's patio, drinking a cup of tea and staring straight at the lens with her chin lifted authoritatively. Anne could almost hear the old lady saying what a fool she'd been more than half a century ago and how Anne shouldn't make the same mistake.

Was it a mistake?

Damn it, she should feel more confident! Anne pulled herself away, going to the refrigerator to dig out some leftover chicken and potato salad.

She wasn't going to take the mosaic down. That would be admitting it hurt too much for her even to look at it. No, she'd leave the pictures up until they lost their power over her, until her memories of Jason mellowed and she no longer felt this throbbing ache inside.

Why had Jason printed these photographs and left them for her? Anne wondered as she fixed herself a glass of iced tea. Since he was gone now, he couldn't have meant them to win her over.

Yet it wasn't like him to mock her, either. Perhaps he'd meant them as a sentimental farewell, a last reminder of what she'd thrown away. Or perhaps he'd intended them as a gift, guessing how much these memories would mean to her.

As she sat alone at the table, staring at the photographs, it occurred to Anne for the first time that she didn't know where Jason had gone.

Her heart sped up and for a minute she felt as if she couldn't breathe properly. Had he gone back to Santa Monica to find another apartment at the beach? Or was he flying abroad even now, perhaps to Japan to start his new book? Even if she wanted to, there was no way to reach him.

Unless he chose to contact her, she had no way of finding Jason every again. Or—

Deanie Parker! The likelihood that he would stay in touch with his cousin comforted Anne far more than she wanted to admit. Of course, she had no intention of inquiring after him—well, not right away. In six months or so, she might ask Deanie casually how Jason was doing. Surely that would be only natural.

She wished she knew where he was right now. She wished she could hear him whistling, eavesdrop on his conversations, watch as he focused his camera on a new subject.

Blast it, she wouldn't go on torturing herself! Resolutely, Anne headed out to the video store so she'd have something to watch that might to distract her.

And if she happened to pick *Oklahoma!* and hum along with the melodies, what did that have to do with Jason?

"WE'D LIKE TO MOVE your publication date up a month." The editor's voice bristled with static over the long-distance line to Mexico.

Jason cupped his hand over his ear to hear better. The only telephone in Juanita's hometown was located in the general store, and it was anything but quiet. A heavyset woman was bargaining loudly for a length of cloth, and just outside the open door two dogs circled each other in the dust, growling threats.

"You'd like to what?" Jason knew he couldn't have heard correctly. On his last two books, publication had been delayed several months each time. Works of photography didn't have the highest priority on a publisher's list, he'd learned.

"We're real excited about this one." The voice was tinny but the words were quite clear. Jason had heard right, after all. "Several of us have looked at the preliminary material you sent. This contrast between a wealthy Southern California community and the poor people who do the dirty work, well, our promotions people think we can book you on some talk shows. And you know what that does for sales.''

Jason wondered what Anne would think if she saw him glibly chatting away on a talk show. She'd probably feel exploited all over again. But he did want this book to be a success.

"We need the rest of the material as soon as possible," his editor continued. "When will you be finished there?"

"I was planning to head back to Mexico City tomorrow and catch a flight out." Jason tried to ignore the shrieks of two barefoot children as they raced up to the counter to buy candy. "But I intended to stop over in California for a few days."

He'd been gone for two weeks. Although he'd been busy meeting Juanita's family and photographing them, his thoughts had never been far from Anne. Did she miss him? Was she even now contemplating a doomed marriage to some fool like Horace Swann, merely because it seemed to make sense? What had she thought of the wall of pictures he'd left behind?

"You can go to California later. We need the rest of those pictures and the text, pronto!"

It occurred to Jason that his editor had a lot of nerve, particularly after refusing to give him an advance because the project "wasn't commercial." But there was nothing to be gained by arguing. After all, this book might be the only way to prove to Anne that he wasn't as flighty as she believed.

With a sigh that must have been audible all the way to New York, Jason said, "All right. I'll see you day after tomorrow."

Anne would just have to wait.

RELAXING ON A CHAISE LONGUE on Ellie's patio, Anne sipped a glass of beer and watched two couples play a good-natured, fumbling game of badminton. A card game was under way a short distance from Anne, and several of the other guests were taking a dip in the hot tub.

In a shaded stroller, Ellie's baby lay dozing, waking occasionally with a loud groan to protest her digestive upsets. Or just plain old gas, if you wanted to be frank about it, Anne thought with a smile. Fortunately, the little girl wasn't a screamer, just a groaner.

"Having a good time?" Ellie plopped into a chair. She'd recovered amazingly well from her C-section and would be going back to work soon.

"Thanks for inviting me. Your parties are always fun. And that chicken on the barbecue smells terrific."

Her friend regarded her knowingly. "You've lost some weight, haven't you?

"Oh, a few pounds, maybe."

"Not eating so well since Jason left?" It was the first time Ellie had mentioned the subject in weeks. "Aren't you going to hire another housekeeper?"

Anne shrugged. "I've been using a cleaning service. It seems to work out well enough." *How could I let someone else live in Jason's room and cook in his kitchen?*

"Heard anything from him?"

"No."

Ellie looked as if she wanted to say more, but her husband, Dennis, came by to ask for some help fixing drinks, and she followed him into the house.

About a dozen people had been invited today. Anne watched through half-closed eyes, pretending to sunbathe as she observed the card game.

Ellie had invited several unattached men and one other single woman, probably to avoid making it look like the point of the party was to pair Anne off. But Anne had a suspicion that had been a primary motive.

One of the men seated at the table had light-brown hair like Jason's, but his eyes lacked the dark fire she was used to, she noted as he dealt the cards. He looked, well, pleasantly bland. He worked with Dennis at a computer firm, she recalled. You certainly couldn't imagine him suggesting a romantic twilight stroll in the Back Bay.

The other fellow, a redhead, struck her as a bit more energetic as he slapped a card down on the table. But maybe too much so. He didn't have Jason's sensitivity; she could see that.

The baby's groans intensified into the beginnings of a wail. Ellie was still indoors, so Anne hurried over and picked up the child.

An angelic smile was her reward, followed by a loud burp. Ah, innocence.

Well, there would be plenty of time to find another man and have her own babies, Anne told herself as she rocked the infant in her arms. Surely it wouldn't be long until she found someone who appealed to her.

Just as soon as she stopped comparing every man she met to Jason...

"I ALMOST DIDN'T recognize you." Jason stood up and pulled out a chair for Jill. She looked smart in her designer suit, with matched Gucci bag and shoes. The restaurant she'd chosen was the perfect setting for her—sleek and hushed despite the crowd at lunch. The predominant sound was the clink of expensive crystal glasses.

"You haven't changed—maybe a few gray hairs." Even her smile was more premeditated than it used to be. Suddenly Jason wondered if he'd ever known his ex-wife at all.

They filled the minutes with chitchat as they studied their menus. She chose the seafood salad; he preferred to try the shrimp crepes, which were outrageously overpriced. But he could afford it, with the hefty advance his publisher had finally coughed up.

He'd decided to look Jill up on a whim. No, it was more than that. For a few years, the two of them had shared their lives. Since the divorce, they'd all but lost contact. Now that he loved someone else, he'd felt the need to see her again, although he wasn't quite sure why.

"Tell me about your new book." It was hard to tell if she was really interested, but Jason dutifully described the premise. Jill nodded slowly as she listened. "I was right. You haven't changed. Still the same old crusader."

"You sound as if you're not sure whether that's good or bad."

She shrugged and sipped the white wine the waiter had set in front of her. "It's okay, I guess. Someone's got to improve the world; heaven knows, it could use it."

"So tell me what you're up to."

She rested her chin on the palm of her hand. Jill was still an attractive woman, Jason noted, and yet he felt no more drawn to her than to a stranger on the street. In a way, she *was* a stranger. He tried to picture the girl he'd met in college, with her long hair and high-flying ideals, but he couldn't see her in this woman sitting across from him.

"First of all, I'm getting married." Jill waited expectantly for his response, and Jason didn't let her down.

"Married? I'm glad for you! Must be a special guy." His enthusiasm came from the heart.

"Ralph's the manager of a major hotel and he's due for a promotion in the chain." Jill went on to sing the praises of her fiancé. She herself had become a designer of linens and had met Ralph when she was hired to create a new line for his hotel.

"Sounds like you two are really on the way up."

Jill paused as the waiter delivered their orders; then she replied, "That's right, we are. The president of the company likes my work, and they may be hiring me to design for them exclusively. Ralph and I could travel together to visit the various hotels. You'd love it, Jason! They've got establishments in Paris, Tokyo, Cairo—all the best places!"

All the best places. Jason hoped she didn't see the irony in his smile as he thought of Juanita's hometown in Mexico. That certainly wouldn't qualify as one of the best places on Jill's list, and yet there'd been a closeness and warmth among the people that came from years of struggling together and sharing joys as well as sorrows.

"It doesn't sound like you're planning on having children." He knew it was none of his business, but he couldn't restrain his curiosity.

"Children? You've got to be kidding!" Jill stared at him over a forkful of salad. "What would I want children for?"

"Some people think they're cute."

"Cute? Dirty diapers and breast-feeding in the middle of the night? Oh, come on!" She was genuinely horrified.

"They're not for everyone," he conceded. "I'm glad you're living the kind of life you've always wanted."

"So am I." She grinned, and for a moment he glimpsed a trace of that younger, more carefree Jill who he'd once thought shared his ideals. "And I hope you find the kind of happiness Ralph and I have."

"Thanks." He didn't feel like telling her about Anne. He knew Jill would approve, but for the wrong reasons—because Anne was successful in a prestigious job, not because she was strong and caring.

Walking back to his hotel after lunch, Jason caught sight of his reflection in a store window. Almost defiantly, he'd chosen to wear jeans today, with a polo shirt and a tweed jacket that he'd removed as soon as he stepped out of the restaurant into the heat of the August day.

Yes, he looked much as he always had. You couldn't see gray hairs in a window reflection, he noted with a half smile.

But Jill was wrong when she said he hadn't changed. He had. Traveling to exotic places and trying to show the world its own face through his photographs still appealed to him. But he was ready for a new phase in his life.

Raising children meant staying in one place for a while and spending time with them. But then, wasn't a home really the entire world in microcosm? Surely there were plenty of insights for a photojournalist in any corner of the world, including the manicured comfort of Irvine.

Jason's step faltered. The need for a transition in his life-style had seemed so obvious to him that he hadn't thought about how he must look to Anne.

Maybe her resistance to him wasn't entirely pigheaded. If she thought he intended to combine having a family with hopping around the globe...

An image of her came to him, standing in the doorway of the kitchen as she had so often. This time she was regarding him and her father with an unreadable expression.

What had he been talking about right before he noticed her? Oh, yes, about wanting to photograph factory workers in three different countries. But that could wait, of course.

Only she hadn't understood that. Maybe because Jason hadn't told her. Oh, damn his own shortsightedness!

At that moment, he would have given anything to sprout wings and fly to California to be with Anne. But he was still finishing revisions on his text, which would take another week at least. And some things simply couldn't be explained over the phone.

Jason's steps dragged the rest of the way to the hotel.

ANNE WIPED BEADS of sweat off her forehead. The one thing she hadn't given much thought to before volunteering was that of course the clinic couldn't afford air conditioning. And today was a real early-September Southern California roaster.

Stretching her shoulders to ease a cramp in her back, she finished jotting down notes in the folder in front of her. The girl who had been Anne's last patient of the day was only seventeen and pregnant for the second time. Amazingly, she'd known almost nothing about the human reproductive cycle and how to avoid getting pregnant.

In the weeks since Anne had begun spending one afternoon a week here, word had spread among women in the area and she'd found herself with as many patients as she could handle. Some had neglected infections; others needed information almost as much as they needed medical care.

We're the richest country in the world, and still people fall between the cracks, she reflected as she stepped out into the now empty waiting room. It was five o'clock, and Anne realized for the first time that she hadn't eaten lunch.

Well, she'd pick up a hamburger on the way home. But the prospect didn't have much appeal. Somehow Anne lacked an appetite these days; maybe it was the heat.

"You're doing a terrific job." The receptionist was a woman in her forties who Anne knew had volunteered to work in this oven even though she could have spent her days at an expensive country club. "One of the women told me she was going to come back next week and bring her two daughters. She's afraid they might get pregnant and she figured they'd listen to you."

Anne leaned wearily against the edge of the desk. "Isn't it ironic? Half the women I know can't seem to get pregnant, and the other half can't seem to avoid it."

"That's life." The receptionist regarded her sympathetically. "You look like you could use a nice relaxing weekend."

"Oh—it's Friday, isn't it?" Anne hoped she didn't sound as confused as she felt. The weeks had lost their shape recently, with nothing to look forward to. "I'm not on call until Sunday. Maybe I'll do something exciting—like sleep late."

"Have fun." The receptionist was getting ready to lock up, so Anne said good-night and departed.

She didn't want to go home yet, to that empty house with the mosaic of photographs waiting for her if she ventured into the kitchen. Well, Anne had been meaning to stop by to see how Juanita was getting along with her new employers. Ellie had relayed glowing reports, but Anne wanted to see for herself.

As she pulled up in front of the cozy bungalow, it occurred to her that the family might be at dinner. Then she saw Juanita's children playing with tricycles in the side yard.

Anne's light tap at the door brought Juanita. "Dr. Eldridge! Please, come in."

"I hope I'm not intruding." She looked around, but the homey living room was unoccupied.

"No—they went to their daughter's house for dinner, and we ate already. If you're hungry, I could cook for you."

Juanita's English had improved greatly, Anne noted as she said, "No, but thank you. I just wanted to see how you were doing."

They sat out on the back porch, enjoying a refreshing breeze and drinking iced tea as Juanita told Anne how much happier her children were now. In the dusk, Anne watched the two little bodies fling themselves about joyfully, shouting and giggling and then turning to their mother for reassurance every few minutes.

Best of all, Juanita added, Ellie's congregation was trying to find a permanent gardening job for her husband. That way he, too, would be able to live here instead of traveling to farms across the state.

In the comfortable silence that fell between them, Anne found herself remembering summer evenings of her childhood—the soft twilight, the sharpened chirps of insects, the sense of security.

Juanita caught her off guard by saying, "How is Jason? When is he coming back?"

Taking a deep breath, Anne said, "I don't know, Juanita. I haven't heard from him. And I doubt if he's going to be coming back."

"He will." The other woman nodded confidently. "He loves you."

It was impossible to explain how she felt to Juanita, Anne reflected. Maybe that was because she wasn't entirely clear how she felt herself.

"Sometimes love isn't enough."

A puzzled frown marked Juanita's confusion. "Yes, but you have enough money. He doesn't have to go away to work."

"Yes, he does, but not because of the money." Anne shifted, suddenly uncomfortable despite the deep cushion on her willow rocking chair. "You know he takes photographs around the world."

It was clear from Juanita's face that she didn't understand why two people who loved each other would allow anything to come in their way, except such dire poverty as had forced her and her husband temporarily apart.

I suppose, from her point of view, we must look like fools, Anne reflected ruefully. *And maybe we are.* Finally, giving in to the hunger pangs that had reasserted themselves, she said goodbye to Juanita and the children and headed for Irvine.

On the way, Anne stopped at a drive-in hamburger joint and picked up dinner. It smelled . . . well . . . edible, anyway, she decided as she drove on.

Maybe it was time to remove the photographs from the kitchen. By leaving them up these past few months, she'd proved her point that they held no particular power over her.

If only there were someone there to know she had proved her point.

Suddenly Anne began to laugh. How ridiculous she would look to anyone who came in and discovered that she was taunting herself with those photographs! She hadn't been indifferent to them at all. Why, she'd hardly been able to force herself into the kitchen. Last night she'd gone out for ice cream rather than run the gauntlet of memories in order to fetch her usual graham crackers and milk.

Oh, Jason, what have I done?

The laughter warped into tears, but Anne fought them back. She'd made her decision and she was going to live with it.

And yet, as she did every evening, Anne found herself half-hoping when she turned the corner onto her street that she'd see Jason's car parked in front of the house.

There was nothing by the curb.

She pulled to a stop and cut the motor. Home. Only this wasn't home; it had reverted to being just a house.

Enough self-pity, she commanded herself sternly, and marched up to the front door with the hamburger sack in her hand.

But her imagination wouldn't leave her alone. As soon as she stepped inside, Anne fancied she smelled something cooking. Fettucine. Cheese and cream and a hint of nutmeg...

She must be light-headed with hunger, because she believed she heard, coming from the direction of the kitchen, the whistled strains of ''People Will Say We're in Love.''

Someone emerged—a tall figure stood silhouetted against the bright kitchen lights. He was built just like Jason.

''Hi.'' That was his voice, too, rich and warm and, well, just right.

''I—I already bought dinner.'' It was a dumb thing to say, Anne noted with one part of her mind, after she hadn't seen Jason for months.

He strode across the hallway and lifted the sack from her hand. ''You call this dinner? Doctor, you're in dire need of help.''

And then strong arms surrounded her, and it finally came home to Anne that he was really here. But it was all an illusion just the same, because he wasn't going to stay.

Chapter Sixteen

"Anne." Jason whispered her name into her hair. "Oh, God, you smell wonderful—just like medicine."

She started to giggle. And she couldn't stop. Hoots of laughter welled up, and she leaned against him weakly. "We're—we're terrific, aren't we? I—I talk about hamburgers, and you make stupid jokes."

"You've lost weight." He ran his hands along her sides. "About ten pounds, I'd say, and I can see why. The refrigerator was almost empty, and your graham crackers had gone stale."

"The photographs..."

"I didn't mean to scare you into starving to death!" Jason held her away from him, his eyes focusing deep into hers. "Why did you leave them up?"

That was a question Anne didn't want to think about. "Oh—just lazy, I guess." Quickly she changed the subject. "Where's your car?"

"It's still at Deanie's. I took a cab from the airport. I figured if you saw my car in front of the house, you might drive off into the night and never return."

"Oh, Jason..."

"Is that your stomach rumbling, or has World War III started? Maybe we ought to continue this conversation after dinner."

Hovering between laughter and tears, Anne agreed.

The kitchen smelled like home again. The track lights overhead were no longer harsh and glaring; the white Formica counters had lost their Saharalike bleakness; the refrigerator no longer loomed at one side like a hungry giant poised to devour the unwary. The air radiated rich cooking smells and a welcoming, indefinable quality that transcended the five senses.

It struck Anne that the photographs on the wall no longer threatened to overwhelm her. They were just pictures, after all.

"I was afraid you might have hired another housekeeper and I'd be forced to bribe her into taking the evening off." Jason dished his sumptuous fettucine onto Anne's best plates. "Or, if it was a man, I'd have to throw him out."

"How could I hire anyone to take your place?" Anne couldn't stop the words from pouring out. "Oh, Jason, it's been horrible! But..."

"Save the buts until after dinner, all right?"

"All right."

Questions bubbled up in her. Where had he been? Why had he come back? What did he want from her?

Across the table, Jason watched Anne as she wolfed down her food. It looked as if she hadn't eaten a bite in the months since he'd left. If he'd had any idea she was starving herself, he would have come back sooner, deadline or no deadline.

He wished he knew how to begin. Perhaps he should tell her about his book—that the publisher was launching a major advertising campaign, that a book club had shown interest and that there was even talk of basing a television movie on the theme.

Or it might be better to plunge ahead, to get right to the heart of the matter. *No, I don't plan to be an absentee husband and father. No, I don't expect you to follow me from one hotel room to another.*

Anne was avoiding his eyes as she attacked a marinated
tichoke heart in her salad. Or maybe she was so devas-
ted by hunger that she could think of nothing else. At the
ry least, she ought to hire him back as her cook, Jason
used.

But he knew her lack of appetite hadn't been due to a lack
f food. Anne could perfectly well afford to have her din-
r catered every night if she wanted. It was his own fault,
r putting these photographs here to haunt her. He'd hoped
at she would finally confront her own heart, but instead
e'd abandoned her kitchen.

Did that mean his quest was hopeless?

"Let's go for a walk," he said when their plates were fi-
lly bare.

"A walk?"

"Down the street and back. It's beautiful out tonight, you
ow—lots of stars just making their appearance, and it's
ol."

Puzzled, Anne agreed.

As soon as they stepped outside, she saw that he was
ght. With its arid climate, Southern California cooled off
e instant the sun went down. The temperature must have
opped by at least fifteen degrees since that afternoon, she
scovered as the evening air washed over her face and
oulders.

In the fading light, the entire world had mellowed to se-
a tones. Children were indoors now, eating dinner or
atching television; the only creature Anne saw stirring was
lone cat that twitched its tail as it observed them, then
alked regally away.

Jason linked his arm with hers and guided her along the
dewalk. Trying to see her neighborhood through his eyes,
nne noticed how similar all the houses were. When she'd
oved here, she'd found the area appealingly modern and
ell constructed, but to him . . .

"I guess you must find this place boring," she said.

"Boring?" He raised an eyebrow in mock amazemen
"Why, Anne—don't you know the people who live in tha
house?" He indicated one of the homes, almost indistin
guishable from the rest.

"No. Why?"

"They're jewel thieves. Notice the stained-glass design i
the upstairs window. Those aren't nuggets of red glass
they're stolen rubies. That's how they hide them."

She smiled. "You'd make a terrific father." *If you cou.
stay in one place long enough.* "Kids love stories like that."

"You think I'm making this up?" He waved at anothe
house. "Those people have orgies in the basement. Hav
you heard of the Hellfire Club?"

"Never have."

"Used to exist in England a few centuries ago. Some o
the lords and ladies in the Age of Reason figured they'
taunt the old notions of religion. They used to meet in an ol
underground salt quarry and commit hanky-panky."

"Commit hanky-panky?"

"Sound like fun?"

Anne had trouble catching her breath. She'd been so bus
with her thoughts this past hour that she'd managed to ig
nore the signals her body was sending her. Now they rushe
in on her all at once.

Jason. How his eyes glowed in the gathering darkness a
he looked at her; how perfectly his lean body fitted again
hers as he slipped an arm around her waist; how tantalizin
his skin felt when his cheek brushed her temple.

She didn't care about the future. Right now he was her
and that was all that mattered.

"How—how do you commit hanky-panky?" she whis
pered, knowing it was an invitation.

"You start with the lips." He demonstrated, the kiss in
tensifying until shivers ran through Anne. She didn't care i
the least that they were standing in the middle of the side
walk, where anyone could see them.

"Hair," she murmured.

"What?"

"Hair. Don't forget about hair." Her fingers stroked his head, fluffing the soft brown hair, feeling the heat from his scalp meet the cool evening air.

"Ears." His tongue found her lobe, then traced the curves and inlets above it. Her knees weakening, Anne sagged against him, giving in to the tickling, tantalizing sensation.

But she had no intention of being a passive partner. This was her Jason, the man she loved and had waited for even without knowing it. They might have only a few days or weeks together—or maybe only tonight—before he jetted off to some new destination, but she meant to make the most of it.

"Throat." As she said the word, she leaned forward to nuzzle the pulse point at his collar. There was something warm and vulnerable about the way he closed his eyes and lifted his chin to give her access. Anne's tongue sought the contours of his throat, and she tingled with pleasure at the groan that welled up in him.

"Shoulders." His hands explored, kneaded, caressed. Until that moment, shoulders had never struck Anne as a particularly sensual part of the body, but he was teaching her otherwise.

"Hands." She brought his up to her lips, kissing the lightly callused palms, tasting the knuckles and fingertips. She could hear Jason's breath coming faster and faster....

"Bed," he said.

"Bed?"

"If we go any farther, we could be arrested."

Damn propriety. Damn the neighbors. Damn what people would say. Still, it *was* getting cold. "Bed," she agreed.

It was outrageous how many obstacles had been erected by unfeeling engineers and architects. Stretches of sidewalk, a front door, a flight of stairs. Why couldn't people just fly over them, the way they seemed to in movies?

Finally, finally, they were alone in the bedroom. Y
Jason didn't appear to be in a hurry. After tossing his jacke
across the back of a chair, he walked slowly around th
room, running his hands across the furniture and pausin
by the window to stare down at the patio.

"I was afraid you'd never let me come up here again." H
swung around to face her. "Anne, we need to talk."

"Not now." She didn't want to hear about his next prc
ject in Japan, or Russia, or the far side of the moon. Sh
didn't want to think about what came next and how muc
it was going to hurt. This one night belonged to her.

When he didn't respond, Anne crossed the room and ur
buttoned his shirt with calm authority. Still Jason r
mained silent and motionless.

"I believe this comes next," she said, and stepped out c
her dress.

"Anne, are you sure...?"

"Are you chickening out?"

"Of course not."

"Well, I think we got as far as shoulders and hands. You
turn."

At first, as the silver light of the rising moon flowe
through the window and touched Jason's face with a strang
new expression, Anne feared he might pull away. Then h
said quietly, "You know what comes next."

Gently, his fingers explored the swell of her breasts, tea
ing the nipples into erectness. Anne let her eyes fall shu
losing herself in pure bliss.

Jason gathered her into his arms and lifted her onto th
bed. As if the moon had invaded her soul and infiltrated i
light through her veins, Anne found herself touched wit
magic.

Every move Jason made was a solemn pact betwee
them—his lips against her stomach, his fingers stroking he
thighs, his cheek brushing her soft center....

Promises made by moonlight lasted only until dawn. But Anne no longer cared.

Like a woman in a dream, she felt her mind merge with her body, so that there was no thought left but Jason. Every breath he drew echoed through her nerve endings. She wanted to touch him everywhere and to be touched by him.

As they explored, tasted, probed, stroked each other, it might have been for the first time. And perhaps for the last. But it was worth it, Anne knew.

This woman inside her, the one she had feared for so long, had become her mistress tonight. And finally Anne knew why women down the ages had thrown common sense to the wind and loved madly, wildly and endlessly.

She met kiss with kiss, caress with caress. They played across each other like currents in the ocean, merging and parting and merging again. It was impossible to tell where he ended and she began.

Waves of passion engulfed her. The moon called to the tides in her blood, and she responded without restraint.

Jason seemed to sense the change in her. Several times he paused to look at Anne in wonder. Each time, she assaulted him again with her silken body, driving conscious thought from his mind as it had been driven from hers.

As their bodies merged, they became one person and at the same time an entire universe. Flames played across the ocean beneath a fiery moon, and Anne cried out with joy.

Jason joined them again and again, sometimes almost roughly, and then with infinite tenderness. New and unsuspected hungers danced and raged through Anne as the two of them were swept up together, higher and higher, until they touched the moon and the world turned silver.

And then there was nothing but the counterpoint of their breathing and the last glorious rays fading over the ocean like the final notes of a symphony.

How could she ask any more of life than this, Anne won
dered vaguely as she drifted into sleep. Her last awarenes
was of a sheet being pulled softly over her.

ANNE AWOKE with the odd sense of having been on a lon
trip to a strange land. Was she really still here in her famil
iar bedroom, outwardly unchanged since the day before?

She turned and saw that Jason's half of the bed wa
empty.

Despite the sharp pang of sorrow, Anne told herself tha
it was only natural he should have gone. It was useless to tr
to hold back the moon or the tide, or to tie Jason down t
the dull routines of everyday life.

On the other hand, bacon had never been known to coo
itself, and she could definitely smell bacon. Wasn't it jus
like Jason to cook for her before he left?

Anne showered quickly and threw on a jade-green su
dress that matched the color of her eyes. In every move
ment, she noted how new and fresh her body felt. Had sh
always had so many nerve endings, such sensitive skin, suc
a yearning to be touched?

Even the scents of Jason's cooking as she descended to th
kitchen seemed somehow different from in her previous life
from the life known by that half-asleep woman who calle
herself Anne Eldridge, M.D.

Anne slipped up behind Jason at the stove and wrappe
him in her arms, pressing her cheek against his back.

"Good morning." He grinned over his shoulder
"Thought I'd get a head start on fattening you up."

"Don't worry. The photographs don't frighten me any
more."

"Oh? Well, I plan to replace them with new ones, so don'
speak too soon."

She drifted over to the table. "Are you going to send then
to me?"

"Come again?"

"The pictures. From Japan or wherever you're going next."

Jason laid the strips of bacon on paper towels. "Actually, I've got something really difficult in mind."

How could he look so incredibly appealing wearing one of Ada's old aprons, Anne wondered. "What's that?"

"Well, have you ever heard of anyone photographing their own wedding?"

She stared at him blankly. "You're getting married?"

"Well, aren't we?"

"I—I'm not sure I see the point." She tried to choose her words carefully. "Jason, I do love you, but ..."

He lifted the frying pan with teasing menace. "I'm getting awfully tired of your buts."

"That's because you never let me finish."

"Okay." He cracked half a dozen eggs into the pan, swirled in milk, salt and grated cheddar and set it on the burner. "You have until this is done—a couple of minutes. Make the most of it."

Why wasn't he taking her seriously? Anne inhaled deeply and poured out her thoughts. "Love isn't enough to make a marriage work. We're both old enough to know that."

"Granted." He stirred the eggs.

"I can't live the way you do. Oh, maybe for a while I'd enjoy traveling around, not having any roots, but then what? That's no way to raise children. And my medical training—I've started volunteering at a clinic for poor women. Jason, they need me. I don't have the right to throw all that away."

"I don't remember anyone asking you to." He added a dash of pepper to the pan.

"So what are you going to do? Leave me here while you roam the world? Or maybe get a job in some studio, taking high-school-graduation photos? How long would it be before you came to hate me?"

Jason transferred the eggs onto two plates, added the bacon and set them on the table. "Would you pour the coffee, please? It's already made."

Anne glared at him. "Did you hear what I said?"

"Yes, but I don't argue well on an empty stomach."

The man was impossible. And outrageous. And right. She was starving, too.

Anne poured the coffee and tackled both her food and her topic at the same time. "Well? Exactly what did you have in mind for our future?"

"We could try sausage for breakfast some mornings. Or maybe kippers. Have you ever had them? They're a kind of salty fish, I think. The English seem to like them." Jason stirred sugar into his coffee with a liberal hand.

"Jason!"

He heaved a deep mock sigh. "A man can't even eat his breakfast in peace. All right, Anne."

Her heart shivered upward toward her throat. Even though she'd been pushing for an answer, Anne suddenly wasn't sure she wanted to hear it.

"You've made a lot of assumptions." There was no teasing in his voice this time. "First of all, I'm not as poor as you think. I won't go out on a limb and say this book will make me wealthy, but I don't need to take a studio job."

Anne clasped her hands together under the table to stop herself from trembling. "That's—that's not really the problem. I'm not so much concerned about finances..."

"Wait." He cocked an eyebrow at her warningly. "You wanted to hear this, so don't interrupt."

She sipped her coffee and waited.

"You overheard me talking about a project I wanted to do on three continents. Well, there's no urgency about doing it now. Maybe I'll never do it. Or maybe we'll have to be apart for one or two months each year. Other couples manage.''

A hundred responses rattled through her mind, but this time Anne shoved them aside. Jason didn't sound the way she'd expected, rash and even a bit flip. He'd obviously thought the subject through, and a glimmer of hope pierced her soul for the first time.

''I want children as much as you do,'' he went on. ''You've probably noticed how much I love kids. Neither one of us wants them raised in hotel rooms or spending most of their lives in day-care. I can't promise a perfect solution. A lot of the time I can stay home with them; sometimes you can; and sometimes they may have to be with a sitter. Other families work it out, and we can, too.''

He'd answered two of Anne's concerns but there was one major one left. ''I'm glad your new book is earning more than you expected. But, Jason, I know you. Your life is all tied up with that camera. How long will it be before you can't stand being idle anymore, before you need to start a new project? Your work is as much a part of you as mine is for me.''

Her gaze drifted, as it had so often these past few months, to the wall of photographs. The composition, the lighting, the printing were highly professional, of course, but there was something more.

Jason's own personality and insight shone through the work. Somehow, through the impersonal medium of a camera, he'd infused his subjects with his own heart. To take that away would be to diminish him, and that was something Anne would never do.

He reached across the table and touched her chin, turning her head until they faced each other.

''Oh, Anne. You're afraid I'll be unhappy, is that it?''

Wordlessly, she nodded.

He yearned to scoop her into his arms and kiss away the misery in her eyes. But this time, finally, he had to win Anne's intellect as well as her love, and so he went on talking.

"I've been reflecting on that myself. And as I said, there will probably be times when I'll need to go away for a while. But there's a lot to be found right here. In fact, there's one project I've been giving a lot of thought to, and my publisher feels it would be popular."

"Migrant farm workers?" Anne guessed. "Or smuggling—oh, Jason, you're not going to do anything dangerous, are you?"

"I was thinking more along the lines of—*The Private Life of a Baby*."

"A . . . baby?" The word caught in her throat. And then a teasing smile lit up her eyes. "Jason, are you trying to tell me you're pregnant?"

A joke was the last thing he'd expected from Anne at this point, and Jason stared at her in confusion for a moment before chuckling. "I wish I were. Then you'd have to do the honorable thing and marry me."

"I certainly believe in honor."

"Well, what do you think?"

She took another sip of coffee, not seeming to notice that it was cold by now. "You appear to have considered all the angles."

"There's just one left."

"What's that?"

"You, Anne." He reached for her hand under the table. "Are you going to hide out in that damn intellect of yours, or are you finally going to do the sensible thing and throw caution to the wind?"

She regarded him gravely. "I think I'll do the sensible thing."

There probably wasn't another woman in the world who would have accepted a marriage proposal with those words, Jason thought happily. But then, there wasn't another woman in the world he wanted to marry, either.

Chapter Seventeen

"I knew it! I knew it!"

Even over the phone, Anne could visualize the expression on her sister's face: pure glee. "If you say 'I told you so,' I'll never speak to you again."

"You'll have to. I'm going to be one of your bridesmaids, aren't I?"

"Of course. I mean, I guess so. To tell you the truth, I hadn't even thought about what kind of wedding we're going to have." Anne balanced the receiver on her shoulder and looked across the kitchen at Jason, who was leaning on the counter wearing a smug expression, as if he were a cat and she were a pitcher of cream.

"Now you sound more like yourself," Lori teased. "Anne, you can't just throw something together in the hospital cafeteria. Weddings take planning."

Anne groaned. "I can't ask Mom to come out for a few weeks to make the arrangements, not with Dad's ulcer flaring up, and I just don't have time. Oh, well. I'll think of something."

"When's it going to be?"

"The middle of October." A vision of the last wedding she'd attended—Ellie's—flashed through Anne's mind. The little church had been beautiful, and so had the reception; she simply hadn't thought about how much work must have gone into it. Let's see, there'd been flowers and champagne and musicians and that long ivory dress and food....

"Well, put Jason on!" Lori's impatient voice broke into Anne's contemplation. "I want to congratulate my new brother-in-law-to-be."

Anne handed the phone to Jason, half-listening to the exchange of good wishes as her thoughts flicked back to earlier this morning, when they'd called her parents. Her mother's quiet joy had radiated over the phone lines. The puzzling thing had been her father's reaction: he'd merely said, "It's about time. When we went on maneuvers in my day, we didn't take two months to do it."

Now, watching Jason grin as he chatted with Lori, it struck Anne that he must have told her father during the reunion that he intended to marry her. What nerve! But then, chutzpah was one of Jason's most endearing qualities.

A minute later, after they'd both said goodbye to Lori and Bob, Anne and Jason sat back down to restore themselves with a second round of scrambled eggs and bacon.

"Lori couldn't stop talking about the wedding," Jason observed, eyeing Anne over a cup of coffee. "Do you think we can still get reservations for Westminster Cathedral? I doubt she'll be satisfied with anything less."

Anne groaned. "Let's elope."

"Right." Chuckling, he flipped two more slices of rye bread into the toaster.

"No, seriously, Jason." Breakfast sat like a lump in her stomach. "I don't have time to plan a wedding. We could drive up to Lake Tahoe and have a combination wedding and honeymoon. Then maybe we could plan some kind of reception when we get back."

Jason stared at her in mock horror. "No way, Anne." She couldn't help noticing how wonderful he looked this morning, the angles of his face softened after a night of love-making, his eyes bright with happiness. Like her own. "I want everybody in the world to know we're getting married. This is important, and it deserves the honor of a real ceremony."

It hadn't taken them long to have their first disagreement—about ten hours into the engagement, she figured. Oh, well, she hadn't expected their temperamental differences to disappear, had she?

Then Anne had a stroke of brilliance. She knew exactly how to make him agree to elope! "Fine. We can have as big and fancy a wedding as you like, on one condition."

"Oh?"

"You do the whole thing." She gestured with her fork. "Find the location, hire the caterer—the whole shot. I'll help address invitations and buy myself a suit and decide on something for Ellie and Lori to wear if they want to be my bridesmaids. And that's all." Anne sat back triumphantly.

Jason didn't say anything for several minutes. Then he muttered, "I guess they put out books on how to do this sort of thing, don't they?"

It was Anne's turn to be thunderstruck. "You mean you'd actually consider it?"

"Why not? I'm between projects at the moment." He shrugged. "I'm good at planning things; that's what makes me such a terrific housekeeper."

"I don't believe it."

"You don't think a man can put on a wedding?"

"Well, of course, but—"

"Don't worry, I'll consult you on the major decisions." Obviously, his mind was already racing ahead. "Maybe a garden setting—October's a beautiful month for a wedding." Suddenly he snapped back to the present. "Now, about the honeymoon. Lake Tahoe is out. We can go there anytime."

Anne sighed. She really did want some time alone with Jason. But it would take a lot of work to clear her calendar. She could arrange for her partner to cover emergencies while ιe was gone, but she hated to dump all her regular office ιsits on him. She'd have to schedule as many of her pre- ιatal checkups as possible before the wedding. And then ιere was her volunteer work at the clinic....

"All right, I'll concede that point," she said. "I think I ιn manage to get free for a week. How about Hawaii?"

From the shocked look on his face, you'd think she'd ιggested they spend a weekend in Tijuana. "Hawaii? For ι week? Anne, a honeymoon is supposed to be the experi- ιce of a lifetime. People around here run over to Hawaii ιr a week every time the airlines offer a discount special."

She had a sinking feeling. "What did you have in mind?"

"There's only one place romantic enough for a honey- ιoon: Paris. And we'll need three weeks at least. Prefer- bly a month."

"A month!" Anne couldn't remember the last time she'd ιad a month off. During medical school, probably. "That's ιpossible."

"What if you got sick? You'd take a month off then, ιouldn't you?"

He had a point, but she refused to give in. "Sure, but I'm ιot sick."

"Yes, you are. In the head. Anne, why don't you bring a ιw patients along so you'll feel at home? Maybe you could ιt guest privileges to practice at a hospital in Paris."

She had to laugh. "Okay, Jason. You win, but only if..."

"I know. I have to make the arrangements." He reached ιver and took out the two slices of toast, which had popped ιp several minutes ago. "No problem."

As she buttered her toast, Anne began to see the advan- ιges of going to Paris. She'd never taken time to travel and ιad always wanted to. "While you're picking up a book on ιeddings, would you get a guidebook, too?"

"Okay." He stretched out, propping his feet up on one of ιe empty chairs. "I'm glad we finally agree on some- ιing."

"Mmm." Anne rested her chin on her palm. "We'll hav
to plan our time carefully so we can see everything. I mean
of course there are the obvious things like the Louvre an
the Eiffel Tower, but I'd like to visit Versailles and the Boi
de Boulogne, and I'm sure there are a lot of smaller muse
ums...."

"Hold it!" Jason straightened up. "I'm not opposed t
sight-seeing, but let's not overdo it. I had in mind some lat
nights in the clubs on the Left Bank, sleeping late, the
lounging around at a sidewalk café for a few hours watch
ing the world go by."

Anne bit off her arguments. "It looks like we're bot
going to have to give a little."

"That sounds fair to me."

They clasped hands across the breakfast table, letting th
crumbs fall where they would. "We might even have a goo
time," Anne said, and they both laughed.

THE WOMAN with the upswept gray hairdo handed Jason
plate of sample hors d'oeuvres—Swedish meatballs, littl
sausages, stuffed mushrooms and barbecued chicken wings
"Of course, you'll want to bring your fiancée in before yo
make your selection."

Jason nibbled at the tasty if not particularly original of
ferings. This was the third caterer he'd visited today. "Tha
won't be necessary."

The woman cleared her throat. "I'm sure she'll want t
approve the menu. Or perhaps the bride's mother could d
it?"

"The bride's mother is in Denver. I'm afraid I'm all ther
is. Couldn't you pretend I'm wearing a dress?" Jason knev
he was bordering on rudeness, but he'd received the sam
reception everywhere.

Florists, photographers—he'd conceded that he couldn'
shoot his own wedding—and bakeries had all asked, wit

arying degrees of subtlety, when the bride-to-be would ac-
ompany him to make the final selection.

They seemed united in believing either that he was incap-
ble of making such decisions or that she'd end up counter-
manding his orders.

"Well, really." The gray-haired woman looked af-
fronted. "Certainly you can place the order if you like. It's
nly that it's customary for the bride to review the menu."

"My bride couldn't care less what she eats as long as it
oesn't talk back to her," Jason assured the woman. "Now,
what do you have in the way of caviar?"

Half an hour later, driving back to Irvine, he had to admit Anne had been right about one thing: planning a wed-
ing was a major undertaking.

He'd never realized there was so much involved. The first
time he got married, Jill had made all the arrangements.
Looking back, Jason couldn't remember much except that
everything was white, which he'd considered rather boring.
This time, he'd chosen a color scheme of gray and ma-
enta, which he was beginning to regret. He'd had to drive
ll over Orange County to find paper plates and napkins in
hose colors.

There'd been the need to line up a minister—fortunately,
Ellie's pastor turned out to be a sympathetic spirit—and a
ocation. There, Jason had gotten lucky. Anne's partner,
ohn, owned a beautiful old house on a quarter-acre lot in
anta Ana and, as his wedding present, had offered the use
f his garden.

Then he'd had to find a printer for the invitations and line
up musicians and coerce Anne into touring jewelry stores
with him. Fortunately, once she was actually confronted
with a trayful of gold and diamonds she'd forgotten her
mpatience, and they'd spent several hours selecting a spar-
ling pair of his-and-hers rings.

Yes, things were finally coming together, but there was a
ot left to do.

Jason pulled up in front of the house and had nearly reached the front steps when he heard the phone ringing. Hurriedly, he let himself into the house and grabbed the phone in the hallway.

"Hello?"

"Jason? This is Anne's great-aunt Myra." The voice might be a bit thin and dry, but it crackled with energy. "I just talked to Janine—Anne's mother—and I can tell she needs her mind put at rest about the wedding."

"Everything's fine."

"I don't doubt it for a minute, but a helping hand never hurt. A friend of mine is driving over your way—" Myra lived in Palm Springs, as he recalled, about two hours from Irvine "—and if you don't mind, I thought I'd ride along."

"We'd love to have you," he said, and meant it. "I don't know if Janine told you, but Anne's too busy, so I'm planning the wedding myself."

"Yes, and a good thing, too, because if it were up to Anne we'd be cutting the wedding cake with scalpels." Obviously, the concept of a man handling a wedding didn't faze Great-aunt Myra. "I'll see you day after tomorrow then, around four."

As he hung up, Jason realized he was going to be glad of the help. And he was looking forward to seeing the feisty old lady again, too.

But before she got here, there was one more point he needed to resolve with Anne. And he wanted to tackle it tonight, so they'd have plenty of time to work it out before Myra arrived.

Anne looked harried but happy when she arrived home from work at six. Jason waited until they were both pleasantly stuffed on roast chicken and then escorted her into the living room, with glasses of white wine to relax them.

"How's it going?" Anne curled up on the couch, tucking her feet under her. She looked younger and softer than she used to, despite her heavy work load, and her green eyes lowed. For a moment, Jason was tempted to forget about the business at hand and take Anne into his arms, but he forced himself to postpone that pleasure.

"Great." He told her about the menu he'd chosen, featuring caviar, lobster and pâté, and about Myra's upcoming visit. "Now, there's one more decision we have to make."

"What's that?"

"The ceremony itself." Jason hesitated, not sure how best to continue.

Anne waved a hand airily. "Oh, the usual will be fine—love, honor and cherish."

"Yes, but I want a two-part ceremony. Before the minister actually marries us, I think we should say a few words ourselves."

She wrinkled her nose. "You mean recite poetry and sprinkle each other with flower petals? I thought that went out with the Sixties."

Jason laughed. "I wouldn't dare suggest you recite poetry, Anne. Listen, maybe I'd better explain my philosophy about weddings."

She took a sip of wine. "I didn't know you had one."

"Neither did I. It's come on me suddenly over the past week." He reached back absentmindedly and rubbed his neck. It had gotten stiff during all the driving he'd done looking for magenta-and-gray paper goods. "You know what normally happens when you go to a wedding? Usually you know either the bride or the groom well but you have no idea how they met or what kind of relationship they have."

"So?"

"Then you stare at their backs while the minister conducts the ceremony, and then down the aisle they go, and you shake their hands in the receiving line and eat some cake and go home. And you don't know anything more about them than you did when you came in."

She regarded him dubiously. "What are you suggesting?"

"I think the people we invite are special, and we want them to feel after the ceremony that they've really participated with us, that they understand why we're getting married and what it means to us."

Skepticism was a mild word for the expression on her face. "And how do you propose to accomplish that?"

"I think we should tell them."

The sound of fingers tapping on the oak end table was the first response, followed by, "You've got to be kidding!"

"Why?"

Anne glared at him. "Jason, I'm not going to stand up there and tell everybody about our private life."

"I don't mean the gory details. But don't you think they'd be interested to know how we resolved our differences and what kind of marriage we plan to have?"

"Of course they would!" Irritably, she brushed a lock of hair out of her eyes. "People are always curious about one another. But that's the sort of thing I'd expect to discuss with my mother or sister in private—not tell the whole world!"

"Hold on a minute." He tried to keep his voice calm. "Obviously, we'll have to decide which details to leave in and which to leave out. I just want us to agree in principle that we'll make some sort of statement beforehand." Then he threw in his ace. "You said we could have any kind of ceremony I wanted as long as I did the work. Isn't that right?"

"Well, yes, but I didn't mean we could say our vows while jumping out of airplanes or snorkeling in the ocean! I meant within reasonable limits."

Jason didn't answer right away. It was hard to handle Anne when she was upset. He supposed he could go along with a conventional ceremony, but . . .

A new thought occurred to him. "You know why I picked gray and magenta for our colors?"

"Because you like them, I assume." She wasn't going to give an inch.

"Yes, but also because my first wedding was white. Entirely, totally, boringly white."

"I haven't bugged you about the colors, have I?"

"And our ceremony was so ordinary I don't remember a bit of it. I don't even remember saying 'I do,' although I'm sure I must have. Anne, this is different. Our marriage is something special, and our life together will be, too, and I want our ceremony to reflect that."

"Oh." She bit her lower lip reflectively. "You know, that's a sweet thing to say. I certainly don't want this wedding to be like your first one, either."

"I thought we might start by describing how we met," he said. "It's kind of funny, when you think about it."

"Yes, I guess it was. Are you going to tell them how you stole my heart with your fettucine?"

He knew better than to show by so much as a grin that he knew he'd won.

THERE WERE a number of things about this household and this wedding that would have been unthinkable in Myra's day. Back then, the bride-to-be certainly didn't sleep with her future husband or, if she did, they made sure nobody knew about it. And she spent her time stitching up her trousseau, not stitching up patients, unless she'd gone off to play Florence Nightingale in the Great War.

However, those things didn't bother a person anywhere near as much as the dress.

You couldn't even call it a dress. Anne had bought herself a suit, the kind a bride might take on her honeymoon, but she was planning to wear it to the ceremony itself.

It was an attractive suit, in the soft shade of gray that Jason had picked as one of the wedding colors. But Anne needed a proper gown, and Myra felt she owed it to her niece Janine, Anne's mother, to make sure the bride got one.

Now, how was she to accomplish that?

Jason was a sterling young man, but he was no help in this department. When Myra broached the subject, he merely chuckled and said, "I'm just glad she's not planning to wear a surgical gown."

The only person who might be able to help was that nice young Ellie, Anne's matron of honor. She'd been over almost every night, for one thing or another, trying in vain to talk Anne into being the guest of honor at a shower, making sure Anne got Lori's measurements for her bridesmaid's dress, helping prepare invitations and so on.

There wasn't much more than a week left before the wedding. Why, Janine and Sutter would be arriving in a few days! Something had to be done quickly about the gown, and Myra seized the first opportunity.

Anne and Ellie had been planning to go shopping that Saturday morning to pick out Ellie's and Lori's dresses, but wouldn't you know it, Anne got called in to the hospital. So Myra volunteered to go along instead.

As soon as she got into the car with Ellie, Myra said, "About Anne's dress."

And Ellie said, "I was thinking the same thing."

They smiled at each other.

"The truth is, I've been nagging her to go shopping with me for weeks, and she kept putting it off," Ellie said. "I think she suspects I wanted her to try on gowns."

"She wears a size nine. I looked through her closet," Myra replied.

"I've got a list of shops." Ellie was obviously a kindred spirit. "But I don't want to wear you out."

"The only thing that would wear me out is having to watch my grand-niece get married in a plain old suit."

The first shop didn't have much, but the second had an excellent selection and a most cooperative manager. Ellie

uickly picked matching pink dresses for the brides-
aids—Jason had approved the color in advance—and
Myra impulsively selected a dignified outfit for herself, with
small gauzy cape that gave her shoulders a filled-out look.

After making their purchases, they explained the situa-
on to the owner, who agreed to let them take several gowns
ome for Anne to try on when they offered to leave a large
eposit.

"I hope she doesn't kill us," said Ellie as the two drove
way.

Myra wasn't worried. Her grand-niece was a mighty
tubborn young woman, but she *was* a woman. How would
he be able to resist these wonderful creations of lace and
atin when they were laid right in front of her?

THIS WAS ONE TIME Anne hadn't really minded having her
aturday interrupted by work. Not that she objected to
ooking at dresses with Ellie. The problem was, the wed-
ing was becoming all-consuming to everyone around her.
ason, Myra and even Ellie talked of little else—except at
ie office, where Ellie kept a discreet silence on the subject.

The phone seemed to ring a dozen times an evening with
SVPs, and the dining-room table was covered with gifts
ent by friends and relatives who couldn't attend.

So far, except for writing thank-you notes, Anne had kept
er resolve to stay out of it. But it hadn't been easy. She
ould hear snippets of conversation that aroused her curi-
sity. Had Jason ordered the pineapple cake or the one with
ayers of chocolate and raspberry? How was he going to ar-
ange the platform for the ceremony? And what kind of
usic had he decided on?

One slip and she'd be a goner. Anne simply couldn't do
ings halfway; she knew herself too well. She had to stay
loof or she'd cave in altogether, and going shopping with
llie might have weakened her resolve.

It was midafternoon by the time she got home. The hou
was quiet. By the middle of the week, her parents would l
arriving, and then Lori's family. Anne looked forward
seeing them, but it was nice to have a moment's peace ar
quiet, too.

She reclined on the couch and leafed through a trav
brochure. Paris! She was glad they hadn't decided on H.
waii, even though she wanted to go there someday, too. B
as Jason said, it would be easy to fly to the islands for
week, whereas they might not go to Europe again for year

Women's voice floated in from outside, and Anne hu
ried to the door in time to hold it while Ellie staggered i
under a load of clothing bags. Myra followed right behin

"You two look as though you bought out the store.
Anne relieved Ellie of several bags. "What's going on?"

She didn't miss the smile that passed between the tw
women. "We couldn't resist," Ellie answered. "We broug
home a couple of gowns for you to try on."

Anne might have known they were up to something!
already bought my suit. Really, what's the sense in buyir
a dress I'll only wear once?"

"This is not the time to be practical." Myra shepherde
them up the stairs. "The least you can do is try the gow
on before you send them back."

Anne didn't want to be rude to her great-aunt. "Wel
okay, but don't get your hopes up."

Seizing the opportunity, Ellie hurried ahead to Anne
bedroom and hung the dresses in the closet. "Come or
There's no telling when Jason will be home, and you don
want him to see you trying on your dress before the wec
ding, do you?"

"Why not?" Anne asked as she kicked off her shoes.

The other two women stared at her in disbelief.

"Sometimes I wonder if you were raised on anothe
planet." Myra shook her head.

"Oh—it's traditional, isn't it?" Anne slipped out of the slacks and blouse she'd worn to the hospital. "But it's traditional for the woman to plan the wedding, too."

"That's different," Ellie said. "I mean, it's not bad luck for the man to plan the wedding, probably because nobody ever thought it would happen."

"Well, let's get on with this."

"Try this one first." Ellie lifted a white gown out of its bag. It was a simple, elegant style with a high neck and a V-shaped yoke.

Anne slid it over her head, grateful for her friend's help in zipping up the back. Then she stepped in front of the mirror.

The dress fit, but the color was too stark against Anne's pale skin and dark-blond hair. "It makes me look washed-out." She turned so the other two women could see.

"I was afraid of that," said Myra. "But don't worry, we have others."

"Even Princess Diana wore ivory," Ellie added as she lifted down another dress.

This one was a rich cream color that flattered Anne's coloring. Trimmed with lots of lace and ribbon, it had puffed sleeves and a Cinderella dreaminess to it.

"Now, that's more like it." Myra folded her arms as if daring Anne to disagree.

Yes, it was beautiful, Anne had to admit. When she was eighteen years old, she'd dreamed about someday picking a wedding dress like this.

That was precisely the problem. The gown was lovely, and she looked fresh and bridelike in it, but she didn't feel like herself. She felt as if she were masquerading as the girl she'd been fifteen years ago.

"There's nothing wrong with the dress, but I can't get married in it." Reluctantly, Anne faced her great-aunt. "I feel as if I'm wearing a costume. Look, I appreciate all the effort you went to, but I'm too old for this sort of dress."

Myra regarded her combatively for a moment and the apparently thought better of it. "You do have a point, suppose."

"That's why we brought this one." Ellie lifted down third clothes bag. "Actually, your great-aunt had he doubts, but I persuaded her that it fit in with Jason's cold scheme, so we should at least give it a chance."

The dress must have been intended for a bridesmaic There couldn't be another bride on earth, even in California, who would choose to wear that shocking shade of magenta.

"It certainly is—bright." Anne regarded the gown doubtfully.

"Well, put it on!" Ellie unzipped the ivory dress, and soon the change was made.

Anne studied herself in the mirror. She never would have chosen this color, even for a street dress, yet it highlighted the rose tones of her skin and made her eyes look brighter than usual. The fabric itself was a very rich, soft silk, cut in clean, classic lines without any ribbons or lace.

"I suppose I wouldn't have to worry about getting hit by a bus," she murmured. "You could see this thing for blocks."

"Light your way home at night," Myra agreed.

"It looks terrific," said Ellie.

Reluctantly, Anne had to agree with her. It was a smashing dress. Why, she'd even be able to wear it again, perhaps on her honeymoon; didn't people dress up for the evening in Paris?

The more she looked at the dress, the more she couldn't bear the idea of returning it to the store. How could she let someone else own this gown that had so obviously been made with Anne in mind?

"Okay, I'm sold." She fingered a fold of the silk. "I'll take it."

Ellie clapped her hands in excitement. "I'm so glad! With the gray tuxedo Jason's planning to wear, you'll look fabulous!"

All Myra could say was "I hope Janine doesn't kill me."

ON TUESDAY NIGHT, Anne's parents arrived, followed the next day by Lori, Bob and the boys. The house throbbed with laughter and giggles and shared confidences. It was impossible not to pick up the spirit of excitement.

Jason's parents arrived on Wednesday. At the airport there was a moment of awkwardness as they stepped off the ramp from the plane, and then Jason's mother caught Anne's hands and said, "I'm so glad he's finally going to settle down. You're wonderful for him; I can tell from his letters."

Jason's brother, Ed, who was single, flew in Thursday morning to be the best man. The trip from Boston was too expensive for Jason's sisters to make, but they sent their love and good wishes.

Delighted though she was to see everyone, Anne couldn't help feeling a bit dazed. When she and Jason decided to get married, it had been a private moment. She hadn't thought about how many other people would be affected. The realization that her marriage was part of a web of relationships that went back for generations and involved people thousands of miles away was a bit daunting.

The night before the wedding, while Jason and the other men were downstairs fighting to conquer the world in a game of Risk and most of the women were playing bridge, Anne's mother came up to her bedroom and sat on the bed, just as she used to do in Anne's high-school days.

"Before I was married, my mother gave me a heart-to-heart talk about the facts of life," Janine observed wryly. "In view of your occupation, I'm sure you know more about that than I do."

Anne finished removing her makeup at the vanity table
and turned around. "Oh, Mom, it's the sentiment that
counts."

"Then you won't mind if I give you a few words of advice." Janine took a deep breath. "Anne, I can't help wondering if you really know what it means, getting married.
You seem so, well, preoccupied with your work, as if you've
kept yourself aloof from everything."

"Mom, it's the wedding I've stayed out of, not the marriage!" Anne protested.

"Yes, but I never saw such a calm bride before. You don't
seem to have the least bit of jitters."

"Why should I? Jason and I love each other, and we're
old enough to know what we want out of life."

Her mother searched for the right words. "I know, but
you sound so—intellectual about it! Anne, this is an emotional time. You should be at least a little scared of the big
commitment you're making. I know you and Jason love
each other, and I'm sure you'll be happy together, but...."
She paused. "I'm not entirely sure what I want to say. Just
that I don't think you've really come to terms with what it
means to get married."

Anne smiled. "Oh, Mom, you always were the sensitive
one in the family, and I've always just clomped ahead. But
I've done all right, haven't I?"

"I only want you to be happy." Janine's eyes sparkled
with tears. "I hope you will be, Anne."

She hurried across the room and they hugged each other.

I will be happy, Anne thought. *With Jason, how could I
help it?*

ON SATURDAY MORNING, Jason went out to pick up the
wedding cake and to make sure the chairs and platform were

set up properly at John's house. The wedding wasn't until three o'clock in the afternoon, but there was a lot to do.

Anne awoke at nine, feeling a touch nervous, but she quickly forgot her concerns in the bustling household. She even cooked breakfast, in Jason's absence, and found herself reassuring everyone around her that the wedding would come off fine.

Maybe her mother had a point. In a way, Anne felt as if she were going to someone else's wedding, even though she and Jason had walked through the ceremony Thursday night with the wedding party and the minister. And she and Jason had spent hours preparing what they were going to say. And they'd gone down to the county registrar's office to get their marriage license earlier in the week. Still, she felt as if they were rehearsing for a play, not a wedding.

It's just the way I am, Anne told herself as she popped another pound of bacon into the microwave oven for latecomers and covered it with a paper towel to prevent splattering. *I'm not the excitable type.*

"Aunt Anne, are you going to have a baby?" Jeb asked as he and Sammy raced in and grabbed biscuits off a plate.

"I hope so, one of these days," she said absently. "Why?"

Jeb shrugged. Then Sammy poked him, and Jeb said, "Well, this boy at school, his sister's getting married, and she's stagnant."

"I think you mean pregnant." Anne looked up, embarrassed, as Great-aunt Myra came into the kitchen.

"Who's pregnant?" Myra regarded her sharply.

"Jeb's friend's sister," Anne said. "He wondered if I was. But I'm not."

"At least you're doing something the old-fashioned way." Myra helped herself to a plate of scrambled eggs from the sideboard.

The phone rang. "I'll get it!" Jeb and Sammy shouted at the same time and nearly collided in their rush to answer it.

Anne lifted the phone off its cradle before her nephews could attack it.

"Dr. Eldridge?" It was the receptionist from the clinic where she volunteered. "I know you're getting married today, but we've got a problem."

Immediately, Anne tuned out the noisy scene around her. "What's wrong?"

"You remember Anita Nuñez? Well, she's in labor and she refuses to go to the hospital unless you'll be there. I offered to drive her, but she won't get in the car."

Anne glanced at the clock and saw it was ten-thirty. She didn't need to be at John's until one. "How far apart are the pains?"

"Twenty minutes, but they seem to be speeding up."

She calculated quickly. "You'll have to bring her down to Irvine. Can you do that?"

"Sure."

"I'll meet you at the hospital."

Anita Nuñez was a heavyset young woman who had previously delivered a stillborn baby at a hospital and blamed the doctor. Anne doubted that he was at fault, but she certainly didn't want Anita giving birth at home and possibly losing another baby.

She explained the situation to Great-aunt Myra. "Please tell everyone not to worry. I'll be at John's house in plenty of time."

"Bring the lady along. Maybe you could deliver her baby during the ceremony. I doubt anyone would be surprised, knowing you," Myra said.

Anne chuckled. "Okay, okay, but this really is an emergency. Ask Lori to pack my makeup and curling iron, would you? Thanks!"

And she was gone, leaving Great-aunt Myra to try to explain to the others why the bride had gone to work on her wedding day.

Chapter Eighteen

With John's and Ed's help, Jason spent about an hour ar
ranging the chairs and setting up the platform and speake
system. Fortunately, the weather had turned out beautiful
sunny with a hint of crispness, and John's yard was th
perfect setting. Tall hibiscus bushes blocked any view o
neighboring houses, and the lawn was a velvety green tha
testified to professional gardening.

About noon, Jason reviewed his checklist. He already hac
the plates and eating utensils on hand. The cake was safe in
the kitchen, and he'd picked up his tuxedo yesterday.

It was hard to believe everything was going so smoothly

As he strolled across the yard, straightening the align
ment of a chair here and there, he couldn't help smiling to
himself at the story Ellie had told about Anne's dress.

He couldn't wait to see what it looked like. Even more, h
couldn't wait to see Anne, radiant as a bride.

If he had any quibble about the past few weeks, it wa
that he and Anne hadn't had nearly enough time together
For one thing, there always seemed to be someone els
around—Great-aunt Myra tried to be discreet, but she wa
their houseguest. And Ellie, much as he liked her, had a wa
of getting underfoot.

Also, Anne had kept busy at work, and Jason suspectec
he knew why. Just as she'd caved in about the dress, sh

would have thrown herself into the wedding preparations if he'd spent much time discussing them. So she'd stayed away.

He missed her, but he didn't really mind. After all, he was going to have Anne to himself for the next month, in one of the most romantic cities in the world. They would make up for lost time and then some.

Jason swung around and regarded the small platform, reflecting that it looked awfully bare. Surely he'd had something else in mind....

The flowers!

Sheer panic shot through Jason. He'd gone through half a dozen florist shops, had settled on the one he wanted and the type of arrangement—but he'd forgotten to call back and place the order!

With a groan, he let his mind race over the possibilities. He could run out and select something himself, but then he wouldn't be here to make sure the caterer and other tradespeople got set up properly.

Ellie had enough on her hands, taking care of the dresses. And he couldn't count on Ed to make an appropriate selection. What his brother knew about flowers could be stuck in a buttonhole.

Maybe Deanie and her husband...but they had the baby to hassle with. Surely there must be someone he could ask who wouldn't be too inconvenienced.

Rosa! She'd been bursting with curiosity over the details of the wedding, as imparted by Jason across the backyard fence, and was planning to bring Juanita. There was still time for her to run by a florist shop.

He raced into the house and dialed her number, hoping he hadn't left early for any reason. Luckily, she was still there, and Jason explained the situation and asked her to pick out two large vases or baskets of flowers.

"Pink flowers, or a deep rose color, something that wi
fit in with the color scheme. I'll pay you back when you ge
here, if that's okay. Can you do it?"

"No problem," said Rosa. "I was hoping you'd let m
help. I'll get Juanita to help me make the selection. We'll b
there as soon as we can."

Hanging up the phone, Jason exhaled with relief. H
knew he was going to get kidded about the oversight; but a
long as the flowers arrived on time, he didn't mind.

His first inkling of trouble didn't come until one o'clock
when Ellie drove up in her car with Lori. Jason glance
down the street, expecting to see Anne's car right behind
but there was no sign of it.

"She had to go deliver a baby," were the first words El
lie said as she got out of the car.

"A baby?" Jason stared at her in disbelief. "She's not o
call today."

Quickly, Ellie explained about the woman from the clinic
"According to Myra, she swore she'd be here on time."

Jason refused to give in to negative thinking. "Then I'
sure she will be. Why don't you go upstairs and get ready
Clear the decks so you can help her when she shows up."

"Right." Ellie pulled some garment bags out of the bac
seat. "Dennis will be bringing the rest of the family in ou
van."

"Great." Jason stood there staring down the street for
moment after Ellie and Lori disappeared into the house
willing Anne to appear.

A car turned onto the block. Could it be...no, that wa
Rosa's car, not Anne's. As they pulled up, he stepped for
ward and held the passenger door for Juanita.

"You wouldn't believe what happened!" Rosa cam
around to open the hatchback. "We went to two shops an
they were nearly cleaned out! They said there's a lot o
weddings this weekend. So look what we got!"

The back of the car was bursting with roses—not tame, odorless florist roses but vibrant blooms in a riot of colors that filled the air with their fragrance.

"My employers are out of town and they told me to cut all the flowers I wanted," Juanita explained.

"It's the best we could do." Rosa spread her hands apologetically. "I'm sorry there weren't enough pink ones."

"That's okay. It's my own fault." At this point, Jason was a lot less worried about the flowers than about the bride. "Let's go and see what kind of vases we can scare up."

With the help of John's wife, two large Chinese vases were soon set up in front of the platform, adding a festive note to the surroundings. They might not fit into the color scheme, Jason decided, but the roses were much prettier than a formal arrangement, and they certainly smelled a lot better.

The house began filling up. The caterer and her assistants bustled about the kitchen, the musicians tuned their instruments, and the photographer looked perplexed at the announcement that the bride was not there yet.

"I'll put in a call to the hospital," John said. A few minutes later, he came back. "She's in the delivery room now. It shouldn't be much longer."

Jason glanced at his watch. It was five minutes after two.

Early guests began to arrive. Ellie volunteered to make sure they signed the guest book, while the musicians launched into a selection of melodies from Rodgers and Hammerstein, as Jason had requested.

The Hernandez yard took on the look of a garden party. More guests showed up, arranging their gaily wrapped presents on the gift table. The minister, looking suitably official in a black suit, chatted with Ellie as she greeted the guests, most of whom she knew.

By two-fifteen, Jason was really worried. He knew Anne wouldn't purposely be late to her own wedding, but the welfare of a patient came first. In a way, he had to agree

with her. And yet, he couldn't help thinking that if she'
been as involved with this event as he had, she would some
how have managed to be here by now.

He could tell that some of her relatives were thinking th
same thing. The guests, of course, had no idea what wa
going on.

The hands of his watch inched toward two-thirty. Wher
the hell was Anne?

THE DELIVERY HAD BEEN a difficult one, compounded by
the patient's fear of losing this baby, too. Her tension had
increased her pain and made it harder for the baby to com
out.

But he *had* come out, a strong, lusty little boy who yelle
his head off, peed on a nurse and quieted immediately whe
placed in his mother's arms.

Wearily, Anne congratulated the woman and made he
way out of the delivery room. Then, for the first time i
hours, she glanced at a clock. It was almost two-thirty.

Two-thirty! She was supposed to get married in half a
hour!

Anne washed up in record time and sprinted for her car
It was ten minutes to three when she reached John's hous
and to her dismay discovered she had to park two block
away. Who'd ever heard of a bride who couldn't find a plac
to park at her own wedding?

She ran the two blocks, ignoring the startled gasps of last
minute guests as they spotted her, and dashed into th
house.

To his credit, Jason refrained from saying, "It's abou
time." Instead, he said, "Lori's got the curling iron ready
upstairs. Did the delivery go all right?"

"Fine." Anne loved him for asking, but she didn't hav
time to say that now. Instead, she sprinted up the stairs.

The next few minutes sped by in a blur. Ellie and Lor
would have received a gold medal if preparing the bride wer

an Olympic event. Lori curled Anne's hair while Ellie applied makeup, and then they both helped her into the dress.

By a quarter past three, she was ready to go. The finishing touch was her bouquet of lace and ribbons. She'd decided she preferred its old-fashioned elegance to having a conventional bouquet of flowers; and, as Lori had pointed out, this way the bridesmaids could keep their versions as mementos.

"Don't worry," Ellie said. "Weddings never start on time anyway."

Then her sister and her best friend hurried out to take their places in the procession.

Anne stood in the front hall, trying to get her bearings. The house felt empty, except for the clinking noises coming from the kitchen. In the morning's haste, she'd forgotten where she was supposed to await her cue. Or what her cue was. Or what she and Jason were supposed to say. Or...

"Scared?" Sutter Eldridge strolled to his daughter's side.

"I—I guess so," Anne admitted. "Oh, Dad, I'm glad you're here. I can't remember anything."

"As long as you don't forget how to say 'I do,' you'll be fine."

Anne clung to her father's arm. What was wrong with her? Her body simply wasn't functioning properly. Her ankles nearly buckled and her knees wobbled as her father guided her out the side door to a shaded area where, she now remembered, they were supposed to await their musical signal. Her heart was thudding much too fast, probably approaching tachycardia, and as for her brain, well, she might as well donate it to science, since she obviously would never be able to use it again.

Calm down, girl. Focus on your surroundings. That ought to help.

From here she couldn't see the guests, but she could hear them. Their chatter had an expectant quality to it. And the

music—it was a medley from *The Sound of Music*. Didn't
that mean something?

The players began a slow version of "Maria," as in the
wedding scene of the movie, and Anne remembered that this
was Lori's and Ellie's cue. She tried to imagine them walking down the aisle as they had Thursday night but this time
wearing their floating pink dresses. What came next? Was
Jason already waiting by the platform? Had he forgotten his
part, too?

Then the music swelled into a stately rendition of "Climb
Every Mountain," and Sutter Eldridge stepped forward with
Anne on his arm.

They moved out from the shady nook and suddenly she
could see everyone, rows and rows of people turning to look
at her, smiling and nodding to each other. She knew almost
everyone, and yet at this moment she couldn't have coughed
up a single name, not even her own mother's.

Marriage. How many millions of brides had gone forward as she was doing now, into an unknown future? As
well as she knew Jason, Anne realized with a start that she
had no idea what lay in store for them. Marriage meant a
whole lifetime—children, and growing old together, and
facing the unexpected. There were sure to be some difficult
times; would she and Jason weather them? This was a huge
commitment they were making. It was like stepping out
blindfolded, not knowing how much light and how much
darkness lay ahead or whether she was really ready for it.

For one panic-stricken moment, Anne wanted to flee.
Then she saw Jason.

He was standing next to his brother, to the minister's left,
but she scarcely noticed anyone else. Only Jason, and the
glow of pure love in his eyes. The panic faded into nothing-
ness, and a bubble of joy rose in Anne, so powerful she
thought she would float the rest of the way up the aisle.

Of course the future was a blank. No one knew what lay
ahead, whether they got married or not. But one thing she

did know: that she and Jason could overcome any obstacles.

UNTIL THE MOMENT when he saw Anne move toward him on her father's arm, Jason's head had been buzzing with details. Did the flowers look okay? Would the public-address system work properly? Did Ed have the rings?

Seeing Anne jolted him back to himself. Jason's first thought was, *that dress certainly is bright!* His second was, *God, she's beautiful.*

Anne glanced up and her eyes met his. He'd never seen her look quite so—ecstatic. And he suspected he looked equally blissful as he watched her mount the steps.

Sutter handed his daughter to Jason with a wink that the guests couldn't see, then went to join his wife in the front row.

As they'd planned, Jason and Anne joined hands and stepped up to the microphone.

"Before we take our vows, we wanted to tell you something about us—how we met and fell in love and why we decided to get married," Jason said. "We want you all to feel that you know us and are part of this special occasion with us."

He glanced at Anne and she smiled at him reassuringly. "I guess you could say it's a bit surprising we ever got together," Jason went on. "The first time I met Anne, I thought she was already married."

"And I thought he was the strangest-looking housekeeper I'd ever seen," she added.

The words flowed easily as they ran over the key moments in their relationship: the discovery that they loved each other; his realization that he hadn't told her he didn't plan to be a jet-set father; and even how she'd agreed to have a big wedding only if Jason would plan it himself.

"So if you don't like the food, you know who to blame," he said, and heard several people chuckle. It was a warm sound, and he knew he and Anne had accomplished what they intended: strengthening the bond between themselves and their friends and family, sharing their happiness.

Then they turned to the minister and the ceremony began. It seemed to Jason to go much too fast. Before he knew it, the rings had been exchanged and the vows said, and he was kissing his bride.

They were married. Really and truly married.

To the tune of "Oh, What a Beautiful Mornin'," they strolled back down the aisle together. Jason had to fight off the impulse to skip, and he suspected Anne did, too.

They'd decided against a formal receiving line, and he was glad. Within minutes, the scene turned into a rollicking party, with good food, champagne and dancing. Anne's nephews were galloping about the lawn with shouts of delight, and Rosa and Juanita chatted merrily with Mrs. Hernandez. Even Great-aunt Myra got a little tipsy, and Jason could have sworn there was a flirtatious look in her eye as she danced with the best man.

ANNE HATED TO LEAVE. She'd never expected to enjoy the reception this much. Looking back, she realized she'd thought of it as something to endure; instead, this had turned out to be one of the most enchanting afternoons of her life. They'd gone through all the rituals she'd always thought were corny—cutting the cake and posing for photographs and tossing her bouquet, which had been caught by John's eldest daughter. And she'd loved every minute of it.

But it was getting late, and they had a plane to catch that evening.

Reluctantly, she began saying goodbye to everyone who meant so much to her. True, she was going away for only a month, but when she came back she would be changed, perhaps in subtle ways, but definitely not the old pigheaded Anne Eldridge.

Now that she'd discovered what marriage really meant, she wasn't going to waste her time disagreeing over petty details. If Jason wanted them to wallpaper the house in bright orange, or plant Venus-flytraps in the backyard, or take up snorkeling, that was fine with her.

"Don't worry about the wedding presents and locking up the house. We'll take care of everything," her mother promised, and gave her daughter a big hug. "Oh, Anne, I'm so glad for you."

"You know what?" Anne blinked back an unexpected film of moisture from her eyes. "You were right. I *didn't* realize what I was getting into. But I do now, Mom."

"It was a beautiful ceremony." Her father slipped his arm around Anne's waist. "Frankly, I wondered what on earth you two were going to say, but, well, I'm glad you did it."

"I feel as if I understand you better now," her mother admitted.

Jason's parents, too, were beaming as they said their farewells. "Welcome to the family." His mother touched Anne's dress admiringly. "That color's a bit shocking, but it looks wonderful on you."

The last word, as usual, came from Great-aunt Myra. "Don't sit around your hotel room writing postcards. And, Jason, don't let Anne get near a hospital, even if she breaks her leg."

Then Jason escorted Anne to the limousine he'd hired to whisk them home for their luggage and on to the airport.

"We cut that a bit close, didn't we?" Anne had retrieved her wristwatch and saw it was getting late. She would barely have time to change into her suit.

"Oh, I'd say we've got about half an hour to spare." Jason began whistling "I Cain't Say No," which immediately made Anne suspicious.

"Just what did you have in mind?" Surely he didn't intend to start their marriage with a hurried fling in the bedroom! Although, having spent the past few hours noticing how handsome he looked in his gray tuxedo, Anne decided she wouldn't mind stripping it off him.

"I think there's a cookie boutique on our way."

"A what?"

"You heard me."

Anne stared at him in consternation. "Yes, but—aren't you full of wedding cake?"

"There's always room for cookies."

"I don't believe it!" She sank back against the seat. "Our wedding day, and he wants to go to a cookie boutique!"

"Look at it this way," Jason said. "They probably don't even have chocolate-chip cookies in Paris. Don't you want to stock up?"

"We'll probably miss our flight!" Anne glared at him. "Of all the crazy ideas..."

"I don't think it's crazy." He rolled down the interior window and told the chauffeur where to stop.

"If you think I'm going into a cookie boutique in my wedding dress..." And then Anne started to laugh.

"What's so funny?"

"Me!" She leaned over and rubbed her cheek against Jason's shoulder. "An hour ago I was resolving not to argue over little things. And here I am, as stubborn as ever."

"I'll say."

"You don't have to agree with me!"

The limousine pulled into a parking lot, passed a group of teenagers licking ice-cream cones, paused at a supermarket for a procession of casually dressed shoppers pushing grocery baskets and then halted in front of the cookie shop.

Anne peeked out the window. As she'd suspected, everyone in the parking lot was staring at the limousine.

The driver came around and opened her door. As Anne stepped out, she found Jason at her side, looking quite at home in his tuxedo.

"Shall we?" He offered his arm.

"Indeed we shall." Anne knew her face was probably as bright red as her dress, but she held her head high as they swept into the store.

After all, Jason might be right. Suppose they *didn't* have chocolate-chip cookies in Paris?

Epilogue

"Why do you think she's crying?"

In the lamplight, Anne regarded Jason with red-rimmed eyes. Cradled in her arms, two-month-old Beth was howling with scarcely a pause for breath, her little round face screwed into a mask of misery.

Jason glanced at the clock. Oh, Lord, almost four o'clock, and Beth had been crying on and off since midnight. He huddled deeper into his bathrobe against the chilly November night.

"I suppose you fed her?"

Anne nodded impatiently. "And I tried the pacifier, but she spit it out. And I burped her, and I played her music box."

"Did you try sitting her up in the infant seat? That calms her down sometimes." Jason couldn't suppress a yawn. Two months without a single night of uninterrupted sleep. He wondered if he and Anne should take turns spending the night at a motel.

"I tried it. Besides, that was last week. This week, she screams at the sight of the thing." Anne's eyelids began to droop, and Jason immediately felt guilty. At least he didn't have to sit there for an hour and feed Beth twice a night.

"We could bring her into bed with us...."

"If she's still screaming in my arms, why should she stop just because she's in our bed?"

That made sense. "I suppose if I pointed out that you're the doctor and you ought to know what to do, I might be in danger of my life?"

Anne didn't have to reply. Her fierce glare was enough of an answer.

"Wait a minute." Stifling a yawn, Jason searched his memory. Unfortunately, his brain didn't function very well at four o'clock in the morning. "I seem to recall there's something else that works."

"Not playing the radio. That was only good the first few days, when she missed the hospital nursery." Anne looked down in dismay at the still-yowling baby. "And to think, she looks like a perfect angel when she's sleeping. Oh, Jason, I know this isn't her fault, it's just her immature digestive system, but..."

"Walking," he said.

"I beg your pardon?"

"The motion of walking. And maybe some fresh air. That *might* work." Jason stretched, feeling the muscles knotting up in his back as he contemplated a future as sleepless as the immediate past. "How well do you like our neighbors?"

"I hardly know them."

"Thank goodness," he said.

Ten minutes later, with clothes thrown on hastily and hair still tangled from lying sleepless in bed, Jason and Anne let themselves out the door. Beth had subsided to whining with an occasional screech, but she looked as though she was working her way back up to a full-fledged tantrum.

Jason shifted the baby's weight so she lay securely in his arms, and they set out along the sidewalk. Sure enough, wails cut through the night, and he sped up his pace. Maybe if he went fast enough, they'd be out of sight before the neighbors were thoroughly awakened.

"I feel like a criminal," Anne admitted as she length-
ened her stride to match his. "Could we be arrested for disturbing the peace or something?"

"It certainly isn't child abuse," Jason muttered. "More
like parent abuse."

They walked faster. Beth took a deep breath, groaned
loudly and fell silent.

Jason's ears continued to ring for several seconds. He realized that his entire body was tensed, waiting for the howls
to resume. But his daughter lay yawning in his arms, trying
her best to stay awake but losing the battle.

"Amazing." Anne jammed her hands into her sweater
pockets as she paced beside him. "Where did you learn that
trick?"

"Deanie's kid." Jason smiled. His little cousin Alexander was two years old now and a bright, inquisitive boy.

"I hear he swallowed half the contents of his parents'
medicine cabinet and had to be rushed to the hosptial,"
Anne said. "Fortunately, he threw most of it up on his
own."

"How on earth did he get into the medicine cabinet?"

"He pulled out the drawers in the bathroom counter and
made stairs out of them."

That won't happen to us, Jason told himself as they
turned a corner. His steps slowed for a moment and Beth
began to whimper, so he sped up again.

He would put a latch on every conceivable cabinet and
drawer in the house. There would be gates at the top and
bottom of the stairs, and he'd lock his photographic chemicals so well even a commando force couldn't break them
out.

There was only one thing wrong—he'd been sure he could
outmaneuver a crying baby, too. Only it hadn't worked out
that way, had it?

Jason forced himself to stop worrying and pay attention
to his surroundings. How beautiful the night was, crisp and

full of stars. Maybe there was something to be said for staying up until four in the morning.

Beside him, Anne stumbled with weariness. He'd forgotten that, while he could sleep late, she had to be at the hospital first thing.

As soon as they were sure Beth was sound asleep, they staggered home. Laying her gently in the bassinet and observing the sweep of dark lashes against the chubby cheek, Jason thought, *our little girl.*

Beside him, Anne shrugged off her sweater. "I'm going to bed."

"I'll be with you in a minute."

He tucked the crocheted blanket over Beth's little body—the blanket had been handmade by Anne's mother—and stood there for a moment watching her breathe.

It seemed like only yesterday they'd come back from Paris. Anne had fallen in love with its broad boulevards and the tang of excitement in the air. Jason had never seen her look more alive—and he'd never been happier.

Adjusting to marriage had been occasionally frustrating but exhilarating nevertheless. And then had come Anne's pregnancy. She'd gone through all the symptoms, from morning sickness to swollen feet. "Now I know why my patients grumble so much," she'd told him one night as he massaged her aching arches.

Jason had done his best to make things easy for her. There'd been plenty of time to keep up with the housework and cooking—he'd become rather possessive of the kitchen and rarely allowed her to cook even when she offered to. And he'd begun a short-term project, a photo essay for a prestigious magazine about the foster-grandparents program at a nearby retirement home.

Anne's medical knowledge hadn't made her delivery any easier. Despite Jason's attempts to assist with her breathing exercises, she'd moaned in a most un-Anne-like manner.

And then out came Beth, beautiful, crying, red-faced Beth. Their daughter.

That night, as Anne slept, Jason went to the nursery and held the baby. Almost instantly, he'd felt a special bond with the little girl.

The first few weeks at home had been confusing, exhausting and delightful. And then Beth had figured out how to scream.

Jason had stripped the library of child-care books, and every one of them said the same thing: nobody really knew why babies cried, and all you could do was hang on until the magic age of three months, when the crying stopped. Although, one book added darkly, some babies had colic for a few months longer.

"Jason?" He looked up to see Anne in her nightgown. "Aren't you coming to bed? I miss you."

"Right away." But he stood there for a minute, just looking at Anne. God, she was beautiful. Every woman in the world ought to have exactly that rebellious lick of hair sticking up where she'd lain on it wrong and that hint of dark circles under the eyes and that forgotten cloth diaper pinned to her shoulder and those laugh lines touching her mouth.

"Let's go," said Jason, and took his wife to bed.

Harlequin American Romance

COMING NEXT MONTH

#197 SUMMER CHARADE by Karen Toller Whittenburg

Rebecca Whitaker's new antique trunk had to contain valuables because it was bringing her nothing but trouble. But *what* was the treasure? If she knew, she wouldn't be keeping company with Quinn Kinser, who was trouble personified. Just how far would Quinn be willing to go to get his hands on the trunk?

#198 SOAR AND SURRENDER by Maralys Wills

Finances unnerved her, aeronautics unhinged her, yet Jenny meant to keep the hang-gliding company she'd inherited. She had the dreams of an eagle, but co-owner Kirk had the instincts of an ostrich! When they're challenged to risk their lives for Jenny's dream, will Kirk be ready to carry her on wings of courage?

#199 WINTER'S END by Alysse Lemery

Chrys's young daughter loved everyone in the small Wisconsin town, and that included Eric McLean, who'd just returned. Chrys, though, had reservations, for she and Eric had once been lovers, a long time ago. A child's love is simple, but it's also magical for a man and a woman united after a long, harsh winter.

#200 FANTASIES AND MEMORIES by Muriel Jensen

Small wonder Destiny felt mutinous. Rafe turned a peaceful summer in Maine into sheer misery. No colas, spicy foods or work. Life would've been easier with Captain Bligh! Was it any wonder she'd jumped ship last time—would she again?

PATRICIA MATTHEWS

America's First Lady of Romance upholds her long
standing reputation as a bestselling romance novelist
with . . .

Caught in the steamy heat of America's New South,
Rebecca Trenton finds herself torn between two
brothers—she yearns for one but a dark secret binds
her to the other.

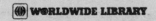

**For the millions who can't read
Give the Gift of Literacy**

One out of five adults in North America
cannot read or write well enough
to fill out a job application
or understand the directions on a bottle of medicine.

**You can change all this by joining the fight
against illiteracy.**

For more information write to:
Contact, Box 81826, Lincoln, Neb. 68501
In the United States, call toll free: 800-228-3225

**The only degree you need
is a degree of caring**

LIT-A-1